Praise for Katie Porter's
Lead and Follow

"Between the red-hot sex scenes, the author deftly explores the pit-falls and possible rewards of friends becoming lovers, leaving readers with the welcome message that life can hand out happy surprises even with things look grim."

~ *Publishers Weekly*

"...[H]ot, hot, hot! The one-of-a-kind plot is accompanied by sizzling rendezvous, and their chemistry is orgasmic."

~ *RT Book Reviews*

"I am definitely looking forward to more burlesque dancing at Club Devant. It's new, different and refreshing. I can't wait to get more!"

~ *Under the Covers*

"Overall a great start to a steamy new series. Very impressed with this new to me duo—Katie Porter. [...] If you're a fan of believable menages (MMF) and sweaty sexy dancing both on and off the dance floor, this is perfect for you!"

~ *Guilty Pleasures Book Reviews*

"*Lead and Follow* is how an erotica novel should be written. This story delivered everything I didn't even dare to hope for!"

~ *Book Lovers Inc.*

Look for these titles by
Katie Porter

Now Available:

Came Upon a Midnight Clear

Vegas Top Guns
Double Down
Inside Bet
Hold 'Em
Hard Way
Bare Knuckle

Club Devant
Lead and Follow
Chains and Canes
Watch and Wait

Lead and Follow

Katie Porter

SAMHAIN
PUBLISHING

Samhain Publishing, Ltd.
11821 Mason Montgomery Road, 4B
Cincinnati, OH 45249
www.samhainpublishing.com

Lead and Follow
Copyright © 2014 by Katie Porter
Print ISBN: 978-1-61921-640-2
Digital ISBN: 978-1-61921-251-0

Editing by Sasha Knight
Cover by Angela Waters

First Samhain Publishing, Ltd. electronic publication: January 2013
First Samhain Publishing, Ltd. print publication: January 2014

Dedication

To PK & AG

Burn for you

Acknowledgements

We greatly appreciate our translation superstar, Andrei Cervoneascii, as he selflessly answered our many questions about the Russian language, although any translation errors are our own.

Chapter One

Lizzie Maynes couldn't help her little strut as she passed through the brass double doors of Club Devant. As always, the music did obscene things to her sense of self-control. Hips. Ass. The tips of her toes. She simply had to move. To dance was to breathe. She winked at Mr. George, the head bouncer, and headed straight in. A few obvious tourists and bored Chelsea boys milled about the red-and-black entryway, hoping to score tickets.

Yeah, good luck with that.

Dima was headlining. He wouldn't know how to perform without a sold-out crowd.

That night, he would perform with Lizzie in the audience.

Keeping the beat with her steps, but with a nervous twist in her gut, Lizzie navigated through the packed nightclub. Her aching knee reminded her why she wouldn't take to the stage with her dance partner of fifteen years. Six months on from the misstep that had shredded her ACL, pain still tweaked her nerves. She had healed, yet performing remained out of the question.

Instead she would watch Dima work the Devant stage—the first time she'd found the nerve to check him out. He'd hold another woman close, guide her, move with her, meet her eyes as if no one else existed. Meanwhile, Lizzie would sip something icy and pretend she didn't hate the hell out of her life.

She pasted on a performance-worthy smile and approached the table occupied by Club Devant owner Declan Shaw, where he held court with patrons, celebrities and his flavor-of-the-week dancers. The girl on his lap was new. She might not work at the club, but she certainly seemed eager to test-drive the ownership.

"Lizzie." Declan's face lit with an amiable smile. "Glad you could finally make it."

"Better late than never?" she asked, taking a seat.

"I figure you're, what, six weeks late? He's been waiting for you."

She cringed and cupped her elbows. "Don't you start too. Watching him move on hasn't been my idea of a great night out."

He only shrugged. His insouciance was the hallmark of a man who'd survived three decades in show business and had the armor to prove it. Lizzie had thought herself that strong too.

Declan lifted the young woman off his lap. After one pat on her gold-lamé-wrapped ass, he said, "Off you go, love. Have Tony buy you a drink."

Her petulant pout turned to a glare when she met eyes with Lizzie. Lizzie glared right back because she was already damn tense. Dismissively, she faced the stage. She'd spent too many frantic hours in competition changing rooms for one girl's fit of pique to wedge under her skin. Catfights over a bottle of fake tanner—that was hardcore.

Hell, she missed it. So badly.

She wondered if Dima did. He certainly didn't seem to, not when he talked on and on about the freedom of dancing at Devant. Just how long was he going to hold out on the obvious, that they would return to the professional ballroom circuit? Resenting him...she wasn't used to that.

How could she not, when he continued on, dancing without her?

Because he's paying the bills. Because, without him, I'd be back at home with Mom and Dad.

Four months of tender loving care had her regressing to a twelve-year-old girl. Escaping had been as necessary as her physical therapy sessions. The two months since her return to the Hell's Kitchen brownstone she shared with Dima...that hadn't been much better. Their goals were changing. *He* was changing—and he'd never been the easiest guy to understand even when they prized the same ambitions.

Her best friend was shutting her out.

Lizzie cupped her elbows. She needed a drink.

"You haven't missed him," Declan said.

Her mental response was that yes, she'd missed Dima more than she could say. For so many years, they'd kept nearly identical hours—whether at home or on tour. Now they spent most of the day divided by different commitments. He danced. She slowly went mad.

Realizing Declan had been referring to the performance, she withheld her initial reaction. "Good."

"Sold-out crowd for the third week in a row," Declan said. "I assume he showed you the review from Kendall Poplinski? High praise."

"Yeah, he was stoked about that."

Whereas Lizzie had been heartsick. The first time in her entire life that the bitchy dance critic found an ounce of good taste, all she did was feed Dima's excitement about this new venture. The worst part had been the flash of disappointment in his soulful brown eyes when he'd looked at Lizzie. The Notorious Poplinski had seen him dance at Devant.

But Lizzie? Nope. Not yet.

She hadn't needed a magic Dima interpreter to figure that one out. Her own guilt, plus knowing she'd be equally disappointed had their roles been reversed, had prompted her to attend.

Declan passed a hand over his head. Fit and lean, he wasn't as old as his closely cut silver hair indicated. Lizzie balked at the realization that she might be nearer to Declan's age than she was to the tart he'd banished from his lap.

"My offer still stands if you want to join him." His Dublin accent had been almost entirely erased after ten years in the States. "I could sell out the club for months with Maynes and Turgenev reunited on my stage."

"Thanks, Declan, really. But we have plans."

"Ah." He took a sip of scotch. "The circuit awaits."

He didn't say anything else, but Lizzie sensed his disapproval. She knew its weight and shape and texture because she was constantly on the receiving end of the same reaction from Dima. Different reasons. Different ambitions for her future. Same sick, liquid feeling that made her want to slam a Jäger and do something stupid.

One injury from one fall and everything had shattered. She'd thought her life built on a firmer foundation than that.

The lights dimmed. A gold-tinted spotlight hit center stage, where the lush red curtains hung ceiling to floor. The club boasted a modest stage with a slight catwalk that bisected two groups of tables. Everywhere was red and black and gold, as if Declan had transplanted a bit of Vegas kitsch to the West Side. The critics called it tacky. The applauding patrons, dolled up and craving novelty, didn't seem to care.

Rihanna's latest single drew to an end. Fabian, the club's MC, stood to one side of the stage. He wore military-inspired boots, black leather hot pants and a frilly pink lace shirt which actually suited his dark coloring. He did a little shimmy before tucking the mic close to his lips.

"Welcome to Club Devant, you dirty bitches!"

Lizzie had to smile. She held no aspiration to dance on that sleek black parquet stage, but she enjoyed the people who worked there. Anymore, finding Dima meant heading to the club. She'd gotten to know Fabian, Declan and the rest out of pure necessity. A little lonely, a little lost, she hadn't needed more than a few minutes to learn names and share stories. Still, getting along with the staff wasn't the same as spending the rest of her career in a Chelsea burlesque club.

"Show some kinky love for tonight's headline performer. Three-time international Latin ballroom champion Dmitri Turgenev and his partner, Jeanne Copeland."

Partner? Shit.

He hadn't won the world title three consecutive years with some stand-in named Jeanne.

Fear became a nasty creature digging into the base of Lizzie's skull. She dug deep for an even brighter smile, knowing the expression would've been joyful and honest had she been ready to join Dima on stage. They hadn't danced together since the accident. Might as well be a hundred years ago. She missed their closeness like she missed rhythm and power and applause.

Oh yes, Lizzie needed a drink.

However, she'd gathered guts enough to show up and didn't want to miss the performance. The bar area was unusually crowded, which meant a wait she wasn't willing to endure. She wondered if that had anything to do with Paul Reeves, the hot new bartender. Rarely did she catalog bartenders' names, but Paul was well worth remembering.

Fabian sauntered stage right with a wave and a few air kisses. The applause kicked up a notch, followed by an Indian-inspired hip-hop track. Curtains parting, the spotlight found a man standing alone in the middle of the stage, his back to the audience.

Shirtless.

Lizzie sucked in a quick breath of air. What the hell was he doing without a shirt on?

Dmitri Turgenev was one of the best Latin dancers in the world, not some sideshow sex attraction. She'd known Devant was a burlesque club, but she'd convinced herself that Dima would rise above it. He always brought years of training and undeniable class to any venture.

Not there. Not then. Despite the up-tempo beat, he turned at half time and strode forward as if he were opening a paso doble, not a playful cha-cha. The play of shadow and light over his bare skin made him beautiful. The way he moved made him a god.

Deities deserved applause as loud as a locomotive.

If even Lizzie was momentarily struck dumb by the wide, gleaming spread of his shoulders and the lithe, sculpted muscles of his lean chest and arms, she couldn't imagine what spell was weaving over the rest of the club. After all, she'd been dancing with him since before his voice changed. Only she knew how shy he was, how reluctant he was to open up about anything personal—a constant point of frustration in their long partnership. A point of frustration that was breaking them in two.

None of that showed when he hit the stage and set it on fire.

The moment was ruined, however, when a skinny blonde with only a little more grace than fashion sense strutted out to meet him. She swished her lime-green spangles for all they were worth, but her feet sloshed around the parquet.

Lizzie squeezed sharp fingernails into her palms. All wrong. Just...*wrong*. Dima was shirtless and bathed in gold and reaching out to a stranger. Only one word thundered through Lizzie's head.

Mine.

They were partners. She belonged up there with him, even when that chorus of *mine, mine, mine* didn't feel professional. It was scary as hell.

She couldn't change the situation, but she could find some means of staying sane. The last six months had proved that.

"Hey, Declan?"

"Hmm?" The man was a flirt and a kinkster, but he was also an amazing artist. Outside of hedonism, the only thing he seemed to take seriously was assessing dancers. The play faded, and he judged them with an astute eye.

He was studying Jeanne that way.

"Tell her she shouldn't wear black shoes anymore," Lizzie said over the thumping music. "Her feet look like lumps of coal on the end of her legs."

"That's what it is. Was bugging me. Well, at least she didn't wear red."

Lizzie grinned past a grimace. She hadn't worn her trademark red dance heels since her injury. If she didn't get back on the circuit—tugging Dima away from this low-rent distraction—she never would.

The performance slid from straight-up Latin ballroom to something...other. Lizzie's stomach fell and her heartbeat sped. The blonde slinked rather than stepped. Even Dima shed his exacting posture for a bit of bump and grind that dragged hoots and catcalls from the audience.

"What the hell is this?"

Declan laughed. "Remy got hold of them, I'm afraid."

"Your choreographer? But we've always done our own choreo."

"Wasn't my idea," he said. "Dmitri asked to work with him. He's been all about exploring new avenues. Surely he's mentioned as much."

"Of course." The words sounded wooden, but spoken so softly, she doubted Declan heard them.

She'd known it would be difficult to watch Dima dance with another woman. That wasn't the surprise. Instead it was some combination of envy, resentment and even arousal. She blamed the imposed distance. She literally couldn't be up there with him, forced instead to admire his hard-earned skill and sweat-sleek body. And her frustrations? *Months'* worth of frustrations? They had nowhere to go. She could tap her toes and watch the lanky blonde trail her hands over Dima's bare chest.

Mine.

What little enthusiasm she'd mustered on that evening dried up like a slice of apple left in the sun.

"I'm gonna get a drink. You need anything?"

With an indulgent smile, Declan seemed to watch her with far too much understanding. "It's my club, love. If I want something, I don't need to ask a guest."

Standing, Lizzie shook her head with a rueful grin. It was a rare man in their line of work who told the truth so bluntly.

She looked up to the stage one last time, just as the song ended. Dima was on his knees. He breathed heavily, with his hands wrapped around the blonde's skinny thigh and his forehead on her hip. A tremor of hot unexpected need shot down to Lizzie's belly.

Bar. Now.

The crowd waiting for drinks had thinned during the performance. She wove through, trying to ignore the weakness in her knees that had nothing to do with her healing injury. She needed a distraction before she threw up or cried or smashed a bottle across the nearest table.

"Hey, Paul," she called to the cute bartender. "Got a G&T for me?"

"Anything for you, Lizzie."

He grinned. He had the best grin on the planet, swear to God. Tan and built, he wore a tight white T-shirt and ragged jeans. His cowboy hat hung on a hook above the computerized cash register. On impulse, she leaned over the bar to check out his feet. Cowboy boots. Excellent.

Paul caught her looking. His gaze darted down to where her cleavage probably made offers she hadn't intended. His grin widened, if that were possible. Hard-boiled sex and a coy sense of humor.

Maybe she'd intended after all. Maybe watching what was left of her old life do a strip club cha-cha with a graceless blonde had forced her to it.

He brought the gin and tonic and placed it dead center on a cocktail napkin before sliding it over. The tips of his fingers came within an inch of her breasts. Damn, he was tall. In the land of dancers, any guy over five foot eight was considered a giant. Paul was well over six foot. The possibilities spun her already dizzy brain.

He licked his lower lip. They'd flirted on occasion since he'd hired on a few weeks earlier, but he flew well past flirting with that deliberate lick.

"Thanks," she said.

"It's on the house. Mr. Shaw's standing order."

"I'll have to thank him too."

She took a fortifying sip. Even though customers waited for his attention, Paul stood there. Tan with golden hair. Eyes like a blue summer sky. Open and interested. She could read a thousand thoughts in that clear gaze.

Anymore, when she read anything at all in Dima's expression, it was disappointment. Aloofness. Heartbreaking hesitancy. As if after fifteen years, they couldn't talk to each other without dance as their language.

17

She downed her drink in three swallows and blinked away the image of Dima's sensual lips and stoic reserve. Paul still stood there, watching her while wearing a bemused smile.

"When are you on break?"

He shrugged. "Now, if you want."

That jolt to her belly turned molten. She exhaled slowly. Bad idea. Totally bad idea, although the tension holding her bones in place wasn't going away any time soon. She liked to think she would've made a sensible decision had she known which way was up.

Lizzie nodded toward a door across from the bar. Dancers' dressing rooms. One in particular. Christ, smashing a bottle would have more subtlety.

Paul fell in step beside her. He'd shoved on his cowboy hat.

Goddamn.

"In here," she said.

The lights were off except for an alarm clock on the vanity table. Lizzie had barely flicked on a small lamp when Paul's hands found her in the near darkness. He kicked the door shut, which freed that deep place where she'd been so nervous. So...not herself.

Just a little fun. The grin that shaped Paul's lips said the same thing.

He tasted of Coke and maraschino cherries. Sweet. Delicious, actually. A scrape of stubble roughed against her cheeks and down her throat. Lizzie dug her fingers into the bulk of his shoulders. He wasn't just a bartender, she remembered. A construction worker. That stray thought shot down to her pussy.

They didn't even undress. Lizzie helped unfasten his jeans, shoving them down to tangle around his knees. She pushed him back in the chair that faced the vanity mirror. His hands climbed beneath her skirt and ripped at her panties. After a crinkle of foil, he rolled on a condom.

Rough guy. Rough hands. Rough, quick fuck.

She straddled his lean hips and sank onto his cock.

"Whoa," she said, almost unconsciously.

"Like that?"

"*Yes.*"

He was big, thick, hard. His breath had taken on a desperate edge. To be able to get guys' hearts pumping had steered her toward Latin dancing rather than her parents' classical ballet. Dima wasn't the only one who liked to show off.

She'd shown off for him for years. Somewhere along the line, his approval had come to mean more than that of a cheering crowd.

The worst part was, she knew Paul was just Dima's type. His tastes occasionally strayed toward guys, and the ones who caught his eye held not an ounce of softness or grace. He liked them all-American with sunny looks and a sunnier disposition.

Great. In her desperation she'd picked a fuck-buddy based on her partner's tastes. She needed to check herself into a mental ward.

One look down at Paul's face, however, derailed that disturbing thought. He was a gorgeous hunk of oh-my-God. She ran her hands across his buzzed head, knocked off the cowboy hat and kissed him long and deep.

This man wasn't Dima. Hell, she didn't want him to be and she didn't want to be anywhere else.

I am such a liar.

Chapter Two

Dmitri knew dancing. When everything else in his life busily turned to shit, he still had the stage. The rush he got off being admired was well worth the balls it took to make the first step.

Without Lizzie, it just wasn't the same. Other women didn't move like her. Didn't smell like her. Didn't feel like her body, shaped perfectly to his hands.

Most of all, they didn't have her wicked smile.

Lizzie's primary purpose in life was to bedevil him until he lost his mind. She'd become particularly adept lately. He needed the woman who had filled his life since he was fourteen. Since returning from her parents' house, however, she'd been nothing but skittish. And hurtful, truth be told. They'd never done anything but support one another, yet until that evening, she'd refused to see him dance at Devant. All he wanted was her opinion. What did she think of this new direction? Was there a slim chance she'd consider joining him?

For Dima, it was something of a last straw. She was determined to break them in two out of pure stubbornness, when he'd taken the job at Devant just to stay with her.

The second he stepped off stage right, he was already on alert. Somewhere out in the crowd, he'd find her—claim her attention, even if it was only for a moment.

Christ, he had to get her reeled in soon. She'd always been a live wire. Now she buzzed with more frantic energy. The focused, determined partner he'd trusted for years was nowhere to be seen in her jumpy behavior and insistence on returning to the pro circuit. That grind was no place for them, not since her injury—yet another problem to weigh on his mood. After all, Dima had been the one to screw up their tidy life together.

She'd fallen right out of his arms.

He'd failed her. Failed the woman for whom he would have done anything. His best friend and closest partner in the world.

Forcing a smile, he made his way into the main area of the club. The creative freedom he'd found at Club Devant was second to none. Being released from the strict guidelines of the competitive circuit tapped into a part of his imagination he hadn't known was there. The hefty paycheck Declan offered in order to pull in the big names wasn't bad either.

That didn't mean he'd gotten used to working the floor.

Declan prided himself on a friendly, open atmosphere, despite the kink. Or maybe because of it. He wished customers to believe they could get a taste of the performers if they were lucky enough. Or hot enough. Or rich enough.

That didn't mean Dima liked it, not without Lizzie at his side. She had been the one to talk when they were interviewed. Cameras loved her sparkle, and she loved meeting new people. It only made sense. That same sparkle turned him inside out, made his whole life brighter. Naturally everyone else would want a part of her.

Dima wanted *all* of her.

Eventually he landed at the table permanently kept for Declan. At the far end, Jeanne nursed a mineral water.

Dima gripped the back of Declan's chair. The club owner was the only man Dima knew who could pull off a sheer dark purple shirt and still look like he used his dick the traditional way. Mostly.

"Good show," Declan said, one arm around the waist of a woman in a tiny shimmering green skirt.

"The cha-cha wasn't over the top?"

"For here? Not at all. And Jeanne's promised to wear neutral shoes from now on, so next time will be perfect."

Best-case scenario would've included Lizzie dancing the cha-cha with him. Always such a flirt. Always so damn good at how she played him *and* the crowd. First he needed to convince her to stay in New York. No more midnight bus trips to God knows where for the privilege of dancing the same routines on a temporary wooden parquet floor. Three championships were enough. He couldn't put either of them through that punishing, body-cruel schedule. After four months at her parents' house, it was his turn to take care of her again. The apartment just hadn't been the same without her.

He made himself smile at Jeanne anyway, since she was blushing a little as she looked at him and Declan. A highly skilled contemporary dancer whose career had been cut short by crippling tendonitis, she meant well.

"Have you seen Lizzie? She said she'd be here tonight."

He was so completely, ridiculously excited by that. *Dumb.* She never held out on him forever. It was part of what made them a unit. Although Lizzie had always trusted him in the long run, his plans wouldn't work if he couldn't even get her to watch him dance in this new way.

Stomach twisting, he knew the answer before Declan opened his mouth. The man's glance darted toward the bar. Wherever Lizzie was, she was with Paul. Probably flirting with him. Occasionally Dima hoped she was doing it intentionally, purposefully trying to drive him crazy. What she didn't realize was that she'd had his full attention for years.

Dima had met the bartender, but hadn't been interested. Some other time, some other place, yeah, he might have enjoyed fucking Paul until they burned each other out. The man was perfection in blue jeans. When Paul had hired on at

Devant, however, Dima and Lizzie had been readjusting to life in the same space—and Dima had been trying to come to terms with his new feelings and the decisions they'd prompted.

When she'd come home to their apartment, she hadn't given Dima a chance to sit down and actually talk. To apologize for letting her get hurt. To really explain his fascination with what had started as a temporary gig at Club Devant. Instead, she'd hit the ground running: physical therapy, new costume designs, a travel schedule for the autumn season. And a parade of new guys. She was as restless as she was hurting, although she steadily ignored what had changed.

Altogether, it was enough to make a man start doubting his choices. Dima had made some huge ones since her injury.

"I've seen her," Declan said at last. He stood up, lifting the chick from his lap and plopping her down in his chair like some living blow-up doll.

"But?"

The other man fisted his hands on his hips. His position took up valuable space in the packed morass of bodies, but no one challenged or even brushed him. Declan was the undisputed king of Club Devant. "But she disappeared halfway through your first act."

Dima made himself shrug as if a pure shot of fear hadn't just cooled his guts. After weeks of hoping she would, Lizzie had decided to see him dance. She couldn't even stay for the whole act before turning to another man.

When she was scared or hurting, she could make some pretty stupid mistakes. Dima had thought that a part of her past—those wicked teenage years when the freedom of touring meant freedoms of all kinds. Apparently not.

"So?"

"So?" Declan echoed. He studied Dima closely. "Fine. Play it that way if you want. When you find my bartender, tell him his break's up."

For Dima, shutting down his emotions as he walked through the busy club was absolutely impossible. He had too much on the line. His muscles tensed, already pooling with lactic acid. He didn't have the luxury of cool-down stretches, only a slimy, oozing sort of fear.

He didn't know what he would find. They'd always maintained a platonic front. Affairs outside of their partnership had silently become off-limit topics. Just...safer. Throughout two years spent with Svetlana Rodchenko, his most recent long-term relationship, Lizzie had managed to keep her distaste for the fellow ballroom dancer at bay. Dima had known her feelings, but he'd been grateful that she hadn't pressed.

Since returning from her parents' smothering brand of care, she'd become increasingly...demanding when it came to his attention. After he and Svetlana had parted ways, Lizzie began amping those demands to exciting, dangerous new extremes. Graphic descriptions of her last date, narrated with her cheeky, wicked smile, had burned into his brainpan—and fueled his jacking off for three weeks.

His hand was shaking as he reached for the doorknob of his dressing room. Sweat from the performance had dried, but a new sheen popped up on his forehead and across the back of his neck. He had an ominous feeling that whatever was behind that door was the start of...*something*.

The beginning of the end, or the end of a fresh beginning.

The flimsy particleboard door opened easily. A perfect triangle of yellow light poured from the corridor into the dressing room.

No matter what recklessness he'd believed Lizzie capable of, the truth was more extreme. He'd known it would be. That didn't make the scene easier to process.

Lizzie straddled Paul in Dima's chair, with her hands at the back of his head. They both froze mid-fuck.

"Well, well."

He shut the door behind himself. His surprise made his voice more gravelly, his accent stronger. He hated that. She'd hear it and know, but maybe she wouldn't hear the hurt underneath.

Lizzie blinked, her eyes unfocused. Her dyed-bright blonde hair was a feathery mess. A scrap of tiny black lace that used to be panties twisted around one of her four-inch heels. Paul's jeans pooled around his thighs, showing off tanned, rock-hard legs beneath the swirl of Lizzie's red dress.

Paul closed his hands over her back, almost protectively. "Hey, buddy, do you mind?"

She could've taken the man anywhere, screwed him anywhere. New York had thousands of motels and hotels. Or hell, there was always the alley behind the club.

Yet she'd brought Paul here, and she sure as hell wasn't scrambling off the hard cowboy. In fact, under Dima's gaze, her hips twitched. Her lips parted.

Feeling tight as piano wire, he crossed to where she sat with Paul still buried deep.

Fuck, Dima didn't have a clue who he envied more. The sudden throb of his ready cock didn't want to differentiate. It'd take either of them. Both. His conscious mind had dropped out somewhere along the way. Eventually he might feel terrible about all this. For now, his only thought was *finally*. Finally they weren't stuck. They weren't frozen in the limbo that had stolen the last half year.

Dima tugged her hair, gently but firmly. Her neck bowed in a graceful arch. He kissed her on the forehead.

"*Privet*, little one." He locked eyes with Paul. Steady blue eyes looked back with a hint of challenge. "And hello to you too. I don't mind. Continue fucking her in my dressing room. I'm sure she meant it that way."

Lizzie's soft gasp shot right through him. Just as hot as he'd imagined, even if it was another man giving her pleasure.

A decade and a half together, one way or the other, and he'd be damned if he could figure her out. At that moment, he sure as hell didn't understand himself.

Turning away was gut-wrenching. He'd never turned his back on Lizzie when she so desperately wanted to be seen.

Only years of training forced his body to obey. He moved past them to the wardrobe in the corner.

The chair creaked behind him. Dima didn't look. If Lizzie wanted his attention, she had it. If she wanted more than that, she'd need to ask for it. He'd be damned if he would guess anymore. They stood at the sharp blade of change, ready to slice through and cut him and Lizzie apart forever. He didn't think he could survive that, but he sure as hell wasn't going to last long in this nowhere land.

He snatched the first set of clothes he found, to replace the sleeveless shirt he'd worn for the second half of his performance. Inside, a roiling swarm of energy buzzed. He always came off the stage popping, especially of late when he became so tense with the effort of protecting lesser partners.

This was more than he'd ever experienced.

The chair creaked again. Dima kicked out of his trousers.

Lizzie gave a little sigh that squeaked upwards to a moan. "Mmm, Dima... You're good to me, aren't you?"

Paul cleared his throat. "Look, I don't know what kind of freak show you two have going, but I'm not sticking around—"

Lizzie's crystalline giggle overrode whatever he'd been about to say. "It's a little difficult to lie when your dick's inside me." She dropped her voice to a faux whisper. "You're even harder than you were before."

Dima shoved a washcloth under water. Cold, of course. Running it over his skin did nothing to cool him off. His blood still slammed a fandango.

Was he really standing for this? Yes. More than that, some small part of him was loving it. The pure wickedness of the situation made his cock ache. While he always planned and strategized, Lizzie tossed wrenches with the best of 'em.

Shifting to the left brought him in line with a mirror. From there he found a perfect, unobstructed view of Lizzie riding Paul. She'd lowered her forehead to his. Her hips worked over him. Big, calloused hands curled around her hips.

Paul glanced at Dima before planting his cowboy boots wide. He fucked up into Lizzie.

Dima jerked his gaze down to the washcloth in his hand as his nerves shot higher. That nod to privacy was ridiculous. Watching didn't mean interrupting, not when they were in his damned dressing room. He found her face in the mirror and didn't look away.

The pair had pressed their cheeks together, staring at Dima's back. They were stroking with tiny movements that appeared no less powerful for it.

She wrapped her forearms around Paul's neck and crossed her wrists. "Lovely, isn't he?"

Paul didn't answer with words, but he grunted. His ass came up off the chair. Lizzie gasped again, this time louder.

Thank God music from the club pumped through the air, this time a jerky, techno-flavored remix of some '80s song. Only Dima and Paul would be lucky enough to hear her sweet noises.

She licked her lips, visibly trying to put on a front—as if she weren't having sex as she chatted. "It's all those hours of dancing. Dima's a stickler for practice. I thought we'd wear ruts in the floor." The perfect line up the side of her calf dug deep as she pointed her toes and hooked her feet over Paul's knees. For leverage apparently, because she arced back. Her breasts rose, perky and full. "It's given him an amazing body. Those shoulders. That gorgeous back."

Paul spread his fingers wide over Lizzie's ass. If it wasn't for the silky red material of her dress, his fingertips would be digging into the delicate skin between her globes. "How many times?" His voice had gone deeper and huskier, edged with something harsh.

Dima swallowed past the tightness in his chest and flicked the washcloth into the sink. He raked his fingers through his hair, but even pulling didn't alleviate the noise in his head. His greed wasn't going anywhere. His hands. On Lizzie. Her lush body, her mouth, her smile. He'd believed he would possess all of those beautiful things eventually, if he were patient enough.

Maybe not. Yet...this was all bloody surreal.

"How many times what?" She twisted her hips in the same move she used when dancing the rumba.

Dima gritted his teeth.

"How many times have you two slept together?" Paul asked on a groan.

She laughed, but the sound was rough. "Only once. A long time ago. It wasn't that great."

Paul watched Dima in the mirror, his face flushed beneath his sunshine tan, but Dima was tired of being used as some sideline attraction. He bent over to push his legs into a pair of workout pants.

"That ass makes me think I should reconsider," Lizzie said, her words a taunt. "What do you think, Paul? Should I give him another chance?"

The centers of Dima's palms burned. He yanked the track pants over his hips and pulled on a tank top and jacket.

There was no staying away from her for long—his partner

and his friend and the key to so many hopes. He stroked a hand over Lizzie's back as he walked by. She shuddered, her head falling forward to expose the delicate bumps of her spine. Her fingertips tightened across Paul's shoulders. The man's darkly tanned hands climbed her sides until his thumb grazed Dima's finger.

"Have a good time, little one. I'll see you back at the flat."

On a silent moan, her lips opened, still slicked with bright pink gloss. They'd gone at it so fast and dirty that her makeup was barely smudged. "Are you going to be alone?"

A devil took control of his tongue. He couldn't pretend they were the same asexual friends they used to be. Not anymore. If Lizzie wanted his attention, he wanted hers right back.

"No. Jeanne made it more than clear that I had an open invitation." After twining a lock of her shoulder-length hair around his finger, he passed the knuckles of his other hand over Paul's shimmering buzz cut. "Tonight, I'm in the mood for a blonde."

Chapter Three

The door slammed and Lizzie kissed Paul. Hard. A lot harder than what a quick-and-dirty demanded. She'd been perched on the edge of coming for minutes, holding back. Holding her breath. Normally she associated kissing with foreplay, but this was more like stress relief.

Dima's calm sexual smolder had flipped her brain, and Paul continued to surprise her.

He released her ass to take her head between his wide hands. The calluses along his palms roughed her cheeks before he tunneled his fingers into her hair. Mouth open, he plunged deep with his tongue. Their teeth clicked but he didn't stop—not the kissing or the relentless thrust of his hard, controlled body. He found her throat and tucked his face there. Lizzie scraped her nails up and down his back, urging without words.

Breathing hard, he asked, "Could he be listening at the door?"

Holy hell, he wasn't done thinking about it. The surprising show Dima had staged must've done a number on Paul. What was she supposed to do with that? Hell, what was she supposed to do with how Dima's body looked entirely new to her? So sexy. So taut and controlled. She'd never reacted to him that way before—purely visceral and primal and not at all some safe, steady partnership.

Her body knew what to do. Some deep, nasty part of her brain knew.

"I wouldn't put it past him." She inhaled as he shifted their angle. Bang. Right against her G-spot. "We share an apartment.

Taking a partner back there is never entirely...private."

"Is he gay?"

Good God, she was blowing apart.

She found Paul's earlobe and bit down hard enough to make him grunt. "No, cowboy," she whispered. So close. He was as frantic as she, all sweat and slick, wet sounds. "He likes both."

Paul smacked his palms on her ass and grabbed. Lizzie just held on while he pumped her with his huge, hard tool. Her climax hit her in a slow roll, so unlike their quick fuck. She arched her neck and let it take her mind. Aching waves of pleasure burned and shook until it released in the form of a tight scream.

Let Dima hear. She hoped it ruined him for that skinny new girl he'd go tackle.

Paul echoed her satisfaction. A moan rumbled out of his solid chest and burrowed into her blood. They sat there panting. Lizzie hadn't been so lightheaded since those weeks doped up on pain meds.

"This job isn't enough to pay my rent," he said with a breathless laugh. "Apparently it has other benefits."

"I'm not a club perk, cowboy." She climbed off him and smoothed her dress.

"So what was it? A cocktease looking for a little revenge against that guy?"

"A cocktease wouldn't have got you off."

He grinned. "True, that."

Scrubbing his face with his hands, he sprawled there in the chair—knees parted, his erection going back into hiding. At the sick lurch in her stomach, Lizzie couldn't tell if she was proud or disgusted by what she'd just done.

Dima had stood by as she fucked another man. Christ.

That thought jolted her all over again. Lingering images of his lean back rippling with muscle shook her to the core.

She'd wanted him.

After fifteen years...*now* her ridiculous mind wanted him? No matter how hot Paul was, or how great her orgasm had been, or how arousing it was to watch Dima's quiet flirtation with the sunshine cowboy, another surprising thought overwhelmed everything else. She'd wanted Dima to stake his claim. Get angry. Throw things. Yank Paul off her and hurl him out the door.

Nope. He'd played as goddamn stoic as always, even if the ridge of his erection had been obvious in his warm-up pants.

Paul stood and yanked on his jeans while she did her best to fix hair, makeup, underwear. Cooled so quickly, she half-expected him to leave without a word. Instead he shoved on his cowboy hat and caught her around the waist.

Damn, he smelled good. Clean but sweaty, musky. Satisfied male. She let him rub a hand up her torso. That idle petting eased some of her regrets, her confusion.

"Hey." His devilish good-boy smile was too powerful to resist. "I get a feeling this was a one-time thing. On a number of levels. So I'll just say thanks." A tiny frown creased between his brows. "And thank him too, okay? What was his name?"

"Dmitri."

"That's not what you called him."

"His Russian diminutive is Dima. It's like Lizzie is short for Elizabeth."

"Dima. Huh." He nodded rather earnestly, as if storing that information. Fascinating that he was still capable of thought. Her brain was as wiggly as her thighs.

She stroked a finger over his left nipple, where it hid beneath plain white cotton. Those earlier regrets transformed yet again. She hadn't seen him naked. No, she'd been too busy gaping at Dima. Even as she wanted to think of that as a wasted opportunity, she couldn't. Watching Dima strip had been wholly erotic in ways that rattled everything she'd believed about their relationship.

She swallowed. "If it wasn't a one-time thing?"

"You have to ask?" Paul stepped back and bowed slightly as he kissed her knuckles. The move was gallant, but the wicked twist of his lips was just plain dirty. "Beck and call, sugar."

Lizzie fished a business card out of her tiny red clutch. "Here. To make the calling part easier."

He took it and frowned. "You danced together?"

"Me and Dima? Oh, sorry. I thought you realized."

"Hell if I knew what that was," he said with a shrug. "So those three championships of his Fabian mentioned? You too?"

A sharp kick of uncertainty made her clam up. What if she wouldn't ever be that woman again? What if she and Dima never rediscovered the forged-strong steel that had made them champions?

"You should get back. I don't want Declan upset with us."

He mock saluted with the card. "Loud and clear, sugar."

She knew he wasn't talking about Declan's potential ire. She simply didn't feel up to strolling down memory lane with the bartender who'd just wet his dick between her thighs. Paul still smiled. He must find some of this amusing or he would've hightailed it already.

Checking her appearance one last time, she watched him in the mirror as he left Dima's dressing room. What a swagger. All long legs and jeans and an ass she wanted to nibble. Nah, she wanted to bite.

If only it could be that simple.

She glanced over to the wardrobe where Dima had changed

clothes. There'd been a moment when she believed he would actually join them. She inhaled sharply at that astonishing thought. By the absolutely fantastic hard-on he'd mustered while staring at Dima, Paul might not be averse. Watching a naked guy didn't seem to be his regular thing—not that she knew much about him—but that only added an extra layer of incredible novelty.

Although...who would she be sharing? Her new fuck with her long-time partner, or the other way around?

Either way, it didn't feel at all like she'd ever pictured a threesome. Maybe that's because porn always turned it into a match where two guys wrestled over a woman. That wasn't anything close to the pictures her depraved brain insisted on creating.

A way to have them both, have it all...

With a frustrated noise, she grabbed her clutch and headed back out to the club.

She didn't want to kill more time at Devant, not having to dodge Paul's eyes and Declan's questions all night. Neither did she feel like heading back to the apartment. Dima would take that girl Jeanne back there, especially if he was pissed at Lizzie.

As if she could tell when he was pissed. Or happy. Or worried. That he had a dick and the capacity for an erection were about the only signs she had of his reaction to that encounter.

She didn't have anywhere else to go. All of her friends were, well, her competition. They'd continued on without her, with the best of them polite enough to assume she'd be back on the circuit in no time.

Her head pounding, Lizzie waved goodbye to Mr. George. When she stood at the club's threshold, she glanced back. Paul caught her eye from across the packed floor. He touched fingers as if to the brim of a cowboy hat before ducking back to work.

She stepped into the vigor of Chelsea on a Saturday night. Without the patience to wait for a bus, she hailed a taxi. No use delaying the inevitable. She needed to go home and sleep. She needed to talk to Dima, maybe even apologize for the way she'd behaved. Apologizing to him wasn't her favorite thing because he never seemed to care one way or the other. Stoic wasn't strong enough of a word for him. She didn't need Freud to know that probably explained why she baited him with sex. Or spoke the common language in dance. At least then she found something hot and vital beneath his cool, reserved shell.

The taxi sped north into Hell's Kitchen.

Pressing her head against the cool window, she gazed without focus at the bright lights. A gentle rain began to fall, which only refracted the colors to smaller slivers. After paying the driver, she raced out of the car and up the brownstone steps. Key code. Front door. Safe and dry. She trudged up the stairs as if a firing squad awaited her in their living room.

More often than she wanted to admit, she'd lain in bed listening to Dima and his occasional one-night stands get it on. Headboard banging. Girl shrieking. Hell, sometimes it'd been another man—their thrusting rhythm even harder, meaner. Only Dima's moans and grunts of pleasure tempted Lizzie to slide her trembling hand down her panties. She'd stroked herself, circling her clit faster and faster, as their rhythm turned orgasmic.

Always she would lie there in the aftermath of overwhelming release, panting, her mind full to bursting with images she'd believed she would never see in person. Justifications jumped to mind quickly, defensively.

Just like porn.

Could've been anyone.

Only an easy way to get off.

She didn't want him. She didn't want to be the one he

made scream.

No way could she handle it. Something too raw had been scraped open. Considering the little display she'd enacted with Paul, she deserved whatever Dima dished out. That didn't make the prospect any more palatable.

She wanted their old life back. Her career. Her partner. No complications. Just the satisfaction of winning and knowing her place in the world. At the top of the second flight of stairs, she smacked her knee out of spite. The ruined knee.

Making plenty of noise in the lock, she allowed enough time for his date to freak out and grab a blanket, if she turned out to be the modest type. With Lizzie's luck, that girl Jeanne would be the sort of exhibitionist who liked screaming and moaning.

Hands shaking. Breath shallow. Inner thighs tender from straddling Paul. Christ, she was a mess.

The apartment was dark. Quiet. Still.

Relief swished down her spine, leaving her boneless. She could shower, rest and regroup before having to face him again. But the back of her neck prickled. She was reaching out to flip on the floor halogen when his voice pierced the dark.

"Don't."

"Shit, you scared me," she said on a squeak.

"Sorry."

She didn't think he was. Otherwise he wouldn't be sitting on the couch in the dark. Open shades in the dining room let in light from the streetlamps, bathing his bare chest in a golden glow. Her mouth had gone dry. She didn't know what to say or how to say it. Two months back in each other's company and they were still behaving as politely as strangers.

God, I miss you.

She cleared her throat. "I didn't think you'd be alone."

"And I didn't think you'd be home so soon. Wasn't he worth

waiting for the end of his shift?"

Ice clinked in his glass as he sipped. A vodka bottle was open on the coffee table. Since when did he drink hard liquor? He was such a health nut, and his parents' slow descent into the throes of alcoholism had turned him into a near teetotaler.

Lizzie frowned. Maybe he wasn't as closed off as she always thought. The drink in his hands was the equivalent of waving a bright red flag. Maybe he was as lost as she was, but that didn't mean sitting down and having a heart-to-heart. She'd survived fifteen years as his partner because of their common purpose. There wasn't much to interpret when training, traveling and winning were their only goals—well, and keeping each other sane in the process.

Now, however. No goals. No way of getting inside his locked-down thoughts.

She tossed her clutch on the desk, knowing its momentum would mess up his careful stacks of bills and papers. Time to try out her theory. "You should know he was good, Dima. You were listening at the door."

Had Lizzie missed the mark entirely, he would've denied it with a look of indignation. He didn't.

She smiled very, very softly to herself and crossed to the back of the couch. Her heels sounded overly loud on the hardwood. None of this made sense. The terrible, taunting refrain of *mine, mine, mine*—it was back. She couldn't tune it out. Dima Turgenev was her best friend. At the moment, poised on possibilities, she wasn't seeing him as just a partner. She wanted a taste of something more.

She slid her hands over his shoulders and down his naked chest. He was tense. Incredibly tense. His little intake of breath encouraged her more than any words.

"You did," she said. "You listened at the door of your own dressing room." His taut stomach muscles bunched beneath her fingertips. "I wonder if you could hear him come over the music."

He swallowed. "No."

"Such a gorgeous low groan," she whispered against his neck. "But I'm sure you heard me."

Another swallow. His heart thundered beneath her palms, which only stoked the fizzle and pop in her blood. Oh, this was not good. *Really* not good. Because the concept of coming on to two men in the same evening—one of them the partner who rarely merited a second look—should've been repulsive. Trampy. Maybe even desperate, knowing she was only trying to prove herself after her injury.

Instead she felt powerful and so sexy. She would've traded every second with Paul had the choice been between riding that hot cowboy and stroking the firm, graceful muscles of Dima's chest. *Since when?*

"I heard you, little one."

"And?"

"And...I'm glad he satisfied you."

Lizzie stood abruptly. Leave it to him to kill the moment. When he danced, he could convey any emotion, *every* emotion— from playful to outright panty-wet sexy. He was as much a talented actor as he was an amazing dancer.

Offstage, he had the reserve of a sealed bank vault. Again she wanted him to break loose. Shout and cuss and call her names and *claim her.* Anything other than the torture of being ignored. Was this why he'd been so quietly pissed at her for not coming to see him perform at Devant? *Damn.* Her fears aside, she should've been there for him.

"Never mind." She turned toward her bedroom.

Dima grabbed her wrist and kissed the tender skin inside. "Me, though? Not satisfied at all."

The rhythm of her heart stuttered. "Oh?"

He dragged her arm down his body, slowly, giving her every chance to withdraw. She wound up bent over the back of the couch, her breasts pressed against his nape, her arms stretched down his lean torso. With their fingers twined, he settled her palm over his cock.

Rock hard.

She fought to speak, knowing the volume would be all off. The rush of blood in her ears was just too strong. "What about Jeanne?"

With a move more suited to the dance floor, he grasped beneath her arms and pulled her over the back of the couch. Lizzie found herself lying on her back, stretched flat across his lap, with his thighs arching her spine. Dima, the man she'd known since he was a preadolescent kid fresh over from Moscow, stared down at her with the intensity he only revealed on stage.

When the stakes were their highest.

"Don't you know, little one? She was the wrong blonde."

Chapter Four

Dima had stretched Lizzie across his knees plenty of times. Hell, he'd flipped her upside down, put his face between her thighs, even smacked her ass, all in the name of good choreography. Like any red-blooded man, he'd noticed her body, especially as they'd both matured. He wasn't dead.

Just the opposite. He was coming alive.

After breaking up with Svetlana six months earlier, and as Lizzie's sexual teasing intensified, he'd had trouble keeping his desires in check. He couldn't help looking at her differently. New fantasies. Darker needs. He wanted to lick her, just to see if her skin tasted as sweet as it was smooth. Yet none of those daydreams held the suspended power of this moment.

Her stomach was a flat plane as she arched back over his thighs. The sleek red dress clung to the tempting swells of her breasts. The skirt hadn't been long to begin with. Now it barely covered the apex of her toned thighs.

Considering the state of her panties the last time Dima had seen them, she might not even be wearing any.

The hot rush of his blood in his ears almost drowned out her raspy, panting breaths. He spread his hand wide over her stomach. When his pinkie grazed the hard thrust of her ribs, his thumb slid into a delectable dip. Her pussy was only a few inches lower. So close.

Christ, how could he be so close? This couldn't be happening.

Beneath his gaze, however, his little one was waiting for him. She watched him with the sort of anticipation that burned in her eyes when they slayed the competition. Fierce. Greedy. Eager.

Keeping a steadying hand on her stomach, he leaned forward to set his empty vodka glass on the coffee table. He didn't drink often. Experience with his parents—too much alcohol and too few goals—had left him wary of the poison.

The evening's events had demanded a little release.

Now... Now he held Lizzie. Nothing would ever be more intoxicating.

He bent his body to hers, pressing his hard-as-hell cock against her side. She didn't move. Just waited. He'd never known her to be a font of patience, but in this, for this moment, she'd found plenty. He couldn't help but hope that held weight. Import.

She'd come to rest with her arms over her head, as if posed. In the dim light, her lips were little more than gleams. He traced the shine of her mouth with his thumb. So small and delicate. So easily hurt, no matter her toughness and determination. The power she burned through, whipping through life, always belied her size. She came off seeming bigger. Taller. More powerful. In reality, she was fragile. Beneath the rough push of his thumb, the flesh of her lower lip was tender.

And her knee.

That sickly twist when his grip had slipped.

Lizzie always pulled herself up from bad bumps and missed lifts, but not from that one. She was, in truth, surprisingly breakable—especially under his hands. Yet he didn't have it in him to pass up the chance to have her. He'd been waiting too long, riding on nothing but tenuous hope.

Her tongue snuck a quick lick at the pad of his thumb. The wet heat seared his skin and snapped him back to their dim living room. His thoughts flew away like a murder of crows, dark and cawing.

"You live to tease me, little one." His voice was rougher beneath the tense weight in his chest.

"Hmm," she purred in her throat. Her smile deepened. "Never noticed that before."

"What is it?"

"Your accent. It's thicker. Like before a competition."

"This is surprising to you?"

"Surprising, no. But I like it." She stretched her arms overhead. "Staid, stoic Dima. Nothing ever affects you."

Plenty affected him. All his tidy strategies, his silent ambitions. Too much to explain. Every fraction of his future included her. Moving on without her was like contemplating chopping off his feet. If she couldn't agree with his plans for Devant, he'd just come up with another. And another. Until recently, however, she hadn't offered any hint of sharing those crazy hopes. She hadn't even come to see him dance. Until that night. When she'd pushed him to the edge of sanity and his cold, deep control by riding some Texan stranger.

No, better to keep the impossible locked away until Dima could get it right. Make sure everything worked out.

She was motionless, watching him, as if waiting for him to make his decision. That decision was easy—so easy, when touching her was possible.

He hardly knew where to start. So much beauty and temptation. Every inch of her deserved his full attention. He'd even crawl inside her brain and start over again, from the inside out. The day he actually figured out what was in that head of hers, he'd retire from dancing and become a guru on women. None could be more complicated than his Lizzie. None could be more perfect.

"You believe nothing affects me? Let me correct you." He

tucked his fingertip behind her ear, into the delicate divot there, where her skin was tissue thin. "Seeing you riding Paul... 'Affected' is hardly the word."

"You could have said something. Done something. Kissed me."

"I did, remember?" He touched two fingers to the exact spot where he had kissed her, right on her forehead. "Just like I always do when saying good night."

"You could have stayed," she said, the words nearly a whisper.

"And wank in the corner while you played with your new toy? No, thank you."

"I would've liked to watch you."

Dima dipped his chin and inhaled. Emotion and control and need churned until he couldn't think straight. She was twisting him into knots. "I can smell him on you," he finally said.

The sugared scent of luxurious bath products, that was Lizzie. She could spend longer in the shower than any person he'd ever known. Tonight, cloaked in the smells of a nightclub and sex, an element of spice clung to her sleek skin.

He bowed over her, keeping one hand at her waist. She couldn't go anywhere. If she tried, he might turn into some feral version of himself, all teeth and growls and furious possessiveness. Holy mother, his world was narrowing to nothing but her. He flattened his other hand on the arm of the couch. The deep breath he dragged into his lungs was scented with both Lizzie and Paul—so heady and strong that he groaned.

"You don't seem to mind," she said.

"I find I don't."

She arched her spine, pushing her breasts higher. He

trailed his index finger along her collarbone, down to the thin material between her tits. The satin of the dress was nothing compared to her skin.

"I'm not surprised his scent's on me." Her eyes drifted to dark slits and she smiled, sweet and sly. "He was all over me. In me."

Dima's breath quickened. He'd be furious if she tried to leave, but hearing her describe her encounter with the tall, rough bartender was unbelievable foreplay. He couldn't have explained it had he possessed his entire mind. Which he didn't.

He stroked down her waist, over her hip. He'd gripped her hips thousands of times. Never like this. Never had his heart hopped up to dance in his throat. So many things he'd like to do with her. To her.

Such a huge leap.

If things went bad...

Losing his best friend would shake his life to its foundation, but he might be on the cusp of losing her anyway. He wanted Devant and the freedom of new challenges. She wanted back on the same tired circuit, as if nothing had changed. Should he lose his Lizzie, he'd rather it be because they went out as champions—both on and off stage. If he was going to hell, he might as well get there running.

Moss-green eyes drifted shut as her body relaxed over his lap. The slope of her shoulders slumped deeper into the cushions as her knees loosened, as if she'd let him do absolutely anything. "Would you rather I don't talk about him?"

"No," he ground out. "Because it doesn't matter. He's not here."

He cupped her hot pussy with his entire hand. His palm centered over the damp scratch of her lace panties.

Her quiet "Oh" went straight to his cock.

"How well did he fill you, little one?"

She gave a contented hum. "So well, Dima. He was big. Very."

His chest clenched. Envy and excitement. Barely controlled. Rather than needing to squash a bubble of jealousy, his arousal jumped. His mind was a mess of confusion, but his body craved more of that gorgeous depravity.

With one flick of his wrist, he tossed her skirt up to pool over her stomach. The black of her panties was an enticing contrast to her strong, pale thighs. He traced a feather-light touch from her navel to the crease between her damp lips. Wetness. Heat. Exactly what he desired.

"Your scream..." He repeated the deliberate touch, pushing a little deeper this time. He was fairly sure her pussy was bare—one of the few tiny mysteries she'd kept lately. Be damned, he was so close to finding out, his hands shook. "Do you always scream like that?"

"Not every time."

She shook her head, which spread her luminous hair against the couch cushion. The gold gleamed. He'd always thought her pretty, even beautiful, but when she'd arrived from her parents' house with bright blonde hair, not her usual dark brown or raven black, something had tripped over inside him. It was like meeting a whole new woman.

"Only when it's good," she whispered. Her voice was quiet but not weak. That constant tingle of teasing made her stronger than she knew. "Only when I come so hard, it's like I lose myself."

That was a challenge if he'd ever heard one. He knew the steps, knew what he wanted to achieve, knew where his body needed to be. At that moment, he needed to taste her pussy more than he needed to keep dancing.

Dima stripped her panties. She let them go willingly,

twisting her hips and laughing a little when he yanked them past her high heels.

Luscious. A tiny track of carefully trimmed hair arrowed down to his prize, one greater than three world championships. Light from the street gleamed off her damp lips. He tucked the panties into the pocket of his track pants. He'd keep those. The scrap of lace could retire in good grace.

"Come on, Dima. You know you want to." Lizzie's hand burrowed deep in his hair.

The intimate touch was something he'd missed. When they were younger, they'd never thought anything of touching. Their entire livelihood depended on physical contact. Even on tour, they leaned on one another. Sometimes literally, like the time they'd fallen asleep in full costume, propped against the corridor wall leading from the dressing rooms to the dance floor, exhausted and waiting to go on.

During the last six months, the space between them was a gulf, absent of touch. He missed it as much as he missed everything about her.

He shook free of that painful lack. "Want to...?"

"Lick me. Right where Paul's huge cock fucked me."

His low growl came without warning. She pushed him and pushed him. Always. Again.

Until he snapped.

He locked his hand around her wrist, pinned her arm above her head. "You're not in charge here, little one. Don't make that mistake."

"No?" Her hips rose off his lap, but he held her still. "It didn't feel like it earlier, when I straddled Paul right in front of you. I haven't felt that kind of rush since we took home our last trophy."

"That was then." He pressed her wrist more firmly against

the padded armrest. "Now, I'm about to make you come so hard that I hear your scream without a door between us."

"Do you promise?"

"I do."

If it took everything in him, hours of attention, he'd wring a scream from that beautiful mouth. It was everything he wanted, to inhale her satisfaction like the air he breathed.

Her grin wavered. Not so bright. More...confused. "You've never broken a promise to me."

"I'm not about to start. Open for me, little one."

She parted her knees so that one brushed the back of the couch. Her wet lips bloomed open. Dima shuddered in tense anticipation. He delved a finger between them before tasting. Her essence exploded across his tongue in a burst of sweetness and spice.

Wrapping his hands around her hips, he boosted Lizzie off his lap and pushed her up. Either surprise or long reflex kept her rigid, as if preparing for a lift. He positioned her just as he wished: half-sitting against the arm of the couch. He grabbed her knees and tugged. Her hips angled toward him. The swish of her skirt dropped back between her legs, but he flicked it away.

Dima settled on his stomach, stretched along the couch. The upholstered softness offered no satisfaction when he pulsed his hard cock. Not enough resistance. Soon, but later.

He didn't start with small licks to warm them up. No point. That wasn't what they wanted. Instead, he claimed her. All taking. All demanding. Lizzie arched deeper and cried out. He locked his mouth over her dripping cunt, drank her deep, delved his tongue into her mysterious secrets. He would make those secrets his.

At first the acrid tang of latex masked her true taste. It only took a few laving moves before a different, sweeter flavor emerged. Lizzie, soft and true. All for him. He licked her clit until he found a rhythm that made her squeal and writhe.

"Harder, God. Please."

Although he sank two fingers into her sheath, he kept his movements slow. He didn't give her the pressure she needed and even pulled back until she whimpered. After one more slow lick, he lifted his mouth.

"Who am I?"

The question roiled up from some dark place—the place that demanded more than the thrill of sex. Claiming her body wasn't enough when that would fade with the last pulses of her release. After all, Paul had done that much. Dima was her partner and he would take what was his.

She tugged on his hair, trying to get his mouth back where she wanted it. "Please..."

But he wouldn't be distracted. Not yet.

"Tell me who you're with, Lizzie. Tell me who's licking your cunt."

Chapter Five

She'd thought his nickname was silly when they first met. Her thirteen-year-old laughter and reflexive, "It sounds like a girl's name," hadn't been well received. He'd maintained an indifferent snit for their whole first week of practice. Not the most auspicious beginning. Since then, she'd probably said his name a couple dozen times a day. It chimed more often in her head, as she assessed the world through his gaze and layered it over her own.

As Lizzie answered his question, she felt as if she'd never shaped its sound before. "You, Dima. You're licking my cunt." She couldn't help her pout. "Or, you were. Do continue."

He stared at her with those gorgeous, molten chocolate eyes, so soulful and perceptive. "When we dance, who leads and who follows?"

"What?"

The two fingers in her pussy shoved deeper. A sudden burst of sensation grabbed her breath, although he gave her nothing harder—nothing like the rough release she needed to blow away all this confusion.

"You heard me, Lizzie."

"You lead and I follow."

"All the time?"

She swallowed. "Sometimes I try to lead."

"When you do, what happens?"

A humiliating reminder of their first junior pairs competition was not what she'd had in mind. Skirt up. Fingers in. Tongue at work. She should've come by now. He never let things just *happen*.

At that first junior pairs competition, only three months along in their young partnership, she hadn't trusted him. She'd tried to lead. Each turn, each grip, each step went wrong. Everyone had been disappointed, including their coach and both sets of parents.

None of that had mattered. One look at Dima's blasted, exhausted face and she'd regretted her behavior. All of his disappointments had shown so clearly for the first time—the feelings he kept tucked inside a mind that had barely learned enough English to order a cheeseburger. Even so, those feelings had only slipped free for a moment before he closed off his expression and walked to the dressing room.

And their single sexual encounter. God, what a train wreck. He hadn't been a virgin, but Lizzie had outranked him when it came to experience. No surprise there. Her teen years had been a series of mistakes even more ridiculous than jumping Paul. So when it came to a drunken, groping fumble that progressed to actual intercourse, she'd taken the lead, working his cock so hard and so eagerly, she'd practically guaranteed a thirty-second fuck. She still couldn't tell what was worse—her embarrassment and disappointment, or knowing she'd made him feel the same way.

Since those hard lessons, trusting Dima had become her whole world. Their magic only happened when he led. They drove each other like cruel taskmasters during rehearsals, pushing to perfection, sharing ideas and fighting and making their union stronger because of that no-holds-barred exchange.

When the lights hit the stage, however, and their bodies found one another, he was in charge.

Too bad it couldn't fall into place like that once the spotlight dimmed. How could she ever trust her future to a man who never opened up? Especially when so much between them remained uncertain? His deep, contemplative silences would be the end of her.

He crooked his two fingers, earning her tight groan.

"Bad things happen," she answered at last.

"Always so hard on yourself."

His grin was soft, nearly apologetic. Such lovely lips, firm and wide. She wanted to kiss the slight cleft in his chin and keep kissing until she learned every inch, every texture.

"Let's just say," he whispered, "that things don't turn out as well as they could." Leaning nearer, he dragged his tongue along the inside of her thigh. His fingers pulsed up and in. She shuddered as he rubbed her G-spot, rocketing her back to that high, hot arousal. "I'm asking you to trust me, little one."

"Dima?"

With a groan, he dropped his forehead to her stomach. "What now?"

"I don't..."

This was harder than she would've guessed. No, that wasn't true. Talking to her partner about the man she'd just screwed *should* be hard. She simply didn't like that she'd crammed herself into such a dumb-shit predicament. Ideally, she wouldn't have needed sex with a stranger to bait the lover she really wanted.

Oh, no. Can't go there.

She inhaled deeply. "I don't want to spend the rest of the night lying in bed, comparing you and Paul."

"Would you?"

"I think so. I've never done this before. Two guys. One night. Hell, you know that."

"I don't know anything of the kind."

Her face flamed. "Well, I haven't."

He nodded soberly, eyes still intently focused. "Fine."

Apparently making some sort of decision—not that he'd ever tell her in advance—he scooted off the couch and helped her to the floor. He propped a throw cushion under her head, urging her without words to lie flat on the hardwood.

The nervous tension in her belly wouldn't calm. This had all the potential for a cosmic, flaming disaster. To have sex with Dima—again, now that they were grown—would change everything. What did she have to lose? She couldn't dance with him, not yet. Every day that he left for the club was another day he slipped out of reach. She'd grabbed his attention with Paul, and had every intention of keeping it. Entirely.

He wore the furrowed expression his features assumed when soaking up new choreography. There was no one better. No one.

She touched his cheek. "I trust you," she whispered.

Easier said than done. Whatever she'd expected fizzled away as he stood and stripped. Clean, efficient movements. She'd seen him change clothes more times than she could recall. Something had clicked off years earlier, so she'd no longer viewed him as a man to be admired, let alone to be lusted after.

Yet she hadn't been putting on an act when goading Paul. Dima had an extraordinary body. Built through countless hours of practice, yoga and a strict regime of healthy foods, he could've been a model in anatomy classes. Every muscle defined. Every stretch of sinew precise, as if masculine grace could be drawn with lines of flesh, bone and skin.

And his cock. Good Lord, he was beautiful even there. Proud and firm, just like his stance. Even a little bit arrogant. Why shouldn't he be?

Mine.

Lizzie licked her lips. He made her dizzy in ways she'd

never thought possible. Not from Dima.

He knelt and straddled her body, facing her feet. The heart-stopping view of his back was illuminated by light angling through the far window. She watched, transfixed, as he levered down her body into a classic 69 position.

Oh God.

Her guts lurched on another hard rush.

Dima propped his weight on his elbows and knees. Before he dipped to taste her once again, he breathed against her inner thigh. "Suck me, little one," he whispered there. "I want you to taste me too."

Inside her, something tight and scared broke free. All the preparation fell away. All the nerves. Never once had she backed away from a challenge, especially not one that stood to produce a fantastic reward.

She drew her fingertips up Dima's stomach, tracing each glorious ridge of muscle as it jumped beneath her touch. Another heady rush of power. Of need.

His mouth closed over her pussy just as she reached for his cock. Heat shot over her nerves like a bomb going off. She grabbed his thick, hard flesh in both hands, grounding herself in the buck of his hips. They would drive each other mad, and they'd do it together.

The head of his prick was swollen and so smooth. She licked until that tender skin was slippery. No friction when she took him into her mouth. Dima's low groan reverberated against her clit. That slight sensation was nothing compared to the quick pulse of his tongue. With a strong grip, he arched her pelvis, opening her more fully to his attention.

Lizzie bent her knees and planted her feet. The dampness along her soles stuck to the cool hardwood. She reached around his hips and grabbed his ass, just as he did hers. Firm muscle clenched beneath her palms as he gently thrust. Melting into the pillow, she let the sinful pleasure ease away the last of her tension.

Her jaw relaxed. She opened fully.

Dima sank his cock all the way to the back of her throat.

Christ, he was big. She tongued every lovely ridge along his shaft, in and out, as he fucked her mouth—and fucked her with his mouth. His tongue was more aggressive now, pulsing and flicking at her electric nerves. He used long fingers to open her folds even wider.

Lizzie sucked on the tip of his cock. Sucked hard. His ass tensed beneath her hands, trying to find that pulse again. She absorbed the sweetness of knowing she could make his body beg with just the hard pressure of her lips. Then she opened again, letting him in deep. He drove down. That sudden feeling of being trapped beneath his thrust jacked her arousal. She raised her hips, seeking an end to the sweet agony that built and built.

So good. She'd never imagined...

He lifted his mouth and bit the inside of her thigh. Just a nibble at first, followed by more pressure. A long, slow bite made her squeal, but that sound was muffled by his thrust. On the next withdrawal, Lizzie let him slide out. His teeth tightened, maybe as punishment. Her nerves bellowed a protest, while her pussy slicked with wetness.

She sucked her fingers instead of his dick, liberally coating her skin with saliva. That done, she let him back in. The satisfaction of being taken was so much stronger in that position. No way to disconnect. Mind and body joined until all she knew and all she thought was need. Dima needed to come and so did she.

With her wet forefingers, she found the pucker of his anus. He was tight but not unwelcoming as she slid inside. He moaned, hips tensing. The falter in his rhythm—from a man who could tap a steady beat in his sleep—was a victory. Lizzie pushed even farther, a gentle in-and-out to counter his gathering frenzy.

He was close. His precome was salty and sharp as she lapped it away. His respiration matched hers. Nearly frantic. She breathed through her nose as he found his rhythm, paired it with the beat of his tongue on her clit. Two fingers, maybe three, slipped inside her pussy. They were in each other, around, entwined, connected at such an intimate level, where all she knew was his sound and feel and taste. Even the air she dragged into her lungs was touched by his musk, his sweat.

Dima rubbed his chin against her inner folds. The sharpness of his evening stubble was nearly pain, but he kept with it, abrading that slick, tender skin, until Lizzie squirmed. Rough hands clutched her hips and kept her immobilized. No number of struggles bucked his fierce hold.

The scratch of his stubble triggered a hot, long-buried memory. It was the first time she'd seen Dima shave. Maybe nineteen at the time, he'd come home from some one-night stand, when they shared their first apartment in Soho—a shitty dive that always smelled of rotten apples. She'd stood in the doorway of the bathroom, berating him for making them both late for practice. Calmly, still wearing that cat-in-the-cream smirk, he'd shaved, never arguing back.

She'd been struck by the urge to be his again. Just one more time. One *good* time. To be the sort of lover who could shape his satisfied smile in the mirror as he shaved. Their one attempt at mixing professional demands with personal desires had been so mortifying that she'd turned away, leaving him alone in the bathroom.

He found her clit once more, trapping her with a gentle vise of teeth. Tongue, over and over. She pulsed her finger in time as his cock hit the back of her throat, stretching her, demanding that she take more.

She was that woman now. He wouldn't be able to look at himself in the morning without remembering how he'd claimed so much, how she'd claimed so very much in return.

Since she'd walked in the door, fire had been building. Now it swept over her in a flash, like fall kindling struck by a spark. Her orgasm slammed up from where he sucked and nipped. She screamed, just as he'd wanted. Just as she'd wanted to. That harsh sound caught around a mouthful of cock. He ground his face against her pussy as she shattered and quaked. The beat of his pelvis faltered. A full-body shudder was her only warning as come filled her mouth.

Lizzie swallowed and swallowed again. She took all that he had and made it a part of herself. She couldn't remember the last time she'd done that. Rarely was anyone worth such a special concession. With Dima, it was nearly as satisfying as her climax. He'd lost control, and she drank her reward with greedy gulps.

Her thighs shook as he slowly licked and eased her back down to earth. Cock, fingers, tongues—all slipped free of where they'd been joined. Dima rolled to one side, with his back to the couch. He flung an arm over his eyes, chest heaving. Lizzie worked her stiff jaw back and forth as she looked up at the ceiling striped by the streetlamps.

"It wasn't as loud," he said, his voice gravelly and very, very Russian. "I liked that scream much better."

The compliment made her shiver, just before her confusion returned. Had to happen. The part where it would be over. The part where her mind would slam back into place.

"Dima—"

"Trust me, remember?"

Before Lizzie could protest, he sat up. His stomach muscles rippled and bunched in a way that left her dizzy all over again. He knelt, gathered her into his impossibly strong arms and urged her to stand. She didn't want to move and certainly didn't have the strength to. Lying there meant not needing to sort through the bizarre evening, nor having to face the consequences.

"Trust," he said against her temple.

He lifted her, as he'd done literally thousands of times. This was no competition lift, with practiced handholds, momentum and the mutual goal of hitting the next beat. This was simply his raw strength pulling her up and close. He was slick with sweat, and even that familiarity was charged with a new intimacy. They'd made each other sweat for years.

Never like this.

He crossed their apartment and into Lizzie's bedroom. A few moments later she found herself snuggled under the blankets. She should say...*something.*

Thank you?

That was great?

Stay with me tonight?

She huddled more deeply beneath the covers and said nothing. It was as if his unexpected tenderness—the man she knew, but in the guise of a new lover she'd just explored—had robbed her of thought.

"*Spokojnoj nochi,* little one."

Good night, she thought in return. Dima, however, had already slipped away.

Chapter Six

Dima used a paring knife to chop and slice herbs for an omelet. That done, he rinsed the blade and proceeded to cut the fruit, but the steady thwack of blade couldn't dim his tension. By the time Lizzie deigned to wake up, he had mounded a too-large pile of diced strawberries at the end of the cutting board.

He was still lost in his own head. In the memories. In the still-wants that plagued him.

She walked out of her bedroom, hair tousled and falling over her face. Scrubbing a palm across sleepy eyes lifted the hem of her oversized Rangers T-shirt. She was a huge hockey fan, to the point of frustration if being on tour meant missing a game. The sport had been one of their early connections, when he'd been new to the US and confounded by its many differences. Hurling English and Russian obscenities across the ice had cemented their friendship outside of the rehearsal room.

Underneath the shirt, she wore only a pair of dark red tap pants. He'd admired the differences in her body last night. Six months ago, she had been competition skinny. Women on the circuit were sticklers about their weight, while trying to maintain the muscle tone required for the grueling demands of dance. Those whose figures more resembled Lizzie's petite, ripe curves worked even harder to stay thin.

During physical therapy, she had gained something like ten pounds of muscle. She'd been powerful beneath his hands and there, in the light of morning with that shirt lifted to a tempting height, she *looked* it. As lush as ever, but with more shapely muscles.

This glance reminded him that she'd worn pajama pants around the house since her return, practically hiding from him.

She wasn't hiding from him anymore.

Those dark red tap pants snugged against the dip of her pussy. The same pussy he'd licked last night. She'd sucked his cock deeper than anyone ever had, man or woman.

He'd needed more, no matter that his orgasm had left him floating and dazed. No denying that. Only Lizzie's hesitation—not wanting to compare him and Paul—had been his stop sign. His dreams had been filled with Lizzie and Paul, both of them twined together. They were inexplicable fantasies, considering how many of his desires started and ended with her. If Paul was going to be involved, he would be on Dima's terms.

"Are you hungry?" He split the egg-white omelet in half, dumped it on two plates and set it on the counter island. The strawberries went in a small bowl with a hefty spoonful of nonfat vanilla Greek yogurt.

She rubbed the back of her hand across her mouth and eyed him warily. If she was worrying he was going to make a scene, she could relax. Every movement said she wanted to keep it light.

Fine with him. For the moment. She had a tendency to bolt, one way or the other. Fast decisions. Quick impulses. If he wanted Lizzie Maynes, and holy Christ he did, he would need to take it a hell of a lot slower than laying her down for another mind-blowing 69. He'd learned a long time ago that she couldn't be forced into anything. Carrying her to bed had been one of the most difficult things he'd done in a long time, but it had been the right thing. If Dima pushed too far, she'd scramble.

Which direction would he push? Where they were headed seemed dark and murky. The last thing he wanted to do was share unformed plans—just hasty desires, really—only to have them fall through.

No, that wasn't right. The last thing he wanted was to lose this woman.

"I could eat," she finally said. With a couple twists and a spin, she braided gold hair out of her face. Not once did she look him in the eyes. She slid onto the barstool and picked up a fork. "I don't think I've ever said, but I missed your cooking when I was gone. I got tired of the salads."

"*Spasibo.*"

He thanked her because her praise was at least *something* in the middle of such an uncomfortable morning.

Could've meant anything, though. Her mom didn't cook. Ballerinas were a whole other breed of dancer. In order to maintain her figure after retirement, the woman pretty much only ate lettuce. She judged Lizzie rather too harshly for having any appetite. Dima only smiled as she savored the ham-and-herb omelet. He liked her appetites. All of them. Especially the ferocious way she'd outright appreciated the feel of his dick pulsing down her throat. Every moan still reverberated through his body like a caress.

Dark thoughts flooded in behind the flash of visceral memory. Had any other woman been stretched out beneath him last night, his morning would be entirely different. He'd have kissed Lizzie immediately, for one thing. None of this dancing around, and none of this wondering whether he should even give his customary greeting.

Screw it. He'd be no lesser version of himself. Having her meant keeping what he valued in their relationship.

He tilted her face up. Her forehead was cool beneath his lips, and he lingered longer than he ever had. "I didn't say good morning. *Dobroe utro*, little one."

Her throat worked over a swallow. The fork clattered against the side of the plate. Eyes lit by streamers of sunlight met his. For once, he couldn't read a damn thing. Pleased, regretful, confused—she could've felt anything. Or everything. He could relate.

"Morning," she whispered.

"Did you sleep well?"

He sat beside her. Keeping calm as he dished fruit onto his plate was difficult. He wanted to paint patterns on her skin with the yogurt and use his tongue to lick her clean.

She pushed a bite of egg around her plate. "Fine."

"What are your plans for the day?"

"I've got a physical therapy appointment this afternoon. Nothing in the morning. Why?"

He leaned an elbow on the counter and turned to frame her within his open knees. Being so near without touching her should have been normal. Without choreography to follow, they generally maintained a friendly yet familiar distance.

Generally.

Sometimes they'd indulged in more intimate contact out of necessity. Touchstones. Competition did funny things to a brain. He couldn't imagine how solo athletes managed. Even if Dima couldn't reveal many of his thoughts, he'd always had that special woman beside him to share each experience— bitching about the judges and being disappointed by small crowds. That meant having the best partner in the world to share in joint triumphs. That meant feeling free to steady both their nerves by touching her lower back just before the opening four-count. And that meant morning kisses and kisses for luck.

After having tasted her, and after having accepted and returned more eager, demanding kisses, he couldn't help but want more.

"Come to practice with me this morning."

She turned away with a little huff of annoyance. "So I can watch you spin Jeanne around the room while I sit in the corner?" The look she shot from the corner of her eyes was as sly as anything he'd ever seen. And Russians knew sly. "What did you say to sitting in the corner while I was busy with Paul? No, thank you?"

She twirled her index finger through hair that looked like spun sugar. Fine and silken and so golden pale. He loved it, especially unbound. She'd complained endlessly at having to slick it down with five types of product for competitions and exhibitions. Silently, he'd hated it too.

"So. Moping around the flat, this is a better idea?"

She stabbed a strawberry. Her mouth bent upside down with her pout. He had the overwhelming urge to take her lower lip between his teeth. "I'm not moping."

"I've never known you to back down from a challenge, little one. I hope this isn't a sign of the future."

Inadvertently voicing one of his deepest fears, that she really was a different woman—less certain, less optimistic— made him face his own plate of food.

"There's no challenge in watching you practice."

"It's Jeanne's bachata. Unacceptably messy. I was hoping you could show her how to sharpen it up."

The idea visibly caught hold behind her eyes. She lit up from within. She wanted to go. Maybe she always had. The right excuse was all she needed.

"Fine," she said, ladling put-upon affectation thick. "I'll go if you need me to."

"I do."

She rubbed her temples. "I'm sorry."

Sorry? Shit. For what? Dima couldn't process the possibilities fast enough. They just hit him up and down his ribs.

"Oh?"

"I should've come see you dance weeks ago. I think...I think I hurt you by refusing. I'm sorry." A hesitant pause. "Though I don't regret what I did with Paul, I should've stayed for the whole performance."

He blinked and breathed and faltered. Back teeth clenched, he pushed his plate aside. The topic was so damn thorny he couldn't weave through. So he focused on the craft they'd shared for a decade and a half. "What did you think of it?"

He said it casually, but her opinion was all he'd wanted. It was nearly as important as her apology. Nearly enough to ease the strange feelings of jealousy and desire when he thought of her with Paul.

"It was different, of course." She offered a shy smile. Lizzie could be shy? "Frankly, I didn't know your body could do that. It was a surprise. And it was..." A furious blush wrapped around her cheekbones. He liked it. The color and the fact that his body had made an impression. Maybe she'd finally seen him as a man. "It was sexy as hell."

"You need to come to Devant today." His own smile felt lighter. "There's plenty more."

The words hung between them. Promise? Come-on? He was losing track of every innuendo. Speaking his mind wasn't a habit he'd ever cultivated.

She broke the silence with a nod. "I'll go get changed."

Two hours later, Dima admired her ass as she sashayed up the back stairwell of Club Devant. The woman's curves just wouldn't quit—and when she was a little annoyed, she poured attitude into her twitch.

Dima managed to control his amusement and his desire before they reached the practice room. He needed to. More rode on the next few moments than he wanted to consider.

The appeal of professional competitions had faded for him about a year ago. Nothing left to sink his teeth into, and no way for him or Lizzie to grow. The permitted choreography had become stifling. Always, they'd received the same backhanded criticisms, even as they won championship after championship. Too theatrical. Too sexual. Apparently certain judges believed there was such a thing as too much connection. What else was Latin dance if it didn't celebrate chemistry? Competition favored precision over sexuality. Such a farce.

Hanging on to that life would've left him a burned-out husk, one of the pathetic old men who sat on the sidelines and made eyes at the new crop of young dancers. His father had been such a man at every single one of Dima's junior competitions. If evolving would keep him from falling into a bottle of vodka, Dima wanted that opportunity.

He needed to make her see that Club Devant was just such an opportunity. That relatively small stage provided enough of an audience to give both of them the performance rush they craved. But first, even before that hurdle, he had to get her dancing again. Practice was the only place to start.

Remy Lomand sprawled in the middle of the hardwood floor, legs spread wide as he stretched. At night and for performances, he spiked his wide, dark Mohawk, but the bright fluorescents of the rehearsal room shone off an unruly mess. The guy looked like he'd rolled out of bed before grabbing the nearest pair of loose-fitting jeans. Not unappealing in the least.

However, the man was trouble. Brilliant, but trouble.

"Ah, you've arrived." Remy's accent slithered with deep Louisiana Cajun.

"With a guest. Lizzie, have you met Remy Lomand?"

"In passing."

Remy hopped to his feet. "If all your guests will be as beautiful, I insist you bring a new one every week."

Lizzie grinned. She held out both hands and let the Cajun take them in his. "Weekly? Do you go through women so quickly?"

"On good weeks, even faster."

Dima didn't like seeing Remy holding on to his partner. The sharp spike that lanced up the back of his head came from sudden, pinching tension. Why now? Why not when she'd straddled Paul in his dressing room? How was he supposed to make firm plans if he couldn't trust his unconscious reactions?

The door opened behind him and Jeanne appeared. Side by side, Dima regretted teasing Lizzie with a comparison. Too many sharp edges, too narrow through the face, Jeanne could never compare to Lizzie—or Paul, for that matter. Dima would take either of them over the slightly space-case dancer any time.

The smirking expression on Lizzie's face said she knew exactly what he was thinking. Her gaze dropped to his dick, and she licked her lips.

Jesus. She'd swallowed him—his whole shaft and his come. Every measured lick had driven him higher and farther.

It wasn't enough.

He would have her. All of her. He'd made up his mind. Now it was a matter of convincing her. Grasping her tight ass and levering her up against a mirrored wall probably wouldn't be the best measure of persuasion. Patience. Goddamn fucking *patience.*

To string his tension even tighter, practice took forever. All because of his gorgeous tormentor. She'd staked a place to watch by the door. Kicking her feet up on the bench was a nicely crafted measure of *can't give a shit*, but with regard to dance, he knew her. The way she tracked their every movement gave her away. Slender fingers twitched to the beat pumping through the sound system. Once in a while, her toes counted out steps along the wood. Totally unconscious. She'd never been able to resist rhythm.

"No. No, no, *non*." Remy's voice cut through Dima's haze. "It's got to be lower. Meaner. Here, Lizzie, help me show her."

Jeanne shoved sweaty blonde hair back from her forehead, retied her ponytail and stood with her hands on her hips. "Come on, Remy. She hasn't done the choreo."

"Oh, no way," Lizzie protested. She flicked her fingers at them. "Off with you. I have to baby my knee. I can't do it."

"You're five months off from your last surgery. Your knee's perfectly fine." Remy's grin flashed white in his swarthy face. "But never mind. Jeanne's right. You probably can't do it. The talented Ms. Maynes is known for her exacting posture. I doubt you can get dirty enough."

Eyebrows a few shades darker than her pale hair shot up.

Dima turned to scoop up a bottle of water from his workout bag. Really, the move was to hide his triumphant grin. Lizzie was about to chew the Southern boy up one side and down the other. Every time Dima hinted that she should dance for Club Devant, she'd sneered at him about sullying the purity of the steps. That if she did anything, she did it right. Among worthy peers.

She rarely backed down from a dare, which went hand in hand with her penchant for snap decisions. Dima had been pussyfooting around their reunion too much to remember that, or he would've used it against her weeks ago.

She stood and offered her hand to Remy. He talked her through the steps he wanted to show Jeanne before offering a demonstration. His palms clasped Lizzie's hips. His index fingers had to be brushing the tips of her pubic bones. He tucked her along the front of his body. Their hips started to swing along to the beat, sinking low in an off-tempo move that screamed sex.

Something hard smashed down inside Dima.

It didn't make any sense. He'd seen Lizzie dance with other

men before, for lessons—both given and received. Even seeing her astride Paul's muscled thighs hadn't produced this heady, possessive response.

"Mmm, that's what I'm talkin' 'bout," Remy said. His mouth was entirely too close to hers. "I knew you had it in you."

"You don't know anything about me."

"I know your dancing. YouTube."

"You like to watch, do you?"

"Naw, that's Declan's thing." He spun their bodies in a tight circle, pausing briefly to indicate the video camera in the far corner of the practice room. "Didn't you see the signs downstairs?"

"Sure. 'You are being watched.' That's not a joke?"

"Nope. They're everywhere. Dressing rooms too."

Damn.

Dima screwed the top back on his water bottle and tossed it into the corner. Turning away didn't help. The entire room was banked with mirrors. If he wasn't looking dead-on at Lizzie as she rocked against the charming choreographer's undulating body, he got a prime view of her laughing reflection.

She hadn't laughed like that with him, not for a long time. They'd worked hard, yeah. Intense, definitely. Even when teasing him with little sexual innuendos, she'd always done so with playfulness in her smile. Something joyful and easy was missing between them.

Laughter.

He knew why, without needing to dig too deeply. After all, he remembered the sickening crunch of bone against hardwood every time he thought of her knee.

He wanted to laugh with her again. Club Devant would be good for them. The way to let go and unwind. He just needed her to unwind with him, not some slick Cajun player.

After having swirled her taste all over his tongue, he couldn't keep his ideas clean. They were raunchy. Filthy. Incredibly exciting.

Seeing her giggle with Paul hadn't produced this same dark tremor. If anything, he'd felt indulgent. He'd enjoyed admiring them together—such a pretty picture. He could step into that picture without any ripples or pain. Was the bartender so easygoing that he radiated that sort of nonchalance? No matter what it was, Dima's jealousy was trumped by desire. He could admit that.

But Paul wasn't anywhere around. And Remy was a goddamn snake.

He strode toward the grinding, smiling pair and snagged Lizzie's free hand in the middle of a promenade. Tugged. Claimed. Brought her into the circle of his arms.

Her breath caught, even as she steadied herself so easily, so reflexively against his chest. "Dima?"

"I'm cutting in," he growled against her throat. "If you're going to dance like that, you'll do it with me."

Chapter Seven

For the second time in twelve hours, Lizzie was in Dima's arms. This should've been easier and less fraught with confusion. It wasn't. The possessive hunger in his magnetic eyes held her prisoner. That reaction was what she'd wanted the night before. For him to get *mean*. For him to stake his claim.

"Dance with me, Lizzie."

It had been six months. Six interminable months.

She replied without words. Hands in his. Close hold. Chin lifted.

And they moved. She breathed as if for the first time. All Dima. He led her and she followed, as they'd taught each other throughout their career. The bachata, however...

Brave. Bold. Exciting.

Lizzie liked the dance, even though she'd only known it from clubs and backstage goofing off. Native to the Dominican Republic, it was only just acquiring a following in professional circles. That meant she could let go of formal training, rules, expectations. So could Dima. His right thigh wedged between hers. He lifted her arms into a high, close hold, and gave her a strange, completely new smile. One that said dancing wasn't the only thing on his mind. In return, she gave him all that her hips had to offer.

She sank into a sit spin, spotting herself with the camera Remy had pointed out.

Dressing rooms too.

Had Declan Shaw been able to watch all that happened with Paul? With Dima standing before them, his delicious prick hard and eager? The thoughts gave her another rush.

Dima led her out of the spin, returning to the grind of his thigh against her pussy. Damn, it was a dirty dance. She tossed her head back, feeling effervescent. Her partner guided her with every step, his arm strong at her back. Maybe it was just the bachata, but she was able to let go. No competition here, other than the way she wanted to blow that girl Jeanne out of the water.

Remy clapped once and whistled. "You like showing off for him, do you?"

"He already knows what I can do."

"I don't think either of you do. C'mon now. He's lovin' this. Dirty it up, baby girl." He held his hand out to Jeanne. "C'mere, girly. Let's take notes from the masters."

Lizzie met Dima's eyes, which were intense and yet oddly playful.

"You heard him," he said. "Let's get dirty, little one."

They both grinned. Everything they'd ever shared on the dance floor amped up, fueled by familiar competition and a sharp new edge of desire. She found the rhythm like a bird catching a fast updraft of air. Soaring. She held on to Dima's shoulders, where hard muscle played beneath her palms. Their torsos came together for a long, slow grind. He took her around the waist, not even bothering with her hands. His heated expression promised he could lead using her hips alone.

She knew it. Knew it like she knew the feel of his body pulsing against hers. Primal and flat-out *sexy.*

He slipped a hand up her back, fingers splayed between her shoulder blades. Lizzie arched into that hold and stretched her arms overhead. Dima grazed his mouth down between her breasts, then yanked her up and into three whip-fast turns.

Letting go, letting him lead, she worked harder than she had in months. She also melted on the inside.

Fantastic.

The track ended with Lizzie beautifully lightheaded. No way could she dance like that and not experience a hefty turn-on. A hardcore bachata affected her as strongly as a fast fuck up against a wall. Athletic. All about the pelvis, where man and woman fit together. She was a sweaty, slightly breathless mess, but damn did she feel good. With two fast spins, Dima dipped her back into a full body layout. He sank to his knee and bowed over her stomach. Both of them panted. Lizzie grinned at his quiet, contented growl.

With a flourish, he drew her to standing and freed her with a spin. The same exit as always, but supercharged with electric sensations. She felt slinky and hot—the first time in months she'd found that thrill on the dance floor. One look at Dima said he was equally dazed. If a humorless Russian ballroom dancer could drool without actually dripping saliva, he was doing just that.

Remy released Jeanne and met Lizzie by the sound system. He took her hand and kissed her knuckles. A sheen of sweat glued the white tank top to his pecs, and his jeans rode low on lean hips and a toned tummy. "We could be great, *chère*," he said softly. "But I think he got it covered."

She wished it could be that simple.

"You're very good," she offered, running the hell away from the idea her desire was so obvious.

He huffed out a chuckle at her polite rejection. "You're surprised, aren't you?"

"By what?"

"Me."

She laughed and shook her head. "Damn, you've got balls. But yes, you surprised me. I thought you were supposed to be a contemporary dancer."

"All bets are off here. I mean, she's supposed to be one too, but here we are dancing bachata."

He flicked his gaze to where Jeanne took a sip of water. Her lack of confidence was obvious. Lizzie twisted her lips, knowing it was completely unfair to gloat about having shown the woman up. The thing was, Jeanne wasn't a bad dancer. In fact she was probably fantastic in her given style. Under the rigors of Remy's fast and sexy moves, however, she was entirely outclassed.

Remy stood at Lizzie's back and kissed her shoulder. "You belong here with us."

Across the practice room, Dima was glaring daggers. Probably the only reason she didn't push Remy away.

"No, I don't think so," she said softly. Although the reasons were becoming hazy, especially as Dima ran his gaze over her.

Rather than press, he shrugged with a *suit yourself* frown. "Take five, *chères.*"

Dima met Lizzie in the middle of the practice floor. He handed her a water and closed tense fingers over her shoulder—just where Remy had kissed. Intentional? He'd locked down his hot-as-fucking expression. Hard to think she could know so little about him after fifteen years.

"Nice work," he said with frustrating nonchalance.

Where had that growl gone? The one when he'd stolen her from Remy and the one he'd pressed between her breasts at the song's conclusion?

"Thanks."

"How's the knee?"

Lizzie glanced down, as if she might see visible proof of what she assessed from the inside. It didn't feel bad, only...a little underused. Physical therapy was doing its job, which included stretches and strength training—not lightning-fast steps. She had a long way to go, but this had been a delicious start.

"Not too bad. I think I'm done for today though. Sally will have my head if I come in worn out for my appointment."

Dima stood too close, breathing through his nose. "I've missed your laugh, little one."

He touched her cheek before backing away, clearing his throat. Lizzie only watched, mouth agape, as he stalked back to his duffle.

God, he was messing with her head. Something was working behind those mesmerizing eyes. Maybe he meant to show poor, injured Lizzie how good settling could be. Fun was fun, and grinding against Dima's hard thigh had certainly been that. However, it wasn't her career. *Their* career. If he wanted to call it quits on the circuit, he'd do it without her. No way was she washed up at twenty-eight.

But to tour without Dima? That thought sent shivers up her back. She took a quick gulp of water.

She stayed, though. As Remy put Dima and Jeanne through their paces for another hour, Lizzie sat back and nursed disquieting thoughts. Although she was tempted to join in again, she'd made her point—and got herself worked up in the process. The sex vibe angling between her and Dima since the evening before was crossing her mental wires.

He and Remy started into a good-natured shouting match. Lizzie had studied Russian since her fourteenth birthday, when she realized that Dima and their Kiev-born coach were talking about her. A smattering of French and German had come later—the languages of the international dance community. She was busy laughing along with their insults when Jeanne threw up her hands.

"I've had it!" She grabbed her bag and stomped out of the

room.

Remy shook his head. "She ain't gonna last."

"I wouldn't either with you two sniping at me," Lizzie said.

"I doubt that, *chère*. Enough for today though, *non*? Sunday is supposed to be a day of rest. My mama would be heartily displeased if she learned I spent the morning grinding with you folks rather than making confession."

That made Lizzie laugh, easing some of her anxiety. She waved goodbye to the Cajun and caught Dima's arm on the way out. He didn't break stride as they walked down the central corridor. Declan's apartment took up the west side of the second floor, with the practice rooms just opposite.

"When do you perform this one?" she asked.

"Two weeks. Friday night opening." His eyebrows pinched into a frown. His concentration face. "I don't think she'll be ready. Too much ground to make up."

"Of course she will. She's got you."

"Sarcasm?"

Teaching a Russian teenager about sarcasm had taken a long time, and even still, he tended to miss more subtle jabs. "Not at all."

They were just coming to the steps when the exit door opened to reveal Paul.

Dima pulled up short. Lizzie didn't hesitate. She gathered the bartender up for a hug that stopped short of the bump and grind she'd practiced that afternoon. Paul caught her with a hand low on her back. With boots, jeans and cowboy hat, he was a Texan wet dream—and an absolute relief after the last twelve confusing hours she'd spent rewriting rules with Dima. He was also another way to keep her frustrating partner's attention. If she had to grasp at straws, she'd do it with Paul.

"Hey, you," she said.

"I'm only here to get my paycheck." He kissed her full on the mouth. Oh, she liked that. Up front and still interested and apparently oblivious to whatever Dima thought. His straightforward attitude was such a relief. "Didn't realize I'd earned a bonus so soon."

"I'm sure you do great work behind the bar." She turned in Paul's arms and threw her partner a sultry look. "You remember Dima, of course."

Wow.

She'd seen lightning storms with less crackle. Maybe some of it was competition, but she didn't get the same sullen *hands off* vibe Dima threw around when she'd danced with Remy. This was deeper. Like marrow and sinew and the salty taste of skin. Paul and Dima sized each other up with a mixture of heat and cool reserve, as if waiting for a move, a sign, a word.

It made her inexplicably proud that Dima took the lead. Relieved, even. Maybe she wouldn't have to attempt impossible mind-reading when it came to his attitude toward Paul.

He extended his hand. "Dmitri Turgenev."

"Paul Reeves."

They shook hands, both solid grips revealed in the hard bunch of forearm tendons. Lizzie shivered. Heat that had barely subsided burst through her body like a volcano blowing its top.

Depraved. So *wrong.*

She wanted them both.

Her connection with Dima was deeper and more complicated, which was probably why flirting with Paul was so much fun. A beautiful, sunny counterpoint to all her confusion. Could having two men actually help her understand one better? Damn, that was screwed up.

"Paul," she said. "Do you have plans for dinner?"

"Not that I know of. You offering?"

She locked gazes with Dima. Her ripped-open feeling was reflected in eyes the color of hot cocoa. About their job, they'd been communicating without words for more than a decade. Disguising a busted lift. Recovering a missed step. Silently slagging off a harsh judge. This had nothing to do with dancing and everything to do with the weird place their relationship had slipped into.

"*Podelishsja?*"

"*Zavisit ot nego.*"

Christ, they weren't having this discussion. Couldn't be.

Are you going to share?

It depends on him.

She slipped her fingertips in the waistband of Paul's jeans. "Our Dima thinks it's cute to speak so that no one else understands. I think it's rude. However, he has grown into a really good cook."

"A miracle," Dima said with a shrug. "Russian cuisine is mostly potatoes, sausage and homebrew vodka."

"Not exactly best for a dancer," she added.

As if testing the waters, Paul nuzzled her temple but spoke directly to Dima. "I happen to like vodka."

Lizzie traced his jaw with her forefinger. Stubble. Just like Dima the night before. She was going to fucking explode, imagining and anticipating. To go through with it might not be possible. Damn if she wasn't going to try. "So, you game? I'm sure he'll make us something fantastic."

Paul let loose a slow, wide grin. "I'm sure he will."

"Eight o'clock?" She gave him the address, followed by a lingering kiss. He was a hellacious kisser. Didn't rush, even when that was exactly what she wanted. The result was a stronger high.

"Eight o'clock," he echoed. "Now if you don't mind, I'm off to brave the mountain of paper in Mr. Shaw's office. He keeps insisting there's a system."

He let go of Lizzie and tipped his cowboy hat. Still, he didn't hurry away. Tall and lanky, he passed within inches of Dima. Again, that crackle and spark. Lizzie held her breath, willing them to touch. To combust right in front of her. Paul only grinned again and walked on, shaking his head slightly.

Lizzie needed air. She turned toward the stairwell, willing strength into her watery thighs. Dima followed close behind. When halfway down to the first floor, he snatched her trailing hand. Gathered her up. Backed her against the wall. Powerful arms wrapped tight, low across her ass and high across her shoulders.

Mouth met mouth. A sudden burst of flavor, different from Paul, harder than Paul. No teasing kiss, this was an embrace that bordered on assault. She could've grabbed the handrail for support, but nothing in the world was steadier than Dima's body. Balance and control. Strength.

He had her, and she reveled in his wildness.

Endless, breathless seconds later, he pressed his forehead to hers. A bubble of energy wiggled out of her abraded lips in the form of a giggle. Surprise of surprises, he smiled again. That was too many to count in such a short span of time. They were like two dirty kids sharing a secret about what went on behind the high school equipment shed.

He slicked his tongue across her lower lip. Once. Twice. He slipped inside. Gently this time. Still as breathless.

"You'll be late for your appointment."

She blinked. "Damn. You're right."

"We'll share a taxi," he said, his no-nonsense voice strained. "And you can help me plan dinner."

Chapter Eight

Until the doorbell rang, Dima hadn't the slightest clue what he would feel. The idea of standing by while Lizzie invited Paul to dinner should've seemed counterintuitive, yet he'd done it. Even...encouraged the invitation. Afterward, he'd kissed the hell out of her in the stairwell when he hadn't been able to wait a second longer.

As soon as he thumbed the intercom button, however, he knew. Anticipation. His muscles bunched hard with the buzzing, prepared momentum he gathered before swinging Lizzie into a lift.

"Yes?" Giving hints as to his nerves wouldn't serve anyone.

"It's Paul."

Dima hit the button to release the street door. "Third floor. Come on in. It's open."

Stepping back into the kitchen area, he gave the potatoes in the skillet a little flip before they burned. Olive oil sizzled. When the front door opened with a click, he turned and smiled.

"*Dobro pozhalovatj*," he said. "Welcome to our home."

He couldn't help the extra emphasis on *our*. Paul might be a welcome visitor and one he wouldn't mind sampling, but he was just that—a visitor. Dima and Lizzie were a unit. His every decision and plan focused on that end. It was only what *sort* of unit they would become that was shifting into new and fantastical directions.

The way she'd danced with him...laughed with him...

It had been too long—heartbreakingly familiar, yet so new

as to make him shake his head.

By the look he slanted at Dima, Paul got the message loud and clear. "Thanks for the invitation."

The man looked good, of course. His usual white T-shirt had been traded for a heather-gray Henley, but he still wore a pair of raggedy jeans. Worn-white patches across the thighs made Dima think of handholds and biting. Dima wanted Lizzie. Craved her. Everything else faded when compared to the desires he could no longer keep in check. That didn't mean he was blind. Paul was distractingly attractive.

The man approached Dima, holding out a bottle of wine, enough for Dima to smell his slightly sweet, mostly spicy cologne. He had an instant flashback to where he'd last smelled it: all over Lizzie before he licked her, relished her wet arousal. His blood surged.

Dima took the wine. "Thanks."

"I hope it's decent. My sister said it was." Paul shrugged. "Lizzie?"

"She's still getting ready." The hiss of the pipes turned off as if on cue. Lizzie would be soaking wet, dripping from her shower. Dima stirred the smallest pot on the stove. "She seems to feel a need to dress up for you."

Paul's smile lit deeply wicked places. Along with his buzzed blond head, the man's bright and shiny grin topped off his perfect American image.

"I'm certainly not going to object." Paul eyed the rest of the apartment. "Nice digs."

A couple quick flips set the burners on low. The food could simmer a while. "Here, let me show you the rest."

There was something strange about showing another man his territory, especially knowing Paul would be inside Lizzie in an instant if she gave him the nod again. The nod that she'd failed to give Dima. Maybe that should have bothered him more.

Maybe he should have been more worried. He only regarded it as a step. A challenge. Their world was changing. He couldn't imagine that process would be easy, but nothing they'd tried together ever was. Yet they triumphed.

The key word was *together*. That was becoming harder to define when their goals were so opposed.

"My sister and I live together too," Paul said as they drifted through the dining room. "Saves on rent. This city's a hell of a lot more expensive than Corpus Christi."

Dima allowed himself to smile. "Lizzie and I haven't needed to room together for a long time. We simply prefer it that way."

"Old habits die hard?" Blue eyes flashed. Paul's grin turned impish.

The growl building in Dima's throat was held back by pure will. The man made him sound as if he were some old T-shirt yet to be discarded in the Goodwill pile. He held down the surge of emotion. Paul didn't know the depths he'd wandered into by stepping into their domain. Hell, even after so long, Dima had moments where he was just trying to keep his head above water. Keep up with frantic Lizzie.

"More like, once a person finds a good partnership, breaking it up is foolish."

Paul's gaze flicked over him in a look that was pure hunger, enough to take the edge off Dima's surprising possessiveness. Paul was novel and, better still, he was a hot-as-hell distraction. Dima's forearms stiffened with the urge to reach out and grab.

The bartender pivoted on a boot heel and shoved his hands in his back pockets as he walked away. "I'm not looking to break anything up. I like my life easy. If that's what you're worried about, you might as well let it go."

"I'm worried about nothing." Dima could hear that his words came out clipped, heavy with accent.

Wide shoulders shrugged. "Fine. No harm, no foul."

They stepped side by side through the archway into the living room. Dima found himself looking at the small room with new eyes. If they all congregated here after dinner, how would they arrange themselves? The couch was comfortable for two, but three would be a squeeze. Especially if two were men.

Dima didn't think he'd mind. Having Lizzie pressed between them, so close that every lovely inch of flesh crushed against him, provided interesting possibilities.

Paul wandered to stand before a bookshelf. Damn, his ass looked good in those jeans. The perfect size and shape to fill Dima's hands, but there was no telling what his opinion might be. On the spectrum of sexuality, sharing an armful of woman wasn't the same as fucking another guy.

Yet Dima would love to see that bright smile wrap around his cock. The intense sensation would force his hands to clench Paul's skull. He looked like a man who'd take a little roughness—like it, actually.

Paul touched a four-picture framed set. "These you two?"

Lizzie had put the display together from pictures of their performance at the Vancouver International. Though Dima had been beyond pissed that they'd come in second for no discernible reason, he hadn't been allowed to stew. He absolutely hated it when they fell short of his goals. Lizzie had practically brained him with pictures until he'd been able to see that yes, they'd had fun doing that dance.

The four she'd eventually chosen were of three poses and a lift, taken by a professional photographer hired for the event. Lizzie's hair had still been dark brown. The silver beaded dress she wore had been so low-cut that she'd needed flesh-colored meshing and tape to hold her breasts in place.

Looking at the pictures as Paul would, Dima didn't see the tape, or think about how Lizzie always needed three hairbrushes and an unfathomable amount of hair product to get her hair just right. She simply looked hot as hell. The way he held her by the hips as she arched back in the spin made the muscled swoop of her legs everything lovely.

He was a lucky man to have her in his life. He couldn't bear the thought of losing her. He wouldn't. No matter what he had to do and no matter what they would become in the future.

"You two look good together." Paul's gaze flicked over Dima from head to toe. "Damn good, but better without the fake tan. Both of you."

"Competition necessity. I'm glad to ditch it."

"How long have you two danced together?"

The chuckle Dima bit down was sudden, sparked by an instantaneous memory. "Sometimes I think too long."

"Nuh-uh." Paul leaned a shoulder against the edge of the bookcase. "There's more to it than that."

"No, I couldn't."

"You can. You will." That sunshine grin was infectious.

Dima walked away, shaking his head and laughing. He had to check on dinner before it burned and they were forced to order in. Paul followed. The small kitchen didn't really provide enough space for two men. The air pressed in on them both, filling with Paul's scent.

The other man stretched his arms to grab the doorframe. The pose accentuated his wide shoulders and the way his ribs slanted down to lean hips. "I know a dirty look when I see one. You ought to know, I'm not letting this go. I can be very persistent when I want to be."

That Dima could believe. Paul would have needed to be either sneakily persistent or damned lucky to entice Lizzie into climbing him after such short acquaintance. Still, Dima couldn't help some teasing of his own.

Testing, rather. He wasn't sure how this night would proceed. A strange tension zipped around the room, but that could be all in his head, left over from this morning's practice. Lizzie had ridden his thigh as if they could fuck while standing, while dancing, while fully clothed and without any need for privacy. How could he simply shake off that feeling? Dima didn't want to.

Under the guise of reaching for the salt, Dima stepped near Paul. Near enough that he could make out the individual gleam of bristly stubble on the other man's jaw.

Paul's nostrils flared as he assessed Dima through slitted eyes, but he didn't move away.

Dima turned back to the stove as he smiled. "You can't tell Lizzie this. It'll likely get me in trouble."

"Giving me ammo? You're a brave man."

"Were you under the impression we're in competition?" Dima showed his teeth. He didn't mean it in a nasty way, but that idea struck him wrong. Frightened him, maybe. If he were in competition for Lizzie, he would need to endure the thought of losing her. That would mean their joint flirtation with Paul had no future at all. The man would be an obstacle to Dima's plans, not a hot prospect.

Paul only grinned. It was becoming more and more apparent he was a good man. Or at least an easygoing one. The vibe he got off Paul was so different than the unease he'd endured when seeing Remy's hands on Lizzie. Dima had been ready to flay the Cajun into thin strips. He'd known on some level that Remy wouldn't hesitate when it came to taking. No rules and no nod to long partnerships. That Paul was willing to take a guided tour rather than shove his way into the apartment, have a seat on the couch and pat his lap, expecting Lizzie to climb aboard—it said a lot about his willingness to share. To have a little fun.

Maybe he was just what Dima and Lizzie needed. Hopefully they could give him something he needed as well. He'd mentioned a good time. Yes, they'd have to work on that. Dima knew he had a competitive streak as wide as the Atlantic, but that didn't mean he was a user. Too many dancers succumbed to the potential bitterness of their industry. They burned bridges, backstabbed and stepped on people as they climbed up the professional ladder. One of the reasons why he and Lizzie had always been so compatible was that they never took that easy, petty road.

Dima never had with a lover either. Fairness. Honesty. It was the only way to deal with people.

"I wouldn't dream of telling," Paul said. "Spit it out before Lizzie shows up."

"How long she and I have danced together? Long enough that I got my first hard-on over her."

Paul's rich, deep laugh filled the kitchen—and was abruptly cut off. His eyes went wide before he turned in the doorway.

Lizzie. After poking Dima in the back, she stood with her arms crossed over her chest and one toe tapping.

If Dima said anything, he'd get dishes thrown at his head, but mad looked good on her. Her cheeks flushed red. Her low-cut dress displayed cleavage that bounced with a huff of annoyance.

"Your first hard-on?"

Paul's mouth quirked. He hopped backward to sit on the counter. "I am definitely staying out of this one."

Dima carefully put down the spoon and took her by the shoulders. The bright blue dress skimmed down from her breasts, hugged her trim waist and ended high on her thighs. The kiss he placed on her forehead was slow and soft. "You look beautiful, little one."

"Dima, darling?"

"Yes?"

"You've lost your mind if you think you're getting off that easily."

Smiling would be a terribly bad idea, but looking at Paul increased the temptation to a ball-clenching degree. The Texan hitched backwards on his palms. He wasn't making any attempt to hide his amusement.

Dima lifted an eyebrow. "It was a valiant attempt, was it not?"

She snuck her fingers through his belt loops and tugged him near. Not nearly as close as he wanted. Not even as close as they'd been in the rehearsal room. Pressed together. Sweating. Dancing.

Holy fuck, *dancing* together once again.

If he wrapped his arms around her back, he'd only need to turn her slightly before she'd be sandwiched between him and Paul. From there, anything would be an option.

She pursed her full mouth into a bud of disapproval. "Details."

Dima knew her well enough to see the humor lurking in the depths of her eyes. "I was fourteen. You bent over in front of me wearing that gauzy pink practice skirt. I liked what I saw, but my reaction wasn't, ah, *sizeable*." He held up two fingers pinched together. "Not a big deal at all."

Pure devilishness took over his mind, to go with his gathering good humor. This was...easy. Nice. Having the three of them all together worked in some way that soothed his soul—a quiet playfulness he hadn't enjoyed since well before Lizzie's injury. Laughing with her at Devant had been a start. This was sexier, more effervescent and all the more tempting.

He leaned forward until his lips brushed the soft shell of her ear. Paul studied them avidly. Dima dropped his voice to an imitation of a whisper. Really, he didn't want anyone to miss a word. "Not now, though. Now it's most certainly a big deal."

More red flushed across her cheeks. This round was all blushing. No huffing mock-anger. Just arousal. She burned hot beneath the fingertip he traced along her skin.

He couldn't resist the impulse to push even further. "As you well know, little one."

He glanced toward Paul. The man leaned forward, smiling, with his chin down. This one twanged with unmistakably filthy intent. He looped his fingers around Lizzie's wrist and tugged her between his knees. "Is that right?"

She bit her bottom lip and looked up at Dima from under her lashes in a move he knew well. She was about to tease him.

He didn't mind in the least. Not that night. Not like when she'd been manic in her attempts to attract his attention after her injury. Silly little one. She didn't need to try so hard.

She nestled back against Paul's chest. "Dima's prick and I became...reacquainted, shall we say? Last night."

Paul's blue eyes burned bright. Although his salacious smile widened, he tightened his hands on Lizzie's shoulders. White, tense tendons on the darkly tanned hands gave him away. "And? Is it big?"

Though Dima usually planned every move, sometimes unmistakable opportunities popped up. Irresistible, even. He stepped closer to Lizzie. His hips tucked against hers. He wanted her to feel the hefty weight of the cock in question. This had nothing to do with choreography. Only need.

Only sex? Holy mother, he wished he knew.

On his way to hold her waist, he brushed Paul's denim-covered thighs with his knuckles. He kissed Lizzie first. Her lips opened under his. She tasted unbearably sweet. Yet the touch was swift. He pulled back, only to lean past her and graze his mouth over Paul's smile.

Kissing him was much like kissing summer. Dima could feel Paul's breath falter, feel Lizzie subtly jump between them. Paul's lips loosened before he kissed back. That was everything. A little firmer, a little more insistent. So much curiosity.

The contrast between their mouths was delectable. Lizzie's softness. Paul's strength.

"Big? Lizzie seemed to think so. You're welcome to find out for yourself."

Chapter Nine

Lizzie held her breath and looked up. Dima's gaze remained fixed on Paul, whose face she couldn't see. Caught, fearing any move would send them both running, she could only wait. The silent challenge arcing between the two men would determine the shape of the evening.

Paul's hands rested lightly on her shoulders, while Dima's hugged beneath her breasts. God, that was intimate. Her heart was racing, pounding so hard. Either one of them would be able to guess how much she wanted this—if they weren't too lost in their own swirling lust.

Leaning nearer, Paul whispered against her ear, "Doesn't dinner smell wonderful?"

She swallowed. "It does."

"Then let's eat."

Dima nodded and backed away, returning to the stove. The sliver of disappointment that wedged between her ribs was nearly painful. She managed, however, to step away from Paul and get dishes from a cabinet.

He hopped down from the counter, although it wasn't much of a hop for his long legs. Her skin prickled as he came up behind her again. "Don't look so crestfallen. I'm hungry." His breath was hot against the side of her neck. He slid a hand down her back and cupped one ass cheek. "And I'm going to need a lot of fuel to keep up with you two."

Lizzie glanced at the stove, where Dima ladled his fabulous rosemary tomato sauce into a soup tureen. He smiled, as if to a private joke. She wanted to tell both of them to quit pissing around, but Jesus, if that wasn't part of the fun.

"Go sit," she said. "I'll get us a drink. Your choice: tea, soda, champagne or vodka."

"He brought wine too," Dima added.

"Forget the wine." Paul licked his lower lip in the way that had tipped her well past gone at the club. "Champagne instead. To celebrate."

"What are we celebrating?"

"I'll tell you later."

He strolled back to the dining room as if nothing had happened. As if nothing would happen.

"Lizzie?"

She frowned slightly. Funny how she never realized how rarely Dima used her name. She was always his "little one". She turned to find him regarding her with something akin to...sympathy. "What?"

"Relax."

"Oh, right. Sure."

She went to the fridge and grabbed their only remaining bottle of *Sovetskoye Shampanskoye*. The most recent they'd opened was after their first and, to date, only television appearance, as guest professionals on a reality dance show. Dima had been so thrilled that night, as if it were the culmination of one of his grand goddamn schemes. It probably had been. Christ if she could tell—*really tell*—what he was thinking. Hard to know when he kept so much locked away. From her. Still. After so many years. Sometimes the frustration was unbearable.

So, yeah. Unspoken television goal accomplished.

Lizzie had blown her knee the following week.

Bottle grasped by the neck, she met Dima where he arranged potatoes and chicken breasts on a serving platter.

"Relax," she said tightly. "Because you're not tied up in knots."

"I am."

"I knew it. This calm thing is an act."

"You'd rather I push? Scare him off?"

He faced her head-on. He'd ditched his usual Russian stoicism for a surprisingly telling expression. A frown creased between brows a shade darker than his honey-brown hair. The full beauty of his lower lip was compressed into a tight line. He was a man working hard to rein in his impulses, all for the sake of the bigger picture. She often resented his control, just as she wondered how successful she would've been without it.

"Here's the truth of it, little one," he said, his voice private and filled with a new, unexpected depth of emotion. "You will be with Paul tonight, one way or the other. With or without me. Tell me, which of us has more to lose if he can't go through with this?"

That was the other thing she resented about his control. He wound up making her feel like an impetuous kid.

"You do."

"So you can help me take it slow, yes? He'll want to play with me or not." He shrugged. "So let's eat. And see what happens."

She sighed. "You never just 'see what happens'."

"I did at rehearsal," he said quietly.

He kissed her forehead, as if nothing at all had changed between them. As if they hadn't exploded in a rush of passion so intense that her dreams had been filled with images, sounds and a restless desire for more. She still felt his body pressed against hers. Sex or dancing—it didn't matter. Moving with him was her definition of rhythm.

He hefted the serving platter. "Just be the undeniable tease you always are."

"And you?"

"You're the one who said I can be persuasive."

She stood in the kitchen holding the champagne, wondering how fucked up it might look from the outside. She and her long-time dance partner were sharing responsibility for seducing a hot Texas bartender. Paul may as well be another of their many shared goals. In more ways than she wanted to admit, they needed an experience like this. They needed *him*. A genial, laid-back man they could share—the shared purpose of seduction, of all things, when all they'd managed since her injury was worrying and sniping and skirting so many new issues.

Five minutes later, with Lizzie's blood as fizzy as the bubbles in her drink, they settled down to dinner.

"Damn, this is good," Paul said as he tucked into the chicken. "My sister and I can't cook for shit."

"What does she do?" Lizzie asked.

"She's a graphic designer, does a lot of work for publishing companies on book covers and the like. She moved up here about, what, five years ago? I followed last year after my divorce." He shrugged—that same male version of fake casual Dima had down pat. "Needed a change."

"Change can be good," Dima said quietly.

Lizzie shot him a *not now* look, which Paul seemed to miss. He didn't need their bickering sessions, not when she wanted entirely more carnal forms of communication.

"Hey, this ain't bad." Paul set his glass down and eyed the bottle. "What is it?"

Dima poured another round, but not for himself. "*Sovetskoye Shampanskoye.*"

Paul grinned. "Say it again."

After complying, Dima's smile was slow and full of calm

ego. His knee pressed against Lizzie's bare thigh. "Soviet champagne," he translated.

"It's nearly drinkable," she said.

Dima made a face. "Don't be mean. It's gorgeous stuff."

"It's like carbonated saltwater, but I'll admit I've acquired a liking for it. Our coach imported a case from Russia when Dima turned twenty-one. Said it was the taste of victory."

Her grin faltered as she realized what that could imply. That their dinner together was victory. That Paul was the prize. Dima rolled his eyes, as if seeking patience and strength from a higher power.

Paul only smiled. His hand found her other knee beneath the table. These two were going to pick her brain apart and flail her with her own desires.

"So how'd you two get to be dancers?" he asked.

Lizzie took a sip. "Oh, the usual." It was lame, but it was also the best she could do. She was pinned between two strong men, each a study in temptation. Their attention was tentative when appraising each other, but it was wickedly intense when aimed at her. What woman wouldn't be flustered by such a situation?

"I'm a construction worker from Texas. I have no idea what usual would mean."

Dima seemed to sense her inability to form coherent sentences because he answered on her behalf—when he *never* answered questions. That was her job. Speaking for them as a pair. Part of it had started because of his teenage struggle to learn English. The other was, well, Lizzie liked it. Dima didn't. They'd always dovetailed. Since lying on the living room floor in a similarly interlocking sexual position, and since dancing together, *finally*, they could again.

"My parents were both professional ballet dancers," Dima said. "Like Lizzie's were. I was eight when the Soviet Union collapsed. The arts community collapsed too. We left five years later, came to New York. When my parents passed their prime, they didn't adjust well to so much change at once. So it was my turn. I'd already been dancing in Moscow, but it became an obsession once we settled here. They signed me up for more hours in lessons than I spent in school."

Lizzie nearly gaped. Dima didn't simply...open up like that. She couldn't help but give his thigh a little squeeze. A little reassurance. He ducked his head and shrugged.

Men. Shrugging. It was an incurable disease.

"Yeah," Paul said. "But don't forget, I've seen you move. You're no ballet dancer."

He flashed a curt grin. "Couldn't help it. I never had the patience for the classical styles. Needed more passion."

Another switch. From openness to outright innuendo. Lizzie found it so difficult to keep up that she nearly choked on a potato. She swallowed quickly, gulping another taste of champagne. "God, you are such a flirt tonight."

"As if it was any different for you," he said. "What did your mother claim about your hips?"

"That they'd been possessed by the devil."

Paul chuckled. "I can attest to that."

The mood around the table had taken a sexier turn, but also a more playful one. She could breathe again—at least until Paul's pinkie finger brushed the satin of her panties.

She shivered. "So after five years of ballet that drove us all crazy, they enrolled me in Latin ballroom classes instead."

"Because the pro dance community's pretty tight, our parents knew each other," Dima finished. "Ta-da. Doomed to a decade of victories."

Paul looked at them both in turn before settling against the back of his chair, hands folded over his stomach. Lizzie didn't know whether his expression was because he was amused by them or with them.

At least his plate was practically licked clean. "That was...fantastic. Thanks."

"No problem," Dima said with a dismissive wave. He stood to clear away the dishes. "There's vodka in the cabinet if you'd like some. None for me though, thanks."

His return to the kitchen meant Lizzie was bereft of both men's touches. The evening was perched on a make-or-break ledge. Either it was going to explode in the best possible way, or Paul would tip his cowboy hat and head home.

He didn't venture farther than the liquor cabinet. Lizzie brought orange juice and ice to make screwdrivers, joining him there. He smelled spicy, utterly delicious. She backed against the wall, watching as he poured the drinks, knowing full well Dima's queen-size bed waited only a few feet down the hall.

What would Paul do if she just...led him there?

Except having him was not the same. She'd jumped him at the club with only herself in mind—or out of her mind, which was entirely possible. To accept a repeat performance would be selfish, done at Dima's expense. She'd hurt him enough lately, with her refusal to see him dance at Devant. She couldn't do that to him again.

"Why doesn't he want a drink?" Paul asked.

"His parents. Like he said, they didn't handle retirement well." She left it at that, hoping Paul would take the hint. His parents' slide toward the worst Russian stereotypes had never sat well with Dima. At all. "So he'll have his disgusting Kusmi tea instead. Don't feel you're missing out, believe me."

Paul nodded and didn't press. Damn, she plain ol' *liked* him. He was adorable, gorgeous, polite. Not much more a girl could ask for. But there she was, waiting for more.

She clinked glasses when he raised his for a toast. The

sharp citrus was a refreshing end to the meal. "You never did tell me what we're celebrating."

After taking a drink, Paul looked her over. Slowly. From her feet on up to her eyes. "Well, first I thought it was because I'd gotten lucky last night. Really lucky."

"Oh?"

"Uh-huh. This hot girl practically jumped me when I was at work."

Lizzie forced her grin into hiding. He wanted to flirt, all stern-faced, and she definitely wanted to join in. His pure and simple safety was part of why she'd latched on to him. Playing along was the least she could offer him in return. "She must have been a tramp."

"I don't think I much cared, to be honest."

She covered her mouth with her hand. "Such high standards."

Paul shrugged and set both of their glasses on the liquor cabinet. He pushed into her space. Hands on her hips. Pelvis angled just right, although the height difference of nearly a foot might take hardcore against-the-wall action off the menu.

"You wouldn't think it, from the way I behaved," he said, his lips against her temple. "But generally I'm a pretty levelheaded guy."

"You seem that way."

"The thing is? I've had a shitty two years. Divorce doesn't happen all of a sudden. It builds up and blows up." His mouth tightened briefly, before he exhaled his obvious tension. "I don't want a damn thing other than a good time."

"For the best, I'd guess. I can't imagine a bar fuck lasting too long."

"Exactly." He wrapped his arms around her low back, bowing her in a deep embrace. "Then...I met her dance partner.

I got an odd vibe off the two of them."

Lizzie looked up, meeting his gaze. A sharp, hot fire lurked in his blue eyes, making that cool color burn. She tried to speak. Tried to swallow. Nothing happened. There was no denying that she and Dima were linked. Maybe that's why Paul hadn't pressed for her attention alone, and why he'd accepted an obviously joint invitation to dinner. He felt it too.

Paul kissed her gently, lip to lip. "See, I got the impression that her partner was as hot for me as she was. Funny, huh?"

"He's a dancer," she said with a grin. "You never can tell."

"Probably true, but the strangest thing about the situation is... Well." He smiled against her mouth. "I'm hot for him too."

"Jesus."

Lizzie shuddered. On tiptoes, she wrapped her forearms around his neck, pressing hard against his chest as they kissed. Tongues surged toward one another, tinged with orange juice and the sharp bite of vodka. Her breathing went from awkward to painful to ecstatic as she dragged ragged gulps of air into her chest.

Paul eased her back against the wall, kissing down her throat. His hands had slid high to cup the undersides of her breasts. She leaned into his touch with a groan. Damn, they were so close. So close to what she'd never believed possible.

"I've never been with a man before, Lizzie," he whispered.

"I'm not too surprised."

He swallowed, Adam's apple bobbing. "It's not something... Damn. I've always been curious. And that was a helluva lot harder to admit than I would've expected."

"Would it help to know you're safe here? No judgment. Total discretion."

"It does actually." A little shake of his head. His beautifully rugged features were dazed. "How crazy is that?"

"Not sure if we're in any position to define crazy, but I like that you believe me." She rubbed her inner wrist against his prickly jaw. "Will you tell me one thing, though? If you've always been curious, why now?"

"Dima's special."

She almost laughed at his quick, matter-of-fact assessment, yet no matter how unfamiliar that thought, it was true. Dmitri Turgenev was uniquely passionate. Perhaps that's what made him so frustrating. She found herself wanting more from the man she admired as an artist, as a friend.

As a lover?

She firmed up her wobbling smile and forced a shrug. "I think he is."

"And the two of you together? Damn."

A nervous, happy giggle tickled in her throat. "Thanks."

"So I'm gonna need your help, okay? His too. Sure I'm new to this, but I'm not naïve. I want..." He grinned again. So goddamn infectious. "I want this to be a night worth celebrating."

"Oh, honey, you don't need to worry about that." She rubbed her nose against his and kissed him again. Already she knew the shape of his lips, the firmness, the strength behind them. Two men. God, what they could do to one another if they let it all loose. "There's something I learned a long time ago about working with Dima. You want to know?"

"Sure."

"Let him lead."

"Is that right?"

Lizzie threw her head back on a laugh, catching Dima's eye where he stood watching from the kitchen doorway. "Tell him."

Dima tossed aside his dishtowel. She'd seen him prowl across the stage, smoldering, always as required by the dance.

His desire at that moment was genuine and so powerful that it raised the hairs on her nape.

He stood directly behind Paul, hands flat on the cowboy's ribs.

Lizzie watched—fascinated and so fucking turned on—as Paul's eyes rolled closed on a sigh. He was taller than Dima by a good four inches, but at that moment, he was theirs.

Theirs to share.

"I lead," Dima said, his voice thick. "The question becomes, are you willing to follow?"

Chapter Ten

Catching Paul between his hands was like catching hold of a thundercloud. Both highly charged and fleeting. If Dima grabbed too hard, the winds would blow him away. Heat seeped through Paul's shirt. The lean expanse of his chest shuddered under uneasy breaths. His ribs were covered with sinewy lengths of muscle. Dima tucked his fingertips along the bottom edge of Paul's pecs, taunting.

Promising.

Walking out of the kitchen to see Lizzie and Paul in an embrace had been exhilarating. An immediate rush of attraction had rocked through Dima's body. They were the perfect picture of everything he desired, without realizing the depth of that want. A curiosity to be sated. Soft and hard, both beautiful in their own ways.

Lizzie waited with blatant anticipation, smiling indulgently. She'd left her arms draped over Paul's neck. "I follow very well."

"Yes, little one," he agreed, swept over with an indulgent warmth. "You do. Most of the time. You can tell our Paul how well things turn out when you do."

Our Paul. So private and possessive. The Texan didn't even flinch.

She leaned into his chest, catching Dima's forearms between them. Paul heaved a quiet breath. Her fingertips grazed his nape right before Dima's eyes. Cream, tan, blonde—all pretty smoothed colors.

"He's never led me wrong." When she looked past their erstwhile partner to Dima, her eyes sparked with a silent message.

Dima was afraid of what that message might mean. Because to be honest, he *had* let her down. That didn't mean he wanted to hear it from her. He liked being there for Lizzie when she needed him. No matter what that meant.

Even when it meant fucking a tall, sexy cowboy.

Not that the idea was a huge sacrifice.

Rather than chase the meaning in Lizzie's eyes and ruin the moment, he smoothed a hand down Paul's chest. Despite the strength thrumming under his touch, he kept it light. Casual. He tugged Paul by a belt loop, turned him so they were face-to-face.

By the expression he wore, the other man wasn't fully committed, as Dima had suspected. Interested, yes. Tempted. Still, there remained a layer of thick trepidation way down deep, like a ghost still wandering the earth—something Paul couldn't shake.

Dima didn't mind making long-term plans. He never had. Stretching this adventure out another few encounters wouldn't be bad at all. Not to mention that Lizzie and her recent running-hard mentality would probably benefit from a slow burn.

He cupped Paul's face in one hand. Stubble abraded his palm in a delicious hint of texture. Hardness and power. He hadn't been with a man in years. Not since before Svetlana. There was something final about this setup. Not that tonight was destined to be the only time the three of them played together, but rather that this marked the end of an era for Dima and Lizzie. Their entire relationship would change after this— even more than it already had.

Either advance...or end.

A terrifying, bone-chilling thought. One he wouldn't allow.

"Will you follow?"

Paul's throat worked over a swallow, and his chest shuddered again. "I'll try. That's about all I can promise."

"Good enough." For now.

The curious part was that Dima wouldn't have accepted the same answer from Lizzie. A tide of demands would've swelled within him, craving concessions they'd never considered.

It hadn't been Lizzie. She still devoured him and Paul with her gaze. If he knew her like he thought he did, she was holding back more than one comment. Good that she realized there was no place for her nervous chatter tonight. Everyone was too skittish.

The edge within him honed to a sharp blade—like standing on stage before the lights went up as energy jerked to levels he'd worked for decades to restrain. He laced his fingers around Paul's thick neck and tugged, pulled him down so that their lips were level. Dima didn't stretch up, which further established his dominance. Paul was the newcomer and the visitor. He would give way. Not the other way around.

The kiss became exploration. Tasting. Orange and vodka taken by sweeps of his tongue in Paul's mouth. Dima hated alcohol, hated what it meant for his family, but from such a sexy source it became dark and delicious. Under his hand, Paul's jaw worked subtly. Slowly. They dove together into the possibilities.

A sigh slid through the air. Lizzie had come around their sides, weaving touches over them both. Dima's back prickled with the lovely trace of her fingertips down his spine. He pulled his mouth from Paul's but still held the man's face—not letting him back away.

"Like what you're seeing, little one?"

Her agreement verged on a moan. "You two look so good."

Paul's mouth quirked into a smile. He hooked an arm low around Lizzie's back. The man seemed to like her ass, from the way he palmed it. "Feels good too."

Dima licked his bottom lip. He took a kiss from Lizzie. She and Paul both tasted of screwdrivers, yes, but different underneath. Something unique. His Lizzie. He could quickly become addicted to her taste.

There was no such thing as getting his fill, but after a moment, he pulled back and nudged her chin toward Paul. "Kiss him."

Her hand snuck under the hem of Dima's shirt to clutch at his waist, even as she stretched up on her toes toward the other man. Dima slipped behind her, filling his hands with her sleek body.

Christ, he loved her curves, but even more he loved that they were underlaid with refined muscles—a testament to her hard work. Her dedication and ambition. He stroked firmly up her sides, all the way to her underarms. She shook lightly against Paul, although it was nothing compared to the way she lifted on her toes when Dima cupped her breasts.

Perky, full and exactly the right shape.

He thumbed the undersides of her tits. In the delicate hollow of her temple, her pulse throbbed beneath his lips. He hadn't spent nearly enough time tending to her breasts last night. Hadn't had the opportunity, which was a damn shame.

Even better, his knuckles brushed against Paul's chest. Every motion that layered pleasure over Lizzie extended to Paul.

Petting down over her waist, he found where Paul's hands looped around her hips. Dima circled those thick, strong wrists. The contrasts were amazing. Lizzie's tender throat under his mouth. Paul's wrists in his hands. Both of them waiting for his choices, his control.

Fuck, it was good.

He slipped his fingers under Lizzie's hem. Slowly, he pulled the dress up until she was forced to stop kissing Paul and lift her arms. Dima stripped off the tiny swath of satin.

When she dropped her head back to rest on his shoulder, she wore a sultry smile and wicked underwear. The lingerie was dark blue with black lace overlay, showing off her breasts and her ass in a way that tightened his balls. He spread his fingers wide over her flat stomach, before tracing the faint line down the center.

"What do you think?" He nestled his mouth against her soft hair but slanted his gaze toward Paul. "Luscious, isn't she?"

Paul's eyes sparked brighter and brighter. He palmed her waist, brushed touches over her ribs. "Luscious is the word." His drawl had thickened. "I want to say something greedy."

She moaned, smiled. "I'd like it if you did."

"I can't wait to lick you."

Dima pressed his forehead against Lizzie's nape, groaned there ever so softly. Her shiver was the response he hadn't known he wanted. Had either of them been out of step in that intimate, untried situation, they'd have seen it. Dance and seduction were twined together throughout human history. He and Lizzie were never out of step when they danced.

"I like the sound of that." She rolled up on her toes, reaching back to loop an arm around Dima's neck. Paul she caught by the belt buckle and pulled him forward. "Not fair that I'm the only one naked."

"You're not quite naked. And you are right that it's not fair." Dima couldn't help but taste her skin. He opened his mouth over the top of her shoulder and nibbled. Harder. "You like it anyway, don't you?"

Her entire body trembled. So did Paul's. Dima's mouth went dry on a rush of possibilities, only to be immediately flooded with moisture. The smoldering passion he found in Paul's eyes suggested so many possibilities. Had Dima wanted to voice something greedy, it would be to suck Paul's cock. He couldn't be sure that would happen tonight.

In the meantime, there were other choices.

He grasped Lizzie's hips and gently pushed her forward. "Sit, little one."

Her eyes went dark, even as her mouth opened as if she'd protest. She nodded. With a hand on Paul's shoulder, Dima led the man behind her.

She sank to the edge of the couch and looked up at them. Still wearing wicked black heels, she made a pretty, pretty picture. Her pink tongue licked her bottom lip even as she carefully folded her hands on her knees.

"Paul," Dima said, his voice sounding pretty damn gravelly. "Strip."

The sexy stud laughed. In the otherwise quiet room, the sound filled Dima's chest. "When y'all said to let you lead, you meant it, didn't you?"

Dima forced his shoulders to loosen. If Paul bucked his choices, there wasn't much he could do. They still had so many tests to pass, while enjoying the thrill of each one. "I'm accustomed to it."

Lizzie reached out to touch them both at the same time, running her fingers up the inside of their thighs. Dima clamped down his bone-deep reaction.

"Please." She wasn't begging, not quite, but the entreaty was sweet. "Paul, I'd like to see you. I didn't get much of a chance last night."

That was enough for him, of course. Dima had yet to meet the man who could withstand Lizzie when she set her mind on something. Paul quickly stripped his gray Henley to reveal a lean torso carved with muscle.

Dima missed watching Paul push down his jeans because he was pulling off his own shirt. The rewarding shock of seeing

Paul's naked body all at once was gut-clenching. His cock was damned good. Thick as hell. Patterned with swollen veins and a hefty, slick head. Dima's own dick swelled in appreciation. He eagerly kicked off his pants. The three of them had tripped over, and there was no holding back.

Stepping nearer to Paul was his only warning. The man didn't shrink away, only darted his gaze between Dima and Lizzie.

Wrapping his hand around Paul's neck, Dima took a kiss, this one hard and sharp. Lips bruised against teeth. Groping down, he found Lizzie's soft hair and wove his fingers deep. He wouldn't risk her straying too far.

Pulling back was harder than he expected. Paul tasted so damned good, even with the layer of bitter vodka. When Dima leaned down to kiss Lizzie, he found a missing puzzle piece. She was simply *right*. That hadn't been what he had in mind. He'd wanted the distractions to keep coming, keep him from looking too hard at how his feelings for her were changing—so quickly, so surprisingly.

He didn't like surprises.

Fending them off was easy when he could stand and touch Paul once again. He took the man's cock in hand.

Paul's eyes rolled shut, his chin dropping low. A harsh shudder shot through the man's chest. He didn't pull away. Instead, hot and sleek together, his cock twitched. A quiet rumble rolled up from his chest. Red colored his cheekbones.

Dima held back his smile and the rush of *win* that loosened his bones. His body throbbed with wanting them both. He ground his palm over his own shaft, trying to push down the surge of anticipation. "Our friend has a lovely cock, doesn't he, little one?"

Lizzie licked her lips. "He does."

"Did it feel as good as it looks?"

Her pinching grip on his thigh intensified. "God, yes. So good inside me."

He roughly scrubbed his thumb down Lizzie's face to her mouth. Outlined her lips. Spread gloss and her own moisture down her chin. Just a little less perfect. He liked that he could do that to her. That she'd let him.

"And taste? Did you get a chance to taste him?"

She shook her head. "No," she said with a softness that had nothing to do with shyness.

He stroked Paul's cock, tugging and jerking. "I think you need to fix that." His gaze flicked up to where Paul's eyes were barely open. "Don't you agree? She needs to suck both of us."

Paul pressed his lips together. His mouth was surprisingly pale amid such vibrant coloring, but still delectable. His nostrils flared on a deep inhale. "You're downright cracked if you think I'm gonna argue with that. My cock. Your dick. Her mouth? *Yes.*"

Chapter Eleven

The night before, Lizzie hadn't wanted to compare her lovers, but it was impossible when faced with them both. Paul was golden sunlight and bulky, working man's muscles. Dima was dark and smoldering with a dancer's defined grace. Both sported long, thick erections, distinguished by Dima's naturally duskier skin tone.

Lizzie took a deep breath and slid her hands up their thighs, one each, needing to touch, to get it into her brain that what she saw was real. Her feast to enjoy. Strong thighs, taut buttocks, flat, carved abdomens—she grabbed a little sample of each. Trailing her fingers down their tummies, she smiled at the arrowed line of hair that flared toward Paul's groin. Dima had waxed his chest for competition since he was seventeen, all sleek and smooth skin.

Their breathing did crazy things to her heartbeat. She couldn't hear over the pulse of blood in her ears—a pulse that was matched by the veins throbbing along their cocks.

She took each in hand, gratified by Dima's relaxed exhale and Paul's quiet gasp. So different in how they approached pleasure. Although Lizzie suspected his nervousness on an instinctual level, Dima acted as if his enjoyment was guaranteed. Always so quietly arrogant. Paul, by contrast, gave off a steady vibe of *good God, how did I get here?*

That meant she wanted to start with him first. Although she worked both using slow, steady strokes, she let Paul have her mouth. He tasted saltier than Dima had last night and smelled faintly of his own distinct musk, but that only edged her curiosity. She was eager for all that made them different.

With the tip of her tongue she traced head and shaft, each ripple and ridge. She took him deep. All the way down. Paul moaned softly, but that sound was cut off. She flicked her gaze up. Dima held Paul by the scruff, kissing him with an open, hungry mouth. They breathed heavily as their kisses made gorgeous wet noises.

Paul grabbed the back of her head with one hand and looped his free arm around Dima's neck, bringing him closer. God, they looked marvelous. Strong and toned, they ate each other with growing relish. Dima broke off and licked along Paul's stubbled jaw, drawing forth another low groan. Paul tightened his grip on her head, and she obliged him by taking the full, rigid length of him again.

Dima reached down and held her there. Maybe Paul would've let her go, but not Dima. He cupped the base of her skull, fingers twined with Paul's, and forced her to deep throat the man they shared. She rolled her eyes closed. She'd never felt so powerful and so vulnerable at the same time, which loosed a flood of wetness between her legs. To touch herself would mean letting go of one her prizes, and she wasn't ready.

Dima twisted her hair in his hand and pulled her back. She inhaled on that slight sting of pain. His dark, expressive desire sent tiny shivers down her back. "My turn, little one."

Whereas Paul was all things new, she licked and sucked Dima with something close to familiarity. That made her attention somehow more personal, not the mechanics of lips on a new dick.

He had leaned down slightly, kissing Paul's firm chest while Paul simply dropped his head back. His Adam's apple bobbed on a strained swallow. Lizzie swiped her tongue down Dima's slit to lick his salty precome. Again with his hand holding her head, he forced her deep.

Since her mouth was doing all the work, she gave in to temptation and slid her right hand between her legs. With her left she continued to work Paul's cock, fully base to tip, using a rhythm meant to keep him excited—not get him off. None of them wanted an early finish.

Dima urged her off his dick. Wiping beneath her chin, she dragged that trickle of spittle up across her lower lip.

"*Ty krasavitsa.*"

You're beautiful.

Lizzie smiled. "I have quite the view too," she said, feeling cheeky. She tingled everywhere.

He took over working Paul's erection and nodded for her to lie back. "Give us a show, little one."

Her smile deepened. Back slightly arched, she reclined on the couch and spread her knees wide. She teased herself just as she'd teased the men, using quick flicks and long, tense plunges into her pussy. All the while she feasted on the sight of Dima and Paul—their kisses, their straining bodies.

Paul pulled back and took a breath. For a split second she was afraid he'd call it off. Dima must've thought the same thing because his hands tightened on Paul's shoulder and cock.

He only grinned. Against Dima's throat he rasped, "I'm not going anywhere."

"Good to hear."

"Would you...?" What was nearly a blush sat across Paul's cheekbones.

Lizzie stilled her anxious pulse. She held her breath, while Dima bit his lower lip in anticipation. He wasn't usually so transparent.

Paul closed the gap between those beautiful male bodies. They embraced, strong arms crisscrossing strong backs. Dima thrust his hips tightly, buttocks clenching, with his cock snugged up against Paul's. Mouths battled in a fierce kiss.

Head thrown back, eyes half closed, Lizzie reached a plateau that was nearly as strong as an ordinary orgasm.

"Would I what?" Dima asked in a raw whisper. "What were you going to ask?"

"Never mind. I'm following."

Dima tweaked his nipple and dragged unforgiving fingers down the ladder of his ribs. "Tell me."

"Would you suck me?"

Lizzie shuddered, her whole body tightening. Dima closed his eyes briefly, shoulders bowed, as if he too had been laid low by that blunt, breathless request.

His surprise didn't last long. He dropped to his knees and splayed his hands over Paul's ass. No gentle seduction, he sucked hard and fast with no preparation.

Paul would've staggered if not for Dima's strong grip. He hissed sharply. "Fuck." Hands shoved in Dima's hair, he stared down at where another man's mouth completely enveloped his erection. Lizzie could only watch, lips parted, as she worked her pussy.

After tonguing the underside of Paul's shaft, Dima swirled over the head. With his fingertips, he edged deeper around the muscles of Paul's ass cheeks. Kneading. Pulling. Paul laced his hands at Dima's nape and held him there, thrusting softly, his hips gyrating in a grinding pulse. Tension popped the tendons along his forearms and bunched his triceps into hard ropes. His abdomen rippled with muscle.

Dima crossed his forearms around Paul's thighs and ass, pulling the man's groin even closer. Paul spread his legs to allow him freer play and moaned when Dima deep-throated him. All the way down. Head buried. Paul grunted, and Dima answered with the same.

Lizzie couldn't hold back anymore. Those paired noises made her think that Paul was going to come in her partner's mouth. The thought alone sent her over the edge. She shoved two fingers in her cunt and fucked herself, back bowing, breasts thrust up as she burst apart.

When her gray haze faded, she opened her eyes to find the men smiling at her. Paul's grin was open and happy— apparently simply glad she'd enjoyed herself. Dima's expression, however, revealed hard power. He crawled forward, knocking her hand out of the way.

"Starting without us?"

"Couldn't help it."

"Girls can be very sensitive after they come."

She licked her lips, still buzzing, and nodded. "Yes."

"Stay still," was all he said before dipping down. He licked her from back to front, lapping up her juices with a taut tongue. Lizzie squirmed when he reached her clit, but he grabbed her hips to keep her from drawing away. Swiping at it, pressing, he heightened her sensation to almost painful levels.

"*Dima.*" She pushed his shoulders.

When he drew up his head, his lips slick and shiny, he still wore that hard-edged smile. "Paul. Your turn."

He held one of her thighs while Paul knelt and pinned the other. They took turns, petting each other's backs as they slurped and sucked at her pussy. Lizzie writhed on the couch. Together they pushed her past her post-orgasm trance and back to the verge of coming.

She panted but didn't fight them anymore. The torture was too beautiful to deny, too intense, as she burned from the inside out.

Just when she thought Dima would send her over the edge, he drew back and chuckled softly. "So hungry for more, little one."

"You know it."

"I think we should be mindful of our guest, especially since you've already come once." He ran his hand up Paul's spine and curled tense fingers around the base of his skull. Paul leaned into that touch, his eyelids heavy and his mouth slightly open. "What would you do to our pretty girl, if you had the choice?"

"Fuck her."

Lizzie inhaled. Dima's body twitched where his hip notched against her inner thigh. She grinned at him, loving how easily Paul's bluntness undid her stoic partner.

Dima recovered quickly. He always did. Mistakes weren't meant to be lingered over, but attacked anew. Conquered. He was bulletproof.

"How?" he asked. "If I had my guess, you'd want access to her backside." He ran his other hand down Paul's front, past his bellybutton, past his cock, to cup his balls. There he gently played, toying, stroking with his thumb. "You can't keep your hands off her lush ass, can you?"

Paul's eyes had zoned to a place of pure pleasure. "Can you?"

Dima angled a sharp, dirty look at Lizzie. "Her ass gave me my first hard-on, but ever since, it's been her fantastic tits."

She blinked. *How long has he looked at me that way?*

Without another word, he released Paul and seized Lizzie's hips. She was so used to the mechanics of momentum and balance when it came to lifts that she forgot how just plain *strong* he was. Over she went, flipped to her stomach. Her knees sank into the couch cushions. After giving her ass a hard swat, he dipped lower to slip two fingers into her pussy.

Bowed low, he said against her spine, "Paul should fuck you, don't you think?" She made a noise in her throat. Dima withdrew and gave her another slap. "Answer, little one."

"Yes. I want him inside me."

"Condoms," Dima said. "Wait here." He padded off to the bathroom.

Paul replaced him, his body flush, pressing her against the back of the couch. He dragged his hands up her torso to cup her breasts. "He's right, you know."

"About?"

"Your tits are fantastic."

She giggled. "Men."

"We're not complicated. A little T&A goes a long way." He pulled back to knead the flesh of her ass. "Damn, you are hot."

"Harder. It's okay."

He pinched and squeezed, hands roaming over her upper thighs before returning to her butt. Mimicking Dima's example, he gave her a quick slap. "You sure?"

"Oh, yeah. I am so fucking turned on."

"You and me both."

The smacks he laid across her ass were sharp, playful—and a far more even cadence than his breathing. He was practically grunting with each stroke. Lizzie eased into every one. Sensation over sensation. She loved the sweet with the rough, and loved it when a man could give her both.

With his mouth snuggled next to her ear, he asked, "How does all this turn out, generally?"

"Turn out?"

"With other guys you share."

Lizzie turned to look back over her shoulder. She reached to touch his jaw and offered a gentle smile. "I thought you knew."

"Knew?"

"You're the only one, baby."

He was so cute when he looked a little knocked sideways. So fucking hot—out of breath, as his muscles gleamed with a sheen of sweat. "Really?"

"We're playing this by ear just as much as you are." She smiled at Dima when he returned with the condoms. "Isn't that right?"

"Playing by ear," he said with a smirk. At least this time his intentions were clear enough to Lizzie. Most times he was completely unreadable outside the usual professional bounds of determination and frustration. She had no doubt, however, that Dima fully intended to initiate their pretty toy—one day, if not that evening. "With a few quiet expectations."

Paul shook his head, grinning, as if he too saw through the game.

Taking Paul by the hips, Dima rolled a condom down the man's long length. He maneuvered between Lizzie and the couch to sit on the floor, his face situated right in front of her pussy. He supported behind her knees. As a preview, he snaked out his tongue and licked her clit. Lizzie shivered, just as Paul nudged the head of his cock between her folds. His hands were like vise grips on her hips.

One mouth ready to suck her mindless.

One cock ready to plunge deep.

Arms braced on the back of the couch, she drew in a long breath. "Goddamn, boys. I'm going to enjoy this."

Chapter Twelve

Dima's world narrowed and expanded at the same time. Two days ago, he never would've guessed he'd be sitting in front of his couch looking up at Lizzie's gleaming pussy. He'd wanted it. Imagined it. What he hadn't imagined was watching as she arched back, about to fuck a hard cock. Skin and flesh and muscles filled his entire vision.

He couldn't help the chuckle that worked out some of his tension. "Your fun is pretty much the point, little one."

Giggling, she dropped her head to look down the stretch of her body at him. "Because you get nothing out of this? Nothing at all?"

Paul's tanned hands smoothed over her stomach before running back down to her hips. "If he tries telling us yes, I'm sure not going to believe it. This has to be one of the hottest moments of my life."

"Paul?" Dima slid his hands up the backs of Lizzie's legs, until he could fold his thumbs along her swollen lips. He pressed inward so the tip of Paul's dick was slightly compressed within the hold.

"Yes?" The response came out sounding strained.

Dima tipped his face up. Flattening his tongue, he started at the base of Paul's shaft and kept going until he could flick Lizzie's clit. The taste of latex wasn't his favorite, but he'd never put her at risk.

"How about you shut up and fuck our girl?"

The fingers wrapped around her hips pinched tight. Lizzie's surprised inhale worked straight to Dima's cock, a surge of power.

Under Dima's keen eye, Paul's prick sank into her. So slowly, every ridge and vein disappearing within her slick lips. Lizzie bowed back into the invasion. The tendons along the insides of her thighs strained. Dima licked her skin. Sweat and a hint of her essence.

He followed that sleek path up to her smooth flesh. Licked her clit once, twice. Fuck, she tasted good and responded even better. Her spine dipped so that she could offer the most access for both him and Paul.

The only thing better was tilting his head to get to both of them. Lizzie's warm, soaking cunt and Paul's thick cock plunging into her. Dima licked them in one move. The jerk and stutter of Paul's rhythm was nearly as gratifying as Lizzie's soft squeak.

He was coming to love the little songs he could evoke from her.

Paul shifted over Lizzie. He scooped up her swaying breasts, pinching her pink nipples between his fingers. "Goddamn, that's good," he growled.

"Slower." Dima caught him by the hips, dragging out his moves. "Let me lick you more."

Paul groaned, but he let Dima control the motion. His ass worked under Dima's grip, sending a wicked shiver through him. His shivers worked out from his mouth and into Lizzie. She shuddered in response. Then Paul. Around and around they went, tucked so closely together it became impossible to tell where each ended.

No matter his intentions, he kept coming back to Lizzie. He sucked and nipped her everywhere. He opened his lips over her clit until he could rock his teeth over the swollen nub. Soft at first, before grinding harder when she moaned. He hunted that sound over and over, taking breaks to lick down the thick length of Paul's shaft.

He took a breath, just watching the lovers working together, sweating and thrusting. He traced a fingertip down the cleft of Paul's ass. The other man only groaned and fucked into Lizzie a little harder.

Dima kept exploring. He teased between Paul's taut globes, circling the tight bud of his anus. The man twitched in a flinching kind of move. So Dima moved on. He wanted the leeway to play as he liked. Wet and slick and oh-so-goddamned hot. He circled two fingers around Paul's cock, holding tight, feeling the slow slam into Lizzie's soaking cunt. He tucked a single blunt finger between the bottom of her clit and Paul's dick.

Fascinating. Beautiful. Mesmerizing.

He'd maintained a hard-on from hell. Nibbling on Lizzie's lips made him throb. Too damn close to coming. He put one hand on his cock, ringing the base and pushing into his pelvis. Holding back the swelling wave.

No way in fuck would he come before Lizzie did.

She folded one arm across the back of the couch, resting her forehead on her wrist. She smoothed over Paul's hands and scraped her nail across her own nipple. Her fingers dove into Dima's hair, stroking. Petting. Her breathing came faster and harder.

"Please," she moaned.

He removed his mouth but left his fingers dabbling in their connection. Interrupting and adding at the same time. "Please what, little one?"

Her hips writhed with more strength. She gave a little sigh that shifted down into a near moan. "I need to come. Soon. Please."

Paul groaned at her blunt words. "Shit. Me too."

Dima couldn't help his smile. He licked them one more time for good measure. Tapped his tongue over Lizzie's hot clit. She gripped the base of Dima's neck. "You both sound disappointed."

"Because it's so damned good." Paul stroked a hand down Lizzie's torso, fingers splayed as if reaching for as much lustrous skin as he could. When he grazed Dima's face, he didn't falter, but rather smoothed over the back of Dima's head. His fingers twined with Lizzie's there.

Dima slid to the side, out from under them both. Paul had plastered himself over Lizzie's back, his mouth nestled against her temple. He wrapped one arm around the front of her shoulders, holding a breast.

In unison they turned their heads to watch him. Identical sleepy-eyed lust darkened their gazes. Dima roughly caressed the muscle-bound span of Paul's upper back. The man's pulsing moves made small tendons and ligaments twitch as far up as his lean shoulders.

It might be pushing the other man too far, but Dima couldn't help himself. He stepped up behind him, carefully adjusting his cock to lie in the crack of Paul's strong ass. Sweat dampened his skin and made thrusting easy. The pressure wasn't enough to come, but sweet Virgin Mary did it go right to Dima's brain, making him lightheaded in the best possible way.

So much of it was the strength in Paul's body. The rock-hard length of his back. He moved like a young god, everything pure and bright.

Sweat dampened the edges of Lizzie's hair as she tossed it over her shoulder. She hooked one hand backward, sliding over Paul's hip and barely grazing Dima. "Holy hell, that's dirty," she moaned.

Paul's shoulders twisted on a shudder. He bowed until his forehead rested on Lizzie's nape. Beyond his thrusts into her cunt, he didn't draw away from Dima's pressure. There'd be an opportunity there. He'd only have to take the right steps.

Leaning one knee on the couch, he kissed them both, one at a time. Wrapped his hand around the back of Paul's neck and took. Sank his fingers through Lizzie's sweat-dampened hair and swept his lips over hers.

Lizzie lifted a hand and tucked it along his jaw. Her eyes drifted shut. Their kiss turned sweet, despite the fact that she was currently being fucked by another man.

Or maybe because of it.

They'd come to such a strange place. Across four months, no matter his mistakes or his plans, Dima had been unable to pull them forward. They had been stuck in a painful limbo. Until their sunshine bartender stepped in. Maybe to help pull them free.

Dima retreated a pace, letting them work together. He fucked into his own hand. "Harder," he ordered. "Harder, Paul. Until she comes."

Lizzie moaned again, louder. Paul screwed into her, his hips twisting. "And me?" he asked. His voice was deep, so rough through and through.

Dima tucked fingertips under the bottom of the man's ass, where hair lightly dusted the tops of his thighs. By contrast, Lizzie's thighs were softer and smoother than cream.

"What about you?" He knew, of course, but he liked the talking. Liked the openness. At any other moment, such openness became too difficult. In the middle of sex, all bets were off. He could say anything he liked.

"I'm going to come soon," Paul groaned.

Dima tucked his smile down, not letting it escape. He liked finding a limit. Even in such a moment, Paul wouldn't beg. "You too. Come. Let her feel how she affects you."

Locking one arm low around Lizzie's hips, Paul gripped the back of the couch. She squeaked a near scream as he used the leverage to slam into her. The lovely, lithe bands of her muscled arms braced her. Her head rocked back, resting against Paul's shoulder—but it was Dima she watched.

Out of the corner of her eyes, she tracked him. He shifted to the side to watch them both. The bunch of Paul's ass as he thrust. The way Lizzie's breasts bounced and her flat stomach clenched and released. Her mouth glistened.

Dima stroked his cock harder, keeping time with them. With his other hand he tugged on his balls. Sensation rocked him up on his heels, but he didn't give up. Barely blinked. The two of them, together. More than hot. Sexier. Filthier in the best sort of way. The hollows of Paul's thighs into his ass were matched only by the flat length of Lizzie's waist. The beautiful moving canvas of Paul's ass was a work of art.

Her eyes went wide. She turned her head to fix on Dima. "I'm coming. Christ, I'm gonna come so hard. *Dima.*"

He grinned. Clenched harder. Stroked faster. "Good. Go with it."

She bit her bottom lip. Her voice spiraled into a soft, choked scream that arrowed all the way down to Dima's guts. Just that quick, he blew over with hot jerks of pleasure. Shivering sensation rammed down his spine, took over his brain in a razor-sharp haze. His come streaked across them both—Lizzie's hips and Paul's ass.

That was apparently enough for Paul. He buried his face against Lizzie's hair and drove his cock into her one last time, coming on a long groan.

The three of them collapsed in a sweaty heap on the couch. With one hand still encircling his shrinking cock and his other fingers tucked into the damp hollow behind Lizzie's knee, Dima started to feel strange.

After he licked and sucked his partner, after he came all over a near-stranger's ass...*then* he started to feel off.

He could almost laugh at himself, if he weren't being attacked by a renewed glut of gut-sick worry.

As if he'd lost his plans entirely.

Which was why he kept his plans and his problems to himself. The sick, wandering worry that came with the lack of a goal wasn't something he'd inflict on anyone else, much less his girl. How could he share anything with her when he trusted his judgment so little?

Lizzie would likely want to snuggle with Paul. Of course she would. No matter the strange turn in their relationship, an old partnership wasn't the same as initiating a new relationship with another man.

Dima shoved the worries down. Refusing to acknowledge fears denied them power. He offered a hint of a smile and brushed a soft kiss over Lizzie's mouth, then Paul's. They both blinked up at him as he pushed off the couch.

"Perfect. Little one, I hope you sleep well." He pressed another kiss to her forehead because he never could sleep right without the small ritual. "Paul, Lizzie can show you what you need."

The other man's smile was nearly bright enough to distract Dima from the sudden darkness that sprang up in Lizzie's eyes, or his disappointment when she didn't say anything at all.

Chapter Thirteen

Lizzie stared up to where dawn had begun to chase the shadows on the ceiling.

Back to normal?

Normal with benefits?

Absolutely no telling.

She could've stayed entwined with Paul, because damn was he a solid hunk of cuddle. Discipline and long years of habit meant she was awake before the sun rose. Throughout high school, she and Dima had put in two hours of practice every day before classes started. Nothing could be more grueling than a four a.m. wake up.

Except facing Dima had every hallmark of an emotional marathon. He was bumping around the kitchen, making tea. Soon he'd start yoga. Lizzie risked a quiet *tsk* of reproach if she didn't get her ass up and join him.

She would, just like she'd search every action, word and look for a clue as to what was going on in his head. Not that she'd find much. He'd shut down pretty damn fast after coming. He might never process the experience well enough to give her an indication of what it had meant to him.

Same as always.

She'd been wickedly disappointed after they won their first junior pairs title—especially considering how badly she'd fucked up the year previous, not trusting him. For her, that win rolled glory and redemption all in one. Dima had only smiled, looking as if he was merely enduring every congratulatory word and hug.

What kind of young man took defeat so hard but refused to show any hint of how victory felt?

The worst part—or perhaps, what kept her searching past his reserve—was that he did feel. She'd caught glimpses through the years. Weeks after that junior pairs win, she'd caught him staring at the trophy in their coach's practice room, his hand pressed to the glass case, head bowed. Sixteen years old, he'd gathered her into an unexpected embrace and whispered, "*Spasibo.*"

Thank you.

The next day, practice as usual.

That was it. That was Dima.

And that's why things were going off course. Initially she'd been cool with his way of doing things. His calm kept her calm. Their goals matched, so why wonder what was in his head? Practice hard, work toward innovation and unison, keep each other sane on the road. Win. His thoughts were completely unreadable, since her injury and since...whatever the hell this was. When they needed to communicate the most, she was back to realizing how little of that he managed.

She closed her eyes. Keeping each other sane had been such a part of their partnership. Sometimes travel meant airplanes, and sometimes bus rides that were, holy crap, centuries long. They'd snoozed in an airport in Dallas once, having missed their connection. Both of them against a pillar at their gate. Both of them exhausted. Shoulder to shoulder, heads listing. He'd been warm and gentle and back to that calm she'd always needed.

The memory that had stayed with her most clearly, however, was on a ride from Phoenix to Sacramento. Some minor competition, but that wasn't the point. It was their first road trip without their parents—a novelty for both of them after so many years of being molded and, to be frank, *scrutinized.*

Watched for signs of fatigue, flirtations with dancers, injury, mistakes, disinterest, cattiness, and "a smile that didn't convince anyone."

That last was her mother's refrain.

The bus ride had been freedom.

When their coach had fallen asleep up near the driver, she and Dima had snuck toward the back. Not for anything sexy. Alone time. Breathing time. The competition in Phoenix had done a serious number on her feet. Bloodied and blistered. Dima had filled a water bottle from the sink in the bus's teeny-tiny bathroom. He'd retrieved a towel, bandages, Tylenol and a tube of antibacterial salve. Seventeen. Only seventeen years old. He shouldn't have known she was in pain. Shouldn't have cared enough. Yet there in the last row of seats, he'd urged her to lay her head back against a wadded-up warm-up jacket while he tended her injured feet. His touch and that lukewarm water had been heavenly.

Over the years, other opportunities had come along for both of them. She hadn't ever considered them. Why would she? He was her partner, and that was enough. That had been…simple.

Staying in bed with Paul would've been less complicated—a lovely morning fuck—but she pushed out from under his heavy forearm. Some things were worth it when they were complicated. If she had any chance of convincing Dima to rejoin her on tour, and to keep their partnership intact, she needed to hold on to the rituals and connections that made them special.

Put the sex away.

God, she didn't want to. She wanted his mouth on her all over again. Glancing back to where Paul lay sprawling, the covers dipping low over his hip, she tugged on her yoga clothes. He could play too. That Paul had pinged as a mere afterthought gave her a shiver.

On silent feet she emerged from the bedroom and found Dima in the dining room. He stood with his back turned, staring out the window that overlooked the street. Yoga pants. No shirt. Hair a sexy tangle. A hard clench of want shot heat out from her belly.

Mine.

Her skin turned to ice.

No.

This was a fun time. A crazy weekend. Nothing like her body's greedy shout—that she should walk to him and drape herself along his beautiful back, kissing the hollow between his graceful shoulder blades. Even if it wouldn't be risking their partnership, she needed more emotional sustenance than he could provide. He'd have her searching for clues for the rest of their lives.

Beyond all that, he was still...Dima. The weekend had opened her eyes to him as a man for the first time, but what new could be had from a relationship so entrenched? With so much platonic history?

"Morning," she said, ducking into the kitchen to grab orange juice.

He met her in the kitchen doorway, a cup of cooled tea in his hand. After his customary kiss to her forehead, he said, "*Dobroe utro.* Sleep well?"

From anyone else, that would've had innuendo or jealousy or something written all over it. Swear to God, from Dima it was only a question.

"Fine. Nice, actually. He doesn't snore."

A tight nod. A tick along his jaw. "He didn't go home?"

"You know he didn't," she said, walking away.

After finishing her juice, Lizzie unfurled her yoga mat and flicked a glance to Dima as he moved the coffee table.

Everything the same. Yet...not. Supercharged in a way that was definitely not their usual morning routine. Her need to goad him only added another layer.

"Aren't you going to ask?"

He grabbed his mat and unrolled it across the hardwood. "Ask what?"

"Whether Paul and I had sex without you."

Eyes intent, he drilled into her with maddening intensity. He thought he had the right to pull that shit with her, never offering up the same information in return. Lizzie tightened her hands into fists.

"You make too much noise, little one," he said simply. "So either you didn't, or he didn't make it worth your while. I can't imagine the latter."

With that, he began his first sun salutation. Lizzie knew doing yoga with a hardcore angry going on would only leave her sore and exhausted. Quiet breathing, calm mind, better results. As she joined him in that familiar sequence, she knew that wasn't going to happen.

She bent into downward dog. Every muscle and tendon creaked a sleepy protest. Between dancing with Remy and Dima, their adventures with Paul, and the arduous process of reclaiming her flexibility, she was a stiff mess. She liked to think she'd be back in fighting form any week now, but sometimes her fears got the best of her. Maybe she wouldn't ever be as good as she once was.

Where did Dima put it all? All the nerves and worries and doubts? That he practiced yoga to relieve stress was another sliver of knowledge she'd gleaned by accident. Their coach had asked, offhandedly, how the exercise was helping with his insomnia. Lizzie had been offended. Apparently sharing such a personal weakness was off the table.

Dima glanced at her as she bent low over her legs,

stretching her hamstrings. "Don't push too hard."

"I know how hard I can push." The words came out more sharply than she intended, but screw it. "Part of my job is to know my body's limits. Unless you don't think I'm capable of that anymore."

"So fucking ambitious," he muttered.

"What?"

"You. Always too fast. You'd storm a machine gun nest to prove me wrong." He shrugged with his eyebrows and arched back, arms stretched. Already a gleam of sweat slicked his tummy and shone along his collarbones. "So go ahead. Pull something. Sprain something. Forget I said anything."

"You can be so damn arrogant. I mean, where do you get off, hmm? Do you think I tore my ACL on my own?"

He froze. So did she.

Fuck.

Injuries happened. They happened even when everything else seemed to go perfectly right. Blame wasn't fair, let alone productive. To imply that sort of mistrust...

No partnership could survive.

He lifted his chin, and his spine transformed into a steel pole. She'd craved a measure of emotion from him, but not the kind she saw in his eyes. Some hurts were too hard to bury on short notice.

"I do my best for you, Lizzie."

He rolled up his mat, not looking at her, and stalked to the bathroom. She only drew breath when the pipes shuddered and the shower sprayed to life.

"Shit," she whispered.

Digging the heels of her hands into her eye sockets, she was surprised to find the scratch of unshed tears.

Anger at her new lover had spilled into hurting her partner.

127

That both were bundled up within Dima undid rational thought. She'd never been turned so inside out.

"Everything okay?"

Paul lounged against the liquor cabinet where they'd kissed, where last night had really launched. Two watery, warm screwdrivers still sat there, unfinished.

She soaked him in. All brightness and easy acceptance. Dressed in those jeans that sat low on his hips, he was shirtless too. Only, the effect was so different. None of Dima's tightly held precision, just a loose-limbed grace that made her want to sink into a safe, welcoming shelter.

He held out a hand, beckoning. She didn't hesitate. Being folded against bare skin and hard muscles was nearly balm enough to forget the hurt she'd put in Dima's eyes. Nearly.

No. She couldn't lie to herself. It wasn't even close.

"How was he this morning?" Paul's voice held a sleepy-soft roughness that melted into her bones.

"Pissed at me."

"For last night?"

"No. I said something I shouldn't have." She pushed deeper into their embrace.

Paul cupped her face and urged her gaze to meet his. "Will you answer something for me?"

"Depends. Give it a try."

"What in the hell are you both doing up so early?"

Lizzie giggled and tucked her face against his chest. "Yoga. The usual."

"Freaks," he said with a smile. His hands traced up and down her back, before gripping the underside of her ass. "But I must say that the results are mind-blowing."

"Should be. Took long enough to get to this point."

"So I suppose inviting you both along to breakfast this morning would be a waste of breath?"

"Why?"

He nuzzled her neck, hands kneading and stroking. Keep this up and she'd never be able to look at the liquor cabinet without thinking of Paul. "Because I had in mind something decadent."

"You have my attention." She ran flat palms up his ribs and gave his pecs a playful squeeze. "Spill it."

"Steak and eggs. Down at Charlie's off the park."

"That dive?"

"Is that scorn I hear?"

She bit her lower lip. "Nope. Not an ounce of scorn. I could go for something not eaten raw or steamed or cooked in olive oil."

"Good." He wore the tiniest frown. It screamed concern on such an otherwise sunny set of features. "How to get him to come along?"

"Ha. That won't happen. He's mad at me and he's the world's biggest stickler for eating healthy." She paused, eyeing Paul with curiosity. "You really want him along?"

The faintest blush edged across his cheekbones. He darted his gaze away.

"Oh, c'mon. Give it up, Paul."

"Last night, had it been just me and you? Would've been great. Really good stuff."

She grinned and flicked his ear. "You blushed 'cause you knew this would come off sounding like an insult."

"Shut up, okay? But yeah. It was memorable because of the three of us. I'm not ready to give that up yet."

"Your good time?"

The uncomplicated grin she enjoyed turned nasty. "You bet."

"I'm not wrong though. He's still not gonna go for it." A sick weight settled over her chest. She'd done this. She'd put her foot in her mouth and ruined something tasty and playful.

Worse, she'd hurt him again. When had she become that sort of partner? Hell, that sort of person? Her bitterness was infecting more than her self-confidence.

"I don't know about that. He's a little intense, but he's still a guy."

Lizzie raised her brows. "Oh?"

"You willing to play along?"

"If this is a lead-and-follow question, you know I don't know you well enough."

He smoothed his hands up her body and cupped her face in that intimate way she loved. Craved. "Nope. Not my job. Hell, I don't know if I'd want that responsibility. Just... Well, it's worth a shot."

Without waiting for an answer, he took her hand and tugged her back down the hall to her bedroom. God, she must look a wreck after their night, and she envied Dima's shower. The expression on Paul's face said he didn't give a shit. He'd lit up in that delicious, priceless way.

He looked her up and down. "Clothes off, hot pants. Time to get nasty."

Lizzie restrained her amusement to a smirk. She stripped for him. Being naked had never been a problem for her, although she knew a hell of a lot of dancers with body images so bad they could barely look in a mirror. In that respect, she'd always been lucky. She was a Latin dancer. Shape was her friend.

Paul pushed her onto the bed and covered her body with

his. The rough scrape of his jeans against her inner thighs made her shiver out a long moan. He kissed and petted her breasts, and shook his head when he gazed at her stomach. "So fucking sexy, Lizzie."

She smiled, hands in his hair, nearly losing the morning's tension on the press of his lips to her navel.

The shower turned off. Lizzie froze. She squeezed her eyes shut, because Paul had left the door open.

She was naked under him, and no way in hell would Dima miss that when he emerged from the bathroom.

Her instinct was to push against Paul's shoulders. Bolt. Get dressed quick. Only, he held her in place, with that nasty smile back in force. Such a contrast on sweet, optimistic Paul did crazy things to her guts.

The bathroom door opened. Lizzie couldn't breathe.

Maybe she could trust Paul after all. He angled a look back to where Dima stood in the doorway, wearing only a towel.

"Join us, Dima?"

Chapter Fourteen

The shower had done little to ease Dima, either his muscles or his head. He'd known Lizzie's accusation would come sooner or later. The truth could not be hidden forever. Ignoring it for so long had done them few favors. No matter what the judges or their coach had said about timing and balance, she'd fallen from his arms—the exact place where she should have been safest.

Seeing his Lizzie, naked and beautifully lush, under Paul... That was surprisingly okay to accept. They were golden perfection wound together. Paul wore jeans dipped low over his hips, showing off the twin dimples above his ass.

Dima forced a smile out of pure will. "Are you certain I'm welcome? You two are quite cozy." The words came out entirely more revealing than he'd intended. A wry joke would have been enough.

Yet he needed to make sure Lizzie wanted him there as well.

His stomach churned with the ugly fact that he had all but withered under Lizzie's approbation. The sharp crack of her angered words had hurt. More than that, they had flayed him open to the bone. Something raw and wounded had spilled out. He and Lizzie had always been a partnership.

He'd never told her about the opportunity he passed up just after her injury. Maybe he should have, but what would that have accomplished? Lizzie didn't owe him, not for that. Instead, he needed to know that she didn't still harbor such painful resentment. He mistrusted himself enough for both of them.

All he'd ever wanted to do was dance. To make his parents proud of him when they couldn't continue their own careers. It had only seemed right after everything they'd done to get them out of Russia and settled in a strange new place. Hell, in a strange way, they had given him Lizzie. Yet nearing thirty, he was a constant half step away from blowing it all. Even if he could forget about six months ago, he couldn't shake the certainty he would bring about disappointment again.

He needed off the circuit. For good. He needed Lizzie safe with him at Club Devant. Somehow. Before all of his limitations were revealed.

However, his high-and-mighty feelings didn't have any sway over his cock. Beneath the towel, his body was waking and readying. How could it not, with the luscious hints of Lizzie's skin peeking out from under Paul?

She swallowed, her slender throat working. Her hand slipped off Paul's ribs and reached for him. "Come to me, Dima." A tiny tremor took her fingers.

That easily, his feet were moving. If Lizzie asked, he'd always do his damnedest. That's the way his mind had been trained—the way she'd trained him.

He slipped his hand into hers. He'd directed last night, and had been glad to, but this morning he needed something more. A sign of acceptance. So he let her tug him down. She slid her hand up his arm and grasped the back of his neck.

Her legs and other arm were wrapped around Paul, but she took Dima's mouth. Everything soft and apologetic. Her tongue slipped over his lips until he opened for her. "I'm sorry I hurt you, Dima mine."

He pulled back. Dark tension still wound up the back of his neck where her fingers were equally taut. Her words weren't exactly the same as an apology for holding him responsible for her injury, but they were better than nothing.

The rapid conclusion all this drove home was how much he relied on having her in his life. Everything had tipped. In his mind, they were no longer just partners. He needed more, while she seemed content with keeping things the way they were—or recklessly courting novelty. What if he couldn't give her either, when he'd willingly given her everything for so long?

He stroked her hair, smoothing back the pale feathery strands. "Yours, eh? How would you take me if you could, little one?"

A softly wicked quirk took her glossy lips. "Any way I could get you."

"And you?" Dima turned to Paul, who he'd certainly not forgotten. Vibrant blue eyes were compassionate and watchful at the same time.

Paul quickly pushed those heavier emotions away. His grin came out to play. "That's a loaded question."

"I don't mean it to be." He scrubbed a hand over Paul's short, crisp hair. "Tell me what you wish this morning."

Red washed across the tops of Paul's cheeks, and the skin around his eyes went tight. His mouth flattened a little. Whatever he was about to say was difficult for him. "I...I want to suck you."

Ah. There it was. No matter his wants, he had struggled with voicing that. Far be it from Dima to deny a reward. He took Paul's mouth in a fast, hot kiss. These kisses were different than the night before, which had been in the moment. They'd been swept away. This meeting of mouths was a deliberate push on Dima's part, even harder than he'd kissed Lizzie. His limbs tingled under a steady whoosh of tension—the good kind.

When he opened his eyes again, he found Lizzie watching them both. Still under Paul, she smiled as heat sparked in her gaze. What a strange, oddly backward situation.

That didn't mean he'd give up a moment.

Standing, he let the towel drop in a slow, deliberate move. He practically expected Lizzie's admiration, but the way Paul drank in the view was an extra-special hit of power. Those jeans-clad hips flexed into Lizzie, and her breath caught. Dima wondered how wet she must be. His mouth actually watered at the thought, but he'd had his lips and tongue all over her the previous night.

Today, this morning...this would be for Paul. A reward. A thank you. The best sort of initiation after all he'd already offered them.

Dima leaned against Lizzie's huge pile of pillows. His elbows dug into her yielding mattress and quilt. Neither Lizzie nor Paul moved as he inched back to the headboard. His legs stretched out flat.

Turning his hand over, he touched first Paul, then Lizzie. Just because he could. "Come here."

Though Dima said it softly, they both obeyed at once. As if they'd done it a hundred times, they arranged themselves without needing to consult. Lizzie wiggled over his legs and nestled against his side. He stroked her shoulders, winding his fingertips into her hair. The muscles at the base of her skull were tight. He'd see what could be done about that.

Paul knelt at Dima's side. Thick thighs folded over his calves, and his hands rested palms up on his knees. His gaze was absolutely locked on Dima's cock, which reared up to meet him. As his tongue flicked out to dampen the corner of his mouth, Paul glanced at them both.

A glimmer of sympathy rose in Dima's chest, warm and gentle. He reached for the other man and touched his waist. Paul's lats flinched. His skin was so hot it verged on feverish.

Dima traced a path up Paul's ribs, over his chest and one not-quite-flat nipple. He cradled Paul's jaw, outlined his mouth.

Eyelids drifted to half-mast that said nothing about sleep and everything about desire. Dima understood. He was feeling covetous.

"What do you think, little one?"

Lizzie pressed an openmouthed kiss to the top of Dima's pecs. The air in the room thickened—harder to breathe, yet more precious for it. "Of what?"

"Will you like seeing this mouth on my cock?"

She shuddered, her breasts rubbing against him. Her hips surged. "Yes. Very much."

"So you'll be making both of us happy," Dima said, this time directing the words to Paul. "You'd like that, wouldn't you?"

Paul didn't speak, but his head jerked in a tiny nod of agreement. Dima tugged, pulling the other man's tense face closer. He took a kiss. Hard. Hot. The thrust of his tongue in the blond's mouth became a mimic of what his cock would do.

He thought he might need to push Paul. Maybe use a little pressure to force his choice. As perverted as that might be, he didn't mind the idea. Paul had already given voice to his wishes. A demonstration of power might work him past the numerous hurdles in his mind.

However, they'd barely separated their lips, with Dima's hand tightening on the back of the bartender's neck, when Paul descended. He didn't exactly take his time, but he didn't speed either, before planting one wet kiss at the base of Dima's throat.

Dima clenched Paul's warm skin and Lizzie's soft shoulder. She stroked over him, petting and soothing. Paul turned his head, kissed her too. The two pulled back and traded a look of silent communication. Dima was too busy maintaining his calm to figure out what it meant. His spine was hard and stiff, his legs burning with the energy needed to keep himself in check.

Lizzie licked his throat until her mouth hovered over his

ear. "You love this, don't you?"

He chuffed a quiet laugh. "Of course I do. I am a man, after all."

She drew back until they looked into each other's eyes, even as Paul ringed a damp circle over Dima's navel and scraped his teeth over the tender flesh beneath. Her expression was curiously difficult to read. Expectant somehow, but he didn't know what she wanted.

"You are," she whispered. "I know."

Would he ever be *her* man? The lonely, echoing thought jabbed in his mind, only to be immediately obliterated in the wet furnace of Paul's mouth.

Dima's head jerked back. His skull thumped against the wrought-iron headboard. He locked a solid grip on Lizzie's hip.

Paul wasn't screwing around. If Dima had been asked to guess, he would've expected a few licks and acclimatizing, perhaps strokes by hand. But Paul had enveloped the head of Dima's cock in his hot mouth, sucking deep. His hands folded around Dima's hips, fingers digging firmly beneath the sharp tips of his hipbones. Tight tension rocked higher. Harder. And fuck it all, but Paul kept sucking.

His flicked his gaze over the whole length of Dima's body. *Amused.* He had his first mouthful of cock, the lean hollows of his cheeks pulling inward, and he only looked amused.

Dima thought his brain might turns circles. Lizzie's lips parted, as if she were sucking along with Paul. Her steamy breath washed over his shoulder.

From Dima's vantage, Paul was mostly shoulders with his jeans-wrapped ass rising behind. Small muscles worked and twitched across his spine as his head bobbed. He pulled his mouth off Dima's dick with a small pop. His lips were glossy and slick.

Pleasure pulsed through Dima's balls, but he held it back.

He rubbed a flat thumb over the side of Paul's face. "Well? How do you like it?"

The other man grinned. He scraped blunt-tipped fingers down Dima's thighs. "Not bad. Helps that you're shower fresh."

Dima and Lizzie both laughed. He brushed back her hair, so that he could see the mossy green of her eyes. "And you?"

She made a quiet purr deep in her throat and undulated against his side. "I like watching." She bent her mouth into an obviously fake pout. "I like *doing* better. I'm left out."

He kissed her, but when she tried to pull away, he sank his teeth into her bottom lip. Gently. Then a little harder because he liked the soft moan she poured into his mouth. Paul's hand wrapped around Dima's cock before he licked a flat tongue over the head. Dima barely managed to hold his hips from flat-out fucking the man's mouth.

With a handful of hair, Dima tugged Lizzie's mouth away from his. "Then get down there and help him."

Chapter Fifteen

Lizzie was finding it harder and harder to focus on what she should do, namely fixing things with Dima. Those thoughts hightailed it in favor of the feast of beautiful manflesh in her bed. This was therapy. This was fun. Considering the unexpected weight in her heart, she needed both.

With her tongue, yes, but mostly with her teeth, Lizzie slid down the lean, graceful, defined expanse of Dima's body. The striated cap of his shoulder. The sweep of his pecs. The exquisite definition of his torso, from lats to ribs to tense, defined abdominals. The man was a work of erotic art. She'd always believed that perfection to be limited to when he danced, but perhaps artificial barriers had been created by habit.

Or fear.

She wasn't afraid now. So wet, she was probably leaving a streak on the sheets as she slinked down. Didn't matter. Her bed. Her men.

Despite the clasp of Dima's hand on the back of her neck, she didn't join Paul right away. Just another moment of watching. Outside of porn, she'd never seen a man blowing another man before last night. Paul did so with surprising gusto. He seemed the sort of guy who dove in hardcore once the decision was made, as he had when fucking her in Dima's dressing room. Built for experiences and sensations in the moment.

So different from her Dima.

"Let me show you," she whispered against Paul's distended cheek. She kissed him there, feeling Dima's defined bulk just underneath.

Paul slipped off and nodded, but he didn't back out of the way. He stayed close enough to kiss. Lizzie grinned and did so, before taking Dima in her mouth, relishing the close shift from lips to cock. Back and forth. She could trade off with them all day. All night.

That she already tasted Dima's salty precome said he was a lot closer than she'd expected. Paul—winning him like this— was probably doing fantastic things to her partner's libido. Power and sexuality.

With that thought came a surprising rush of possessiveness. She wanted to make an impression on Dima. One that had nothing to do with their profession, their long years together, or the hasty, unfair words she'd lobbed at him that morning.

"Relax your throat," she said to Paul. "Keep this angle so you can take it deep."

She returned to Dima's cock and sucked him into her mouth. Paul had already juiced the thick, veined shaft, so it was an easy thing to slide all the way to the hilt. Dima hissed and his hips surged. Paul grabbed the back of her head, holding her there, until she couldn't think beyond the way her mouth, her throat, filled and stretched. Deeper still. Tears watered, and saliva dripped from one corner of her mouth.

"Fuck," Dima groaned before yanking them both away. A manic darkness clouded his eyes. "So good."

She smiled past a surprising blush and wiped her mouth. Satisfied at having made that strong impression, and having earned the reward of his praise, she needed to bring Paul back in. Paul kept it from being a power play—kept it just plain play. "Your turn. Think you can deep throat our Dima?"

"Why go in by halves, eh?"

With a sure grin, Paul changed positions. Taking a

gratifying degree of initiative in his own pleasure, he spread Dima's legs and settled between them on all fours. His hands braced on both of Dima's hips, pinning her partner to the mattress. Lizzie hid a flicker of amusement when Dima looked ready to protest. Only briefly. Then he seemed to settle in for the ride. Good. He was too tightly strung to be in charge all the time.

She wanted him to learn that, to trust that.

Paul sucked him just as she'd demonstrated. Sure and strong all the way down. Slow and lingering all the way up. The contest between those toned male bodies was told in grunts, sharp breaths, but even more so in the little ripples of tight tendons and bunched muscles. Paul's forearms and triceps stood out in relief as he gripped Dima's lean hips. Every ounce of passionate expectation was shown in the squeeze and flex of his cut abs.

That Paul could take charge did gorgeous things to Lizzie's arousal. She was watching gladiators in a sweaty duel—if gladiators face-fucked one another. Smiling fully, she sat back and admired Paul's technique, playing with her nipples. Sure enough, Dima's entire shaft disappeared each time. He seemed torn between watching her hands at work on her breasts and Paul as he swallowed cock like a goddamn pro.

She wiggled behind Paul, draped lightly across his back and held his head down. Fully down. At first he seemed ready to fight that pressure. Only he wasn't the man she was used to knowing. Paul inhaled through his nose. Every muscle relaxed as he settled in, with Dima's prick tucked down his throat. He groaned, and Dima answered with a growled curse of his own.

She met Dima's eyes again, barely recognizing the look she found. Heavy-lidded. Needy. *Vulnerable.* That wasn't him at all. Yet there he was, prone and restrained by the most erotic hold.

"Paul wants to take us to breakfast," she said conversationally. Silent laughter bowed Paul's back beneath her

141

body. She released her hold only long enough for him to catch his breath and dive back in. He returned to that deep, deep swallow. "What do you say, Dima? You up for something naughty this morning?"

"Yes," he gritted. She saw why, as Paul used his construction worker's hands to separate Dima's firm ass cheeks. Such a defenseless position for a man to be in, spread that way, knees fanned out to either side. Only the sure two-handed grip Dima maintained at the base of Paul's skull proved he wasn't entirely a passive performer in this bit of erotic theater.

Lizzie crawled up Paul's body, her breasts flush against his arched back. She worked her hands down his chest and flat, rock-hard tummy until she reached his fly. Opened it. Slipped her fingers inside to free his straining, throbbing dick.

"You could fuck him, you know," she whispered. "Dima would love to be your first. He'd take it as a compliment."

Paul made a soft humming sound in his throat, but it was truncated as he took Dima deep once again. He was picking up speed, face-fucking by his own design. He didn't have much farther to go, if Dima's straining neck was any indication. Both of them fought to set the pace.

"I have a bottle of lube right here in my nightstand," she continued. "Or I could lick that fresh-washed asshole until he was slippery and open for you."

"Little one?"

"Yes, Dima?"

"Shut the fuck up."

"Hmmm...nope. Don't think I will. Paul likes this too much. Don't you, Paul?"

She wrapped around his body to catch a side view as he smiled around Dima's cock. That he enjoyed teasing Dima as much as she did made her relax. She had an ally in loosening him up.

"Don't worry, Dima mine. I think Paul here wants to finish what he started. Yes, Paul?"

He groaned around another smile. Dima started in on a stream of Russian curses, his hips pulsing under unyielding hands. As if by instinct, Paul loosened his hold to give Dima more freedom to maneuver. She knew what a stickler for control her partner was. Bound in any way, physically or mentally, he was more likely to get frustrated or lose his hot, tightly reined temper than get off.

She kissed her thanks between Paul's shoulder blades, licked away the sweat and began to stroke him in time with his attention to Dima. "I want you to fuck me. As soon as he comes, Paul, I want you inside of me. You kiss will still taste like Dima when you drive this beautiful cock home."

To emphasize the point, while the boys kicked up the pace, she tugged Paul's jeans down even farther. She unwrapped a condom and rolled it down to sheath his heavy erection. His hips were grinding the air. She bit the flesh at the top of his buttocks and held on as his mouth bounced over Dima.

Paul breathed heavily through his nose. Sloppy wet noises filled her bedroom, and the air was laced with sweat and sex and the need for an explosion. Dima's explosion.

"Little one," he growled. "Here. Now."

As much as she enjoyed nibbling Paul's ass, she was Dima's to command. How long had that been the case? She crawled up the bed, ready to resume the same cuddled-up position.

Dima had other ideas.

Ideas he hadn't shared. She might've thought to get more upset if his dominance in bed wasn't such a damn turn-on.

"On your back."

His voice was a low, heavily accented rasp that sent shivers of nervous anticipation up the backs of her thighs. Dima never hurt her—hell, never intentionally—but he expected things of her that could push her limits. Throughout their partnership, she had been the public face while, behind the scenes, always testing her resolve, he matched his daring to her ambition. They urged each other to greatness.

If only...

No, she didn't want to stray toward useless daydreams when a very real, very incredible fantasy stretched out on her bed.

Lizzie shut off her brain and obeyed. It was easy. The brief moment of control she'd had, watching the men in their sexy contest, teasing them both, was over. She settled into her submission with the ease of returning home. Dima led and she followed. Another shiver played across her skin but landed nearer her heart than her slick pussy.

Dima relinquished his hold on Paul's nape. "Arms overhead," he said.

Lizzie barely reached them up before Dima revealed his intentions. He looped his forearm to encircle the insides of her elbow. Hauling her slightly sideways, he angled her head to rest in the crook of his shoulder. Her upraised hands dangled uselessly just out of sight. She arched, stretching her breasts in that long, voluptuous pose.

"This is your reward, Paul," Dima said softly. "This girl. Those tits are for your mouth, which has to be tingling."

Lizzie couldn't see Dima's face from her position, but she had a clear view of how his sexy taunts affected Paul. He looked as submerged in the strong aura of Dima's pleasure as she was.

"Don't forget her ass. The hot little ass you love so much. You can clasp her sweet flesh just like you're doing mine, but she won't fight you. She'll take every stroke because she wants it that hard from you." He paused. "Even if she can't say so."

"Dima...?"

His free hand closed over her mouth, holding fast. Completely restrained. She struggled once, but his arm tightened across her elbows and kept her immobilized.

"I told you to shut the fuck up, little one. Now we'll only hear your teases and your screams if I want us to."

After the tiniest flash of panic, she relaxed on a damp rush of *oh, holy fuck.* She found Paul's eyes, where he had slowed—but never stopped—to watch the new development. A silent question waited there, as well as concern she needed to alleviate.

I do my best for you, Lizzie.

Christ, he always did. No matter what happened, Dima would not intentionally allow her to be hurt. She knew that like she knew how to breathe.

She blinked at Paul, nodded as much as she could.

Dima relaxed too. The granite-solid muscle beneath her head eased as he accepted her permission too. "Make me come, Paul."

The blue-eyed man with a body built to fuck like a piston returned to his sexy task. He pulsed Dima's prick in and out, jerking them both back to full salutes. The two sturdy tendons along his buzzed nape stood out like ropes. Sweat lined his forehead and upper lip, which was taut around Dima's thick shaft.

Lizzie couldn't look away, couldn't say a word. Breath from her nose moistened Dima's hand where he clasped her so firmly. She wanted to touch between her legs, but all she managed was an impatient wiggle, thighs clenching and releasing.

"Close, Paul. So close for us. Make me come so you can do

the same for our Lizzie. She's here waiting for you." Dima pushed his mouth against her ear. "Open your legs," he rasped. "Let him see his reward."

She complied, which only made Dima's hips twitch faster, up into Paul's mouth. She moaned against the hand holding her silent. A tingle invaded her forearms and fingertips where Dima held her arms completely still.

A low rumble gathered in his throat. He gripped her bottom jaw as his orgasm seemed to build from somewhere in the middle of all three sweaty bodies.

"Swallow me, Paul." His words were feral. His hips worked a hard counter to Paul's steady mouth. "Show me how much you love sucking me. Your first cock. Your first mouthful of fuck juice—"

He jerked and shoved, unloading on a low, deep growl. Lizzie caught the quickest flash of Paul's expression—pure satisfaction—before the man pounced. Never as lithe as Dima, but so goddamn powerful. He lay over her and attacked with one swift movement, filling her so fast that she screamed against Dima's hand. She arched, but two sets of implacable hands held her still. Paul pinned her lower body with his legs and grinding pelvis.

Just as Dima had teased, Paul grabbed her ass and used her cheeks for leverage. Every thrust hit her like a rocket firing into space. Dima had removed his hand from her mouth. The crown of her head pushed against Dima's shoulder. He padded her with his muscles, urging her on with dark words that wove between English and Russian. She heard them even as Paul fucked her, even as Paul kissed her—his tongue tasting of Dima. He was everywhere.

"Race him, little one. He's ready to blow, but you can beat him to it. Better than anyone else who ever tried. My superstar. Come for him, Lizzie. God, come for *me*."

Her orgasm hit her like slamming into a wall at a dead run. Motion and feeling and momentum suddenly stopped, suspended, as pleasure too hot, too frantic, burst across every nerve. She was pulling out of her own skin. And *screaming*. Her hoarse, raw-throated bellow filled the tight bedroom. She was completely unmoored, despite two strong men who held her captive, one with his relentless pumping cock, the other with his lovely filthy mind.

Dima grabbed the back of Paul's head and pulled him down, forehead to forehead. "Have you ever been so perfect at anything? At any moment? Make this perfect."

"Aw, fuck."

Paul's tight, scraping fingers stung Lizzie's ass. His cock was as hard as being fucked with a pipe. She shrieked again as another climax swept over the last. She twisted against Dima, fought against Paul, as pulses of light fused to white behind her eyes. One last thrust and Paul joined her, his groaned curse animalistic. She opened her eyes just in time to see the men kiss, roughly, as Paul shuddered the last of his pleasure.

He collapsed between them, half sprawled on her and Dima, with an exhausted laugh chugging out of his chest.

"What's funny?" Dima asked quietly as he stroked damp hair back from Lizzie's temple. He had yet to release her hands. Not so firmly, but still...holding.

"I think there was an agreement in there somewhere. Don't you, Liz?"

She stretched down to her toes. "Sure do."

"Agreement to what?" Dima's accent was so thick. He'd gone to some primal place. A default mode. He really did have the most delicious voice.

"You accepted Paul's invitation to breakfast," she said on a giddy exhale. "Time to go do something really naughty."

Chapter Sixteen

Not much compared to spring in New York, unless it was walking with a view of Lizzie's ass. Hands slung in his pockets, Dima followed her and Paul underneath a stretching canopy of trees that shaded a residential sidewalk. Together, the fair couple ducked a group of wise-mouth tweens tumbling off a stoop.

At the corner, they stopped. Lizzie looked over her shoulder. Her arm was looped through Paul's. Late-morning sunshine draped over the pair like gold cloth, emphasizing their brilliance. Lizzie's grin glowed and she wore a tiny jeans skirt with a wide-necked T-shirt. It draped off her shoulder with a tank top underneath, showing off the creamy skin he'd tasted less than an hour ago. Paul wore the same jeans, but he'd borrowed a shirt from Dima. Slightly too snug, it clung to thick biceps.

In an instant Dima knew that image would shine forever in his mind. No matter what happened.

The two of them looked like they belonged together. So perfectly gleaming, they were painful to watch, as if their combined warmth could melt the world.

Still, he told himself he had no worries. Though he walked behind, there was no such thing as left out. Not when Lizzie held out her hand and smiled at him.

What a picture they must make as a trio. Lizzie's lush breasts rubbed against Paul as she walked, yet she twined her fingers through Dima's in an intimate hold. He couldn't bring himself to care. They were happy together, and for the love of the Virgin, they were in New York City. In Chelsea even. There was no better place for them to slide by without notice.

Paul and Lizzie kept up a steady stream of chatter as all three crossed the street against the light. If anything, she was playing tour guide in that way of hers. Always she attached a personal story to whatever she pointed out. She kept them both amused the entire way—although Dima had heard most of the stories already and had been there for the rest.

Only two streets down from Club Devant and a block away from the dive where Paul intended they pretend to eat, they came to Chelsea Park. They cut through diagonally, as leafy patterns dappled Lizzie with artful patterns. In the heart of the park they found a makeshift dance hall. An overly muscled vato rapped along surprisingly well to a Latin-flavored background track. Also with him was a skinny-armed buddy who beat a rhythm on an upside-down paint can. A baseball cap on the ground sparkled with a few coins and few bills. A loose semicircle of people ringed the musicians.

Paul stopped, his arm around Lizzie's shoulders. "This is like what you dance to, right?"

"Some." Dima traced a pattern across Lizzie's palm. "This is meatier. We dance to prescribed music, without so much flair."

"You mean on the dance circuit, Dima mine." Lizzie slanted him a sly look. Her toes were already tapping along to the beat. "I remember rehearsals yesterday being quite a bit...what was it? Meatier? I like that. You could dance to this on stage if you wanted."

"In the club, you could as well," he said quietly.

"So, what, it's not your thing?" Paul asked Lizzie. "I assumed that's why you're not dancing together."

She made a face. "I was injured. Only recently starting to feel better."

Dima hid a grimace. She spoke as if the hiatus of their

partnership could be explained so easily. So much more had built a brick wall between them. Ironic, considering how close they'd been for the past thirty-six hours.

"I've never been much of a dancer," Paul said.

"Oh, really?" Dima couldn't help his sardonic smile. "Because I happen to know you have quite the sense of rhythm."

Paul laughed, and so did Lizzie. It warmed Dima to be able to give them that, even if he wasn't moved to laughter himself.

"Fine, yeah," Paul said. "But I've never known the steps."

Lizzie wound her fingers with Paul's. "Moves are extraneous. It's not like I'm going to demand an *assemblè devant* in a park."

"Devant? Like the club?"

"Funny." She made eye contact with Dima, who shrugged. "Maybe we take it for granted. *Devant* means out in front. I bet Declan thought it was clever."

His blond brows lifted. "I assumed it was something kinky I didn't quite get. Deviant, you know?"

"Nope. On the up-and-up. Mostly." Lizzie twirled out, tugging him along with her. Even on a casual trip like this, she wore dance heels that turned her calves into works of art. "Now, all you have to do is feel the music."

With a few words whispered in Paul's ear, she slung her arms up over his shoulders. Their bodies plastered together like coming home. He instinctively pushed one thick thigh between hers. His hands rested low on her hips, unsurprisingly making a beeline for her ass.

A smile on his mouth, Dima pushed his hands back in his pockets and retreated a step. Yet another scene that would imprint him for life.

He could still hardly believe he'd had them both.

It didn't take long before Lizzie tutored Paul in long, grinding movements. Their hips slid together, playing, taunting. The easy rapport they shared made Dima think he should back off and let them develop a normal relationship.

He was not that good. He was greedy, through and through, and he'd keep both as long as he could. When it was all over he'd still have Lizzie. He'd make sure of that. There was no giving up the ground he'd already claimed, the concessions she'd already made. No going back to what they were when something so much bigger hovered just out of reach.

So many unknowns still remained. He hated unknowns. If she couldn't trust him, couldn't forgive him...

Lizzie spun around, nestling her ass against Paul's pelvis and wiggling her hips in a move more suited to Club Devant than any formal competition. If only she could realize that. Her innate sexuality could take them places he'd never even thought of.

By the time Lizzie finished with Paul, he was panting slightly and staring at her with that familiar heat. They'd gathered something of an audience, drawing the notice of the crowd that had been listening to the music. Dima tossed a ten in the vato's hat, shrugging silently as Lizzie and Paul tripped away, laughing.

He caught up with them in just a couple strides. They hadn't noticed he'd been lagging behind.

At the door to the restaurant, Paul held the brass-handled glass open with a wide flourish. Lots of black-and-white checks filled the interior, from the tiles across the floor to the backsplash behind the giant flat-topped grill. The booths were all red vinyl, topping off the slightly '50s kitsch vibe.

Dima slid into a booth by the plate-glass window. Paul automatically sat across from him. For a moment, Lizzie hovered at the edge of the table as if she didn't know where to go. Decision made, she hopped in next to Paul and tucked her shoulders under his.

He ought not to blame her for the choice. If given the opportunity, he'd have enjoyed teasing and tormenting the blond god. He wouldn't have been gentle as he dug his fingers into Paul's thighs, either.

Dima had never claimed to be a reasonable man. He was a petty, small bastard and damn it all, he wanted Lizzie sitting next to him. As if she were his girl, not his partner. The bone-deep grind of his teeth spiked pain down his jaw.

The menu was a single laminated sheet. "Where are the lighter items?"

Paul and Lizzie exchanged an amused look. While Dima didn't wish to be so self-centered as to think it was at his expense, he could see no other option.

"There is no light stuff," Paul eventually supplied.

The air was thick with grease and the scent of potatoes, but Dima had assumed there would be other options in this day and age. The stupid, small problem ate at him.

Just like Lizzie's words from this morning still niggled and ate at him. Just like he blamed himself for the months they'd lost. Every time a woman's heels clicked on a dance floor, he expected the sickly crunch of bone to follow. Tears and bellows of pain were inevitable. Lizzie hadn't just cried from the pain, but with the panic of uncertainty. He'd only been able to hold her and murmur nonsense words until the paramedics arrived.

How could Dima expect her to let his failures go if he couldn't let them go either? So much had always weighed him down, from his parents' expectations to his own. Anyone he dropped had a long way to fall.

He'd been contemplating making Lizzie his partner in more than just dance? What a fool.

A tiny brunette waitress appeared. With the pad in her

hand flipped open, she smiled as if greeting old friends. "What can I get you?"

"Coffee for me," Paul said.

"Same," Lizzie chirped.

"Please, a cup of coffee." Dima pinned his gaze on the pair at the other side of the table. "As it seems to be the only thing I'll be having this morning."

Paul grinned. "You've got to try the bacon omelet. I think they put half a pig in it."

"I don't think that's nearly as enticing as you mean it to sound."

"C'mon, live a little," Lizzie said.

She rubbed the toe of her shoe along his calf. If she believed she could manipulate him with a half-assed caress like that, he would need to reeducate her.

"I take care of myself. Much as I take care of you."

Her eyebrows went up, but she said nothing.

Paul glanced back and forth between them both and waved the menu. "I think my favorite is the hash browns though. Perfectly done. Crispy on the outside, soft on the inside."

Dima was as locked and ready as if he were about to begin a tango. Supercharged. Stretched near to breaking.

Lizzie leaned forward and splayed her hands on the glossy table. "Do you have a problem, Dima?" she asked, her voice so low it neared a growl.

"That display, in the park." He narrowed his eyes. "And yesterday, using me to show off for Remy. You danced with more passion and vitality than in the last two years on tour. You'll dance like that for fun, but not when it could mean a second career for us?"

"We have a career, as soon as my therapy is done."

The waitress snapped her notebook shut. "I'll just come

back in a few," she said before she scuttled away.

Paul sighed, but only put his arm across the back of Lizzie's seat as if settling in for a long wait.

"Your therapy could be done if you weren't scared." From what must be the deepest recesses of his brain, he spilled out heated words. "You're scared I'll let you down again. That I'm not as invested as you are."

"You're full of crap." Her eyes flashed with the most passion he'd seen from her during daylight hours. "You're the one who wants to stay in that dive. I'd have expected more ambition from you!"

This. This was what he'd missed. Not the fighting, but the engagement. The feeling that they were connected. Only feeling it while his cock was in her mouth made him realize how much they'd lost. Even sniping at each other in a grease-laden diner felt better than two months of frozen hell.

He fisted his hands on his knees beneath the table. She'd withdrawn her foot. "Do you have any idea what I've given up for you?"

"Nothing." Her mouth turned down into a genuine pout. "You slid right into Devant as if you didn't even miss dancing with me. So yeah, thanks for visiting me at my parents' house. Believe me, I appreciated the distraction from Mom hovering. But that isn't the same and you know it. How could you decide to just...*quit*? Quit us?"

He reached out, snagging her hands between both of his. Her fingers were cold, which made sense because he was a rock in a midwinter field. Everything had been colder in these months living a half-life. "I missed you. You are my partner. But I won't have my decisions thrown in my face as if I've done something wrong."

Just as he'd expected, she tried to pull away. Paul put a hand behind her back. Though the other man was rubbing softly, the sympathetic look he threw Dima said he was also keeping her put.

Lizzie pursed her lips, her posture aggressive. "What decisions? To throw away your training? To give up on our partnership?"

"No, to give up on Svetlana."

"Not my fault you broke up with that cow."

He turned the words over in his head once, twice. He'd held few secrets from Lizzie. He hadn't liked keeping this one, but it had been his burden. It had been his call. She'd needed all her strength to recover without hearing his dilemmas.

"Sveta offered me the lead in her new show."

She pulled on her hand again, but he wasn't letting go. Instead, her eyes drifted shut—as close to hiding as she could get without physical movement. "The one on Broadway?"

"Yes."

"I..." The lovely dark green of her eyes had clouded with confusion. "What happened? Tell me."

"Word about what had happened to your knee didn't take long to get around. You know how fast bad news travels."

He stared down at the glossy red polish on her fingernails. Maybe earlier that morning he would've found pleasure in the thought of her nails on his flesh, as her stinging need urged him on. At that moment, however, he would've looked at *anything*. Anything to distance himself from what he needed to admit.

"I sat in the ER waiting room. They wouldn't let me see you yet." The diner's savory scents mingled with that sharp memory, twisting his stomach. "Svetlana called me. She made her offer. Tried to convince me to become partners on stage as well as off. Broadway was what she dangled. Our own show."

Lizzie's brow wrinkled. "You passed it up?"

He flicked a glance at Paul. How strange to think they were playing out such intimacies both with and before him. "I did, and I ended it with her on the day of your first surgery."

"You'd been with her for two years. I didn't like her, but..." More confusion, with something near to sadness. "Why would you do that?"

"Don't you understand yet, little one?" His heart pinched. They were lost. Both of them. He knew only one thing. "I will never go anywhere you aren't eventually willing to follow."

Chapter Seventeen

Lizzie stood beside Mr. George at the entrance to Club Devant. He smoked a cigar and nodded on occasion to the notable faces who slipped through the velvet ropes without hesitation. Other curious guests and ticketholders waited for Mr. George to feel like doing a little work. Lizzie could've gone in right away, but she lingered while calling herself all manner of chickenshit.

More than a week had passed since their weekend and since Dima had left the diner without eating. As a featured headliner, he wouldn't be performing on a Tuesday night, but she knew he'd be there. They couldn't share an apartment and not know one another's comings and goings. Having for the most part avoided her since walking out of that disastrous breakfast, he would be inside somewhere. Talking with the other dancers. Mingling with patrons, even though he hated it. Practicing with women who weren't Lizzie.

Although she would've liked to avoid him right back, she hadn't seen Paul either. She missed them both. Negotiating the currents of their threesome had meant a living-on-the-edge weekend. Now she had none of it. No danger, companionship, fun. It highlighted all the more exactly how limited her world had become since her injury.

Back on the circuit, her mind kept saying. All this unsettled crap would fit back into the right shape. She'd have her friends back, her partner, her life.

Yet...where had those friends been when she in a hospital room, so doped up on painkillers that she'd sung along to a block of '80s vids on VH1? Where had they been when Dima was, apparently, fending off a stringy Russian witch who scoped for dance partners in the ER waiting room? Where were they when endless questions spun her brain like a top?

Nope. Nada. After more than a decade as a touring professional, she had left the circuit with exactly zero by way of non-Dima-shaped friends.

"He turned her down," she said absently to Mr. George. So much a fixture of Club Devant, talking to him was like talking to the massive red-and-gold neon sign. She could never tell if Declan had designed the place ironically, or if his odd Irish sense of style decided this was how an upscale sex revue should look.

Mr. George only nodded. "Course he would."

Lizzie glanced at him sharply. Surely he didn't know what the hell she was talking about. *She* barely did. "I mean, who would do that? Turn down an opportunity like that?"

He shrugged. "Not me. Which means you're talking to the wrong guy. In or out, Miss Lizzie. Unless you like nosy bitches shooting eye daggers at you. Yeah, I'm talking about you, you skinny tramp. Get back in line."

Although she had no idea who the woman was, Lizzie waved toodles with her fingertips and headed inside with her decision made. She would at least see Paul. If Dima happened to be there...well, maybe it was time they talked. So far, *not talking* had been a disaster.

Tuesday night was relatively quiet, despite the people Mr. George made stand on line outside. "Relatively quiet" meant she could see Paul. The swarm around the bar was a little less densely packed. He wore his cowboy hat and a white wife-beater T-shirt, making plain ol' cotton look obscene. Big smile for everyone—even the men, she noticed. That made her smile too. No matter what this experience meant for her and Dima, she hoped it had opened doors for Paul. Maybe he would simply have more...options.

She wiggled through the crowd and behind the bar. Standing behind Paul on tippy-toes, she grabbed his cowboy hat and shoved it on her own head. Without missing a beat with his cocktail shaker, he glanced over his shoulder with a grin that said he knew who he'd find.

"Hey, gorgeous. You here to help me with the dishes? I'm behind."

"Me? Dishes?" She giggled and started loading a batch of glasses into a huge plastic tray. Already she anticipated watching him lift the heavy thing and haul it back to the kitchen.

"Been a while," he said conversationally.

"Yup. Sorry."

"Any news?"

"News?"

He shot her a *don't be dumb* look and took a twenty from a well-endowed brunette. She waved off the change.

Lizzie laughed behind her hand. "You must make some hellacious tips."

Licking his lower lip, he ignored the next round of orders and cornered Lizzie against the counter. "That I do."

"Arrogant ass."

"Don't say that word. I'll get grabby."

"I wouldn't call the cops on you. Pinkie swear."

"Hey, Lyle, you got this for a second?"

The other barman waved with a towel and returned to handing a redhead three glasses of white wine. She hardly looked steady enough to manage.

"Cool. C'mon, we got a minute or two." He pulled her into

the corridor between the bar and the kitchen. Lizzie flipped her hair, hoping to distract him from whatever he was hinting about. Probably Dima-related.

God, she was tired of being scared all the time. No such luck.

Paul's smile didn't stick around. That now-familiar concern shone from his eyes, which were shadowy in the club's dim lighting. "So, spill it. What's up with you two?"

"You haven't been here?"

"Nope. I have a new gig in Westchester, renovating a big, drafty old colonial. A good two months' work. I was out there this weekend for the interview. Tonight's my last regular night."

"Wow." Lizzie rested her hands on his biceps. She squeezed. Damn, such a rocket and already burning out. Had she really thought it would be any different? After all, shagging him in a dressing room wasn't the best start to a potential relationship. Nor was sharing him with her dance partner. "I'm...damn, Paul, I'm happy for you. A bit disappointed you won't be around, but I'm glad you'll be doing what you love."

His mouth tightened. "Save it, Lizzie."

"Huh?"

Leaning closer, he was near enough to share breaths—his calm but heavy, hers truncated. She wasn't used to seeing Paul upset. "If you'd wanted to see me so bad, you'd have found me. Dima or not. We both knew that wasn't going to happen, not after what he said at the diner."

"He didn't mean it. I know he didn't. He's still angry for what I said that morning."

"No way. He doesn't seem like the guy to open up like that if he didn't mean to."

"You call that opening up? Seriously?"

"You don't? Jesus, open your eyes. Because, sure, guys

make statements like that all the time. As for the do-what-you-love shtick, you don't get to talk about that stuff when you're wallowing too."

"Where do you get off?"

With a sad shake of his head, he touched her shoulder, petting the bare skin revealed by her purple spaghetti strap top. "I'm not angry, Liz. Promise. I just know where I play in all of this, but I don't think you do." A customer yelled for his attention, but he waved him off. "It's time to be honest. You can know a person for years and still not know them. Not even see them."

"I don't get it."

He exhaled heavily. "I told my wife of six years that, on occasion, I fantasize about men. I thought all her anti-gay shit was just Texas talking. That our marriage would hold. Hell, that she loved me more than that. It was only fantasy, anyway. Wasn't like I was gonna go pick up a rentboy."

"But she...?" Her heart sank for him as the lines on either side of his mouth tightened. Without his smile, he seemed a little older, a little less like Paul.

"We gave it time in counseling, gave each other space. That was all we could manage. You know what? At the end, it hurt like fuck." He straightened and grabbed the nearest bottle of Jack, pouring them each a shot. "Yet...I'm here. I'm in love with this town, and I've already had a helluva time. If you put too much of yourself in a box, you'll regret it. I would've had I stayed."

She downed the whiskey, needing another three or four to quell the restless pain in her gut. "What does this have to do with me and Dima?"

"Could you go back to just being friends?"

Hell no.

Mine.

The words were so quick and clear that she grabbed the counter. Fear rushed in behind it, equally powerful. It was easier with Paul there to say the things she and Dima couldn't say to each other. To carry on without him was a terrifying prospect.

To carry on without Dima at all...

He gave up a Broadway show. He gave up his girlfriend. For Lizzie. What insanity thought that was a fair trade, especially when he hadn't ever told her? He never talked, but telling her at least a little bit would've been enough to keep her holding on forever. Instead she'd spent months reading tea leaves and trying to figure out why he'd chosen to perform at Devant.

He'd done it to stay with her, without changing a damn thing about how they'd lived.

"You have a lot to think about, and I have to work before Declan takes my head off." Paul stood up straight and crossed his arms. "Now you get to ask where he is."

Lizzie grimaced. "Where is he?"

"Some dark-haired Russian chick has him holed up in a corner booth by the stage."

Ice. Pure ice. She fumbled for a second shot, abandoning the bottle when Paul took control. Even an extra dose of JD didn't melt the fear. What if Dima had given up? He laid himself out there so rarely, no matter how clumsily. He'd done so with gusto at the diner. Now he was cozied up to Svetlana—his bitchy, skeletal back-up plan—in a corner booth.

"When do you get off?" she asked, her voice rough. Tears pressed against the backs of her eyelids. "Work, I mean."

Paul glanced at an art deco wall clock. "An hour."

"One last romp before you head for Westchester?"

"Lizzie..."

"What?"

"Do you think that's such a good idea?"

"I don't have any others. I need to get him away from her and out of here. I promise, I'll talk with him in the morning. We'll smooth it out and make it work."

Paul's mouth twisted up in a bunch. "You sure?"

"Yeah, just not...shit, not tonight. I have to sort through this."

No matter that she'd had more than a week. Watching Dima walk out of that diner, his back ramrod straight but his neck bowed low, should've triggered *something*. Something stronger. More certain. Maybe an all-encompassing need to call him back and make it right. Why hadn't that happened? Jesus, what if she wasn't ever going to be able to feel anything but intense friendship, even desire and possession? He was her whole world. A piece of her was broken if she still wanted more from him.

After what he'd sacrificed on her behalf... Dima deserved better.

"So you'd rather sort it out after doing two guys?"

She playfully slapped his arm. "Shut up! It's not like you don't like it too."

"Never said otherwise. Besides, those regrets I mentioned? I don't have any when it comes to what we've done." He exhaled slowly. "So. Okay. You go work on him. I'll come check on you both when I'm off my shift. Make sure you're still speaking before my dick gets any ideas."

Lizzie wanted to protest—of course they'd still be talking—but Paul had returned to the bar, and she wasn't certain at all. She leaned against the wall and admired his back, his ass, his long legs. In her head, Dima wasn't ever going to be just a friend again, and Paul wasn't ever going to be her lover, free and clear of complication. She'd muddled them too closely in her memories. Dima could stand tall on his own, but Paul was too new. He would always be a living, breathing reminder of this heartache.

Before she could chicken out, again, she forced her sluggish body back into the main room of the club. Declan's newest hire, Jack, was on stage. He was a wiry, graceful jazz dancer with a spray of fluffy hair at the top of his head, while the sides were much more close cut. He practically owned the audience. Every flashy move and giant gesture played to their applause and their silences. He told stories with his body. Made her watch, made her wait, made her feel.

She'd never known anything like it on the circuit. She'd been respected and adored by judges, but that wasn't the same as feeling five hundred people *breathing* with her. They breathed with Jack. Stiffness was all Lizzie saw in the mirror when she tried to loosen up. She'd been a pro for too long, until even the sexiness and sensuality of Latin dance had become proscribed.

The wild cheers and applause said Jack was well received. Not that it mattered when Lizzie spotted Dima. With Svetlana. Practically in his lap. She'd lost weight, if that was possible. Her hair was most definitely a wig. And, ugh, the fake tan. It looked garish and plain *wrong* on a Siberian woman who'd probably been born as pale as a three-day-dead trout.

Did wanting to rip her nasty wig off and burn it in the table's lone votive constitute a personal or professional jealousy? Lizzie couldn't tell the difference anymore. She just wanted the woman disintegrated.

"Hello, Svetlana."

"Hello, Elizabeth."

Dima shifted. His body language said uncomfortable but his face remained stoically detached. God, she wanted to shake him. "Will you have a seat, Lizzie?"

She took more room than she needed, pushing her leg against Dima's. It was a compromise against what she really wanted, which was jabbing her heel into Svetlana's calf. "You're looking...well."

"You haven't put on so much weight as I expected." Svetlana pursed her bright red lips and sipped tonic water. "You know, with the injury."

"Is that something new you're doing with your hair?"

Dima grabbed her hand under the table and clasped it. Yet he quirked his eyebrow only slightly. How often had he given her a similar warning through the years? *Back off*, it said. *We're grownups.* She sure wished she believed that. Nothing had changed since they were in junior high. Only these catfighting combatants wore more makeup and higher heels.

All she could think was that Dima had chosen her over Svetlana. Terrifying, but also glorious.

To be this man's choice...

She cleared her throat. "Paul got a new job." If she looked at the stage, she could pretend all of this was normal. It sure as hell wasn't. Her heart was beating so hard that she couldn't even hear the blaring music, let alone the words she mouthed. "He won't be around regularly. Thought you'd want to say *schastlivo*. Be happy and all."

Still, she needed to see that reaction. His reaction. Lust flared in Dima's eyes, going slightly wider with shock. The hand gripping hers tightened nearly to crushing force. If she reached between his legs, would she find him already hard?

He let her go. "Sveta and I have a great deal to discuss."

She'd always hated when he used Svetlana's diminutive. It was too intimate.

That intimacy was back.

Lizzie was going to be sick. Or pass out. Or stay this disturbingly numb for the rest of her life.

Whatever would've happened was cut short by Paul's

arrival. Lizzie shot out of the booth. She made hasty introductions before tugging his arm. Flee. Run away. Be done with pretending there was anything more to be had with her and Dima. It had been a dumb idea when she started this whole mess, and it was even dumber now, when he seemed poised to make use of his skinny Russian escape route.

"Not gonna happen," she whispered to Paul. "I can't make this right."

"You can. Tomorrow. Remember?"

She hadn't replied before Paul brushed past her and slid into the booth. Right beside Dima. Svetlana had clung all the more tightly with Lizzie's intrusion, but Paul's intimate posture actually made her sit back. Darkly penciled eyebrows lifted high. She looked to Lizzie for explanation. *Too bad, lady.* Whereas Paul seemed to look to her for assurance.

"Promise, Lizzie?" he asked above the din.

She nodded, a little dazed—although what she really promised remained out of grasp. How was she going to make this right? At least she could talk to Dima. Try to. Her best friend. Her partner of fifteen years. Yes, she would talk to him seriously and be as open as he needed. No secrets anymore.

Yeah, right. Plenty of secrets remained, because right in plain sight, Paul leaned over and whispered in Dima's ear.

Chapter Eighteen

"Fuck me or be fucked. Your choice, but it has to be tonight." Paul's voice cracked through Dima's skin in small, short zings.

Welcome to the land of the surreal. Svetlana still sat to his side, her hand on his upper arm, though much more loosely. The bulk of Paul's body warmed his other side. In front of him...Lizzie. Everything hinged on her, whether she realized it or not. She shone like a beacon, a bare sliver of risk between home and being dashed on rocks.

Did she mean this as a farewell? More than a decade of partnership and she'd shatter them both. She couldn't even do that alone. She offered him Paul, no matter what Dima had said in the diner.

He hadn't been fair, either. To drop it and run, lay low for a week, then sit with Svetlana. He hadn't invited her, but he sure as hell hadn't sent her away either. However, when faced with the choice between her and the combined shimmer and sexuality of Paul and Lizzie... There was no choice.

Saying good night to Svetlana took on a hazy feel, like he swam through smoke. The whole time, Paul and Lizzie waited behind him. Paul's vibe was slightly smug, while his little one was as unreadable as ever. She was two seconds from bolting. Maybe she would've gone already if not for Paul's strong arm hooked around her waist.

Even the cab ride continued like that. Dima sat up front, watching Paul and Lizzie in the rearview mirror. He'd expected them to begin without him, but they sat primly, only their thighs pressed together and their hands linked. Lizzie rested her head on Paul's shoulder, but her eyes didn't falter from Dima's.

She would always be his. Even if they were apart.

In the apartment, no one turned on lights. Dima led the silent procession to his bedroom. An orange glow from a streetlight poured through his slanted blinds.

Lizzie looked so lost. She stood by the bed, her arms crossed over her chest. They'd done this before in laughter and fun, never mind the intensity. This was more like a punishment or an obligation. Although the wrongness sat heavily between Dima's shoulder blades, he could no more stop than he could make sense of what would be best for all three. Need clouded his judgment. He should be stronger, but even that admonishment didn't stop him.

Tiny shadows ringed under Lizzie's eyes, and he wondered how the hell he'd not noticed. Because he'd been all but ignoring her, afraid of this, that all he'd find was the excitement of the sex, not the connection he missed so much.

Afraid he'd settle yet again.

But fine. If Paul was leaving and this was all Lizzie offered, he'd make sure it was the best damn fuck of their lives.

"Kneel," he snapped, pointing at the floor in front of him.

Damn, they both did, though Paul's eyebrows lifted in a sardonic tilt. The sharp rush of power woke Dima's cock. Hunger worked him hard.

He stripped fast, because a slow tease was beyond him. Grasping his cock, he held it between their up-turned faces. Paul reached around to grab Dima's ass, his fingertips straying to the pucker of his anus. He opened his mouth, took Dima's cock first. Lizzie next, as they passed it back and forth, their tongues twirling and sliding.

He wanted to grab Lizzie's hair and jerk her head down on

his dick until her eyes watered and she looked up at him with such pretty pleading. See how much of them was left.

"God, you're both so good at that." He rubbed his hand over Paul's bristling buzz cut. "Did you ever think you'd suck cock so well?"

Paul released his hold with a wet smack. "I don't know about well." The grin he flashed was completely cheeky—the thing Dima would always remember about him. "But I'm having fun while I do it."

"C'mere."

Dima yanked him up to a deep, mean kiss. He couldn't take all the happy, as he battled the all-so-wrong feeling in the air. When their lips slid, pulled, and when Dima's teeth tugged on Paul's bottom lip, he could make it go away—until Lizzie stood next to them both. Dima couldn't *not* kiss her. Denying himself a taste of his little one was like going without oxygen.

Though perhaps he'd soon find out what that was like.

"Strip," he ordered. "Paul, your clothes off too. Lizzie, flat on your back on the bed, legs spread so I can see that pretty pussy."

She liked that. He could see it in the way her breathing shortened and jerked, the way her breasts bounced as she stripped off her shimmery black tank top and wiggled out of her tiny silver shorts. She obeyed him to the letter, spreading her legs wide enough that her toes clenched the corners of the mattress. Her pussy gleamed and shone with wetness. Graceful hands fisted in the sheets at her side.

Fuck, she was gorgeous. The proud rise of her breasts, the soft dip of her toned stomach. She considered him through lids heavily shaded by thick lashes, her wide smile long gone. Her pale peach lips were tight with anticipation. Even that added to her appeal. She was nervous but she was lying there because he'd told her to. She was everything that was perfection.

After grabbing a couple things from the nightstand, Dima knee-walked onto the bed, between her feet but not quite touching. He pulled Paul up behind him, and the big man wrapped his arms around Dima's waist. His hands slid, touched, eased some of the stiffness—and thank God for it, because Dima thought his cracking, popping energy might start to escape out his skin.

"Is this what you want, little one?" Dima purred, intentionally low and rough. Reaching behind, he wrapped his hand around Paul's thick erection. "Do you want to see me take this cock up my ass?"

She jolted visibly, her lips parting. "Let me see. Please, Dima mine."

His smile felt decidedly cold. "Oh, but I'm not yours. Not so long as he's fucking me."

She started to make words, but her eyes fluttered half shut. She only shook her head. Her gaze dipped to the empty stretch of mattress between them.

"Paul, would you like to see Lizzie touch herself?"

"Fuck, yes." The man's chin dug into Dima's shoulder. His hands clenched.

"Obey, Lizzie."

She did, immediately. One hand went to her breast and the other cupped her pussy in a hard clench.

Dima had never seen anything more erotic. A pure, powerful hit of his sweet girl.

He rolled a condom onto Paul and lubed him up. The trick would be holding himself back. Not letting her see exactly how messed up he was. All his plans had toppled, everything out of line. How could he be expected to make logical decisions when real life paled in the face of Lizzie? When she turned everything incandescent with a stray glance and a few touches?

When she actually meant to shine, she left him breathless, unmoored, humbled.

Paul grunted when Dima closed his fist around his cock, but he didn't flag. The muscular cowboy was as huge as Dima had ever seen, swelled and aroused.

Dima leaned his head back to nestle his cheek against the other man's jaw. Stubble met roughness. It was hard to tell where each of them left off. "You've fucked women up the ass, yes?"

Paul groaned on another stroke of Dima's well-lubed hand. "Yes," he hissed.

"Just like that." He bowed forward. His fists planted on the outside of Lizzie's hips, but still he didn't touch her. He couldn't. Not yet.

He knew what she hoped for, in her soft pant and the way her hips tipped toward his mouth, but not this time. He couldn't link them until he could take all of her—everything he'd wanted for so long.

There'd be no stopping him this time.

Paul wedged a hand over Dima's ass, holding him open. Dima hissed at the first nudge of Paul's cock. The slight sting. The deep and dark pressure.

Taboo, dangerous, goddamn gorgeous.

Dima dropped his head back at the invasion. It had been years since he'd taken another man, even without Lizzie watching the whole time. Her eyes burned with fascination, her lips open and glossy. The soft stroke of her fingers over her wet pussy distracted Dima until Paul was seated hip deep.

God, he was so much. Overwhelming. Especially when Paul shuddered and bent his forehead to the nape of Dima's neck.

"Good," he growled. "Good, fuck. Oh, so good."

Dima couldn't help a small smile. That was what he got out

of bottoming, a feeling that he'd given his partner a gift unlike anything else, that he'd taken Paul's world and completely shaken it up. He would forever be the first man Paul had fucked, which was only the icing on the cake.

"I'm glad you like it." He smoothed one hand behind him, caressing the back of Paul's head. Testing the thrust and fill, he flexed his ass. "Now fuck me."

Paul huffed a short breath. "I'm so not going to last long."

Lizzie liked that. Her eyelids drooped, and she pinched one of her dusky nipples. "Dima's perfection, isn't he? Worth your first time."

"God, yes."

"That's it." Dima moaned quietly. "Deep as you can."

Paul started slow, his cock stroking languorously, but his pace didn't stay that way. He drew long, juddering flourishes of pleasure from Dima. Hovering over Lizzie while Paul pulled in and out of his ass was only the crowning touch. He grabbed handfuls of twisted sheets, holding back the blooming pleasure as Paul slid over his prostate. Good was such an understatement.

Lizzie grinned. "Right here, Dima. Did you ever think?" Her fingers dipped into her pussy. She lifted them to her mouth, licking, before touching them to Dima's lips.

Salty, clean and sweet at the same time. His Lizzie, no matter how this worked out. He sucked two of her fingers into his mouth. His tongue darted all around, cleaning her taste away. Taking it into himself.

He was riding so high on a wire. Sparks threw out, shining down his body. Paul worked his ass. Lizzie was so close, all soft flesh and toned muscle. He dove his hand into her hair and angled her neck to reveal another curve—one meant for him to take and mark. He locked his teeth on that vulnerable tendon and bit down.

"That's what you don't get," he whispered. "I did think. Over and over."

This moment wasn't quite it. The taste was slightly off, like slamming down the wrong drink—something nearly as good, but not what he wanted.

He traced his mouth down to her breast, bit the tight bead of her nipple and licked it with the flat of his tongue. "I've thought of fucking you more times than I can count."

Something about that worked on Lizzie, because her hand stuttered in her cunt and a low groan stuttered out of her slender throat.

Dima locked his hand over hers. Wetness slipped between their fingers, her pussy trapped beneath. "No," he said sharply. "I didn't say you could come yet."

"Fuck, that's dirty," Paul muttered.

He thrust once, twice, slamming harder. Sharp pleasure rocked all the way up Dima's spine, but he held back the orgasm tingling in his own balls. He had a plan. Of course he did.

Paul's hands froze, locked deep around Dima's hips as he came. Two more surges coincided with a stream of curses from the easygoing man. Another rush of exhilaration swept Dima's vision dark. The power was all that mattered. He'd be Paul's first forever.

Now it was time to take what he intended. He couldn't get the condom on fast enough, even while Paul was panting and withdrawing.

Lizzie knew what was coming. Her hands rose over her head to the headboard. The pose stretched her tits up in a pretty picture. Pure submission. She bent her knees, the better to shelter him. Her throat worked with a swallow.

"Dima." Her voice was so soft that he wondered if he'd imagined it. "My turn."

One rock forward was all it took.

His cock slid into her tight sheath. Arms twined together, his elbow just over her shoulder. One of her feet rose to hook over his ass. Fucking her was like being at peace in his own mind.

Finally.

Chapter Nineteen

Lizzie had long ago put "sex with Dima" into a faraway corner of her thoughts, where things like one-night stands dwelled.

But this...

This bright, hot memory would blaze for the rest of her life.

Dima's first full thrust slammed her back against the brass headboard. She groaned and gripped even tighter, just to keep pace. That slight shift of arm and finger was the only leeway he allowed. The rest of her belonged to his hands, his mouth, his thick, pounding cock.

He stretched between her legs. The sure, strong length of his body determined their pace. He took hold of her calf and hooked it over his shoulder. After licking the inside of her knee, he softly bit her inner thigh. She shuddered, just as he changed the angle of his hips and hit her G-spot. The first tingles of *oh, yes, there it is* began to gather low, low in her belly.

Lizzie wanted to grin at him, to marvel with him. They could be so damn good. Except Dima was fucking her with more determination than she'd seen him attack any challenge. No finesse, despite how graceful he could be. This was all about power and faultless rhythm. A grim cast to his mouth made him nearly frown. Two lines furrowed between his dark, dark eyes. Shadows took so much of his light, and the anger shimmering between them stole his laughter.

God, she missed him.

She turned her face to one side, blinking back emotion that had no place in that moment. Paul had knelt by the side of the bed, his head pillowed by his forearms crisscrossed on the mattress. Just watching. He was smiling with a gorgeously dazed expression, as if his every fantasy were in the midst of coming true. Despite the shadows in Dima's bedroom, Paul remained a sunny center of light.

Lizzie reached out to touch his brow. She needed that. No matter what fierce pleasure Dima wrung from her body, she needed the safe port he was not.

Dima grabbed her hand and flung it around his neck. "Hold on to me. *Me.* Don't let go."

She would've fought back if not for the gruff, unexpected pleading in his voice. So much emotion there. So surprising. Her heart tightened around a protective twinge. She'd cared about him for years, but that moment cemented something vital and surprisingly tender. Something well beyond simple caring.

"I've got you." Finding his earlobe, she licked the entire curve. "You've got me. You lead and I follow. Take us there, Dima mine."

A strangled sound dragged her attention to his throat. She lifted her head and latched her mouth on his taut skin. He'd see her mark the next morning when he shaved, wear it all day when he practiced at the club.

"Again," he grunted as he shoved deeper. His lean dancer's hips were brutally strong. Lizzie rocked back with every pulse and grind. She scratched her nails along his shoulders and sucked until his demand for more and more sank into a hoarse moan. "Tell me you're close, Lizzie."

"You know my body better than I do," she panted. "You know I am."

Braced on his knees, he wrapped an arm around her lower back, bowing her breasts to his mouth. His other hand clasped and kneaded. He tugged one nipple to a hard point and suckled. The stroke of his tongue matched that of his prick.

Lizzie slid her taut fingertips down his slick, straining biceps until the texture became rougher. He kept his chest waxed for performances, but his forearms glittered with pale brown, sweat-sleek hair. From boy to man, he had always been hers, but never like this. Never as if their skin would soften and their breath would fuse two people into one.

He spoke against her second nipple. "So wet, little one."

Apparently to prove the point, he slipped free of her pussy. Lizzie cried out. Filled...and *empty*. Just like that. He dragged his hand up from between her legs, painting her stomach with her arousal. Two times, three. Without taking his eyes from hers, he thrust out his arm and smiled only slightly when Paul edged forward to lick his fingers.

"Yes, you are so close," he said. "But most of the time, close isn't good enough."

Lizzie shivered at his foreboding comment, but she had no time—no inclination—to parse his meaning. Dima was a puzzle, but their pleasure was not. She trusted implicitly that he would see this to the explosive conclusion they both craved.

"Paul, you still with us?" he asked.

"Right here." Lizzie didn't need to see his face to hear the grin, but she looked anyway. He nodded once, a little sign of encouragement. "May I be of assistance?"

Dima's wide mouth twisted. That same determination. That same darkness. "Lube. Your fingers. Our Lizzie needs her ass fucked too."

With that he brought his mouth down on hers with surprising force. His tongue pushed inside. She grabbed his head with both hands, feeling his jaw work beneath her fingertips. More delicious hair, this time the bare scrape of stubble. She rubbed her mouth, her cheeks, her inner wrists along his jaw, savoring that tingling burn. Every nerve ending had gone numb, poised between pleasure and release, and she needed it hard, harder still.

They drank each other. Just the two of them. Until Paul's fingers, cold with lube, found her asshole. She breathed into Dima's mouth and arched. All she could do was anchor herself with a firm grip on the strong cords running from his shoulders to his neck. He lifted her feet until her knees neared her shoulders, holding them to one side with his powerful left hand. The pose exposed her pussy and asshole—and kept his right hand free.

"God I love a flexible woman," Paul whispered, his voice awed.

"Shit, yes," came Dima's reply. He seemed to catch himself, reining in his appreciative lapse. "You're going to be still, little one."

"Dima, no. Can't— Oh!"

Paul's finger pushed inside. First one. Two. Oh, fuck, *three.*

Sweet Christ. Her body was opening to another man's touch, but she couldn't take her eyes off Dima. He knelt above her, hands at her ankles. He was like a conquering warrior— just waiting for Paul to find the perfect slow, sliding rhythm. Shadows arrowed between Dima's pectorals. Shoulders and arms had been perfectly molded by years of holding her, lifting her, guiding her. His taut stomach defined what it was to be a fit, ripped man. His erection jutted up from his groin, thick and long, all beautiful phallic power.

Paul shoved deep. Lizzie squeaked in surprise. Dima caught her throat in one hand. "You're going to be still," he repeated. "Understand me?"

She tried to speak, but he pressed on just the right spot to block her air and surged inside.

Gray swam over Lizzie's vision. Her thoughts blew apart. Dima was relentless. His pause in the action had dried her a little. So much more friction now, glorious and sharp with pleasure. He cracked past her conscious mind and threw her into a place of pure, greedy sensation. She fought for it, strove toward it, even as she knew it was beyond her ability to bear.

The gray darkened to a thicker haze. Her blood sizzled and her heartbeat became Latin drums in her skull. Dima's huge cock beat the tempo of thrust and withdrawal. Paul's worked an intimate counterpoint, with his three fingers quick and sure. And Jesus, that muscular hand still held her throat, truncating another inhale as she climbed right to the edge of the cliff.

Dima grabbed her jaw, anchoring her. "Little one," he growled. "Come back to me."

And suddenly she could breathe again. The air rushed in on a cool, glorious gasp. Dima. She found Dima. Dark eyes nearly black, nostrils wide, expression pained as he fucked her. Nothing held back. In her mind Lizzie began to chant *no, no, no, no. Too much.*

"Make me happy, little one," he whispered, every syllable a fight for breath. Sweat rolled down his lats and his elegant ribs. "Let go. Let it all go."

Her climax would not be denied, not with that softly pleading command—as if he needed her release more than she did. She burst apart on a shriek she'd never recognize as her own voice. "Dima. Yes. Dima, oh God."

The words slurred, but not before he grabbed her legs right where they met her body. Palm to hipbone. Leverage. Power. Distantly she felt Paul slip away as Dima's mind drifted toward bliss. She loved seeing it happen. Dark eyes rolled closed. After a sharp, grunted, "Fuck me," and a last hard thrust, his expression lost its tension. His lower lip went slack on something close to a smile. Pure wonderment. He was shaking as badly as she, like they'd just practiced to the point of total muscle collapse.

He withdrew and sank to all fours, reminiscent of the pose

he'd struck to receive Paul, but his fight was gone. All the tightness. He slumped to her side, his hands coming right to her waist. Neck bowed, he tucked his mouth to her temple, still breathing hard. "My Lizzie," he whispered, feather soft.

Slowly, as Dima's sleepy exhales counted the rhythm, she straightened her legs and blew out the last of the stiffness. Only a floating rush of satisfaction remained.

The faucet in the bathroom turned off. Paul emerged wearing a towel around his waist. The hair at the back of his neck was damp. "You're so beautiful," she heard herself saying.

Beside her, Dima grunted something that may have been an affirmative. She petted the back of his head, down his nape and up again. Soothing them both, away from the eye of the storm. He may have drifted out to sleep and back—or maybe not—while Paul cleaned up.

"If you say so," Paul said with a chuckle. He sat on the edge of the bed. Boxy stomach muscles folded together like perfect origami. His thighs were *lovely.* "I gotta scram though. Not that I wouldn't love to cuddle."

Lizzie felt drugged. Nothing worked right, which was an odd sensation for a dancer. Not worthy of panic like an injury, but that she could disconnect for a while. What a gift.

"We can make room," she said. "Even for a big boy like you."

"I have to be in Westchester in..." He looked over to Dima's glowing red alarm clock. "Shit, four hours."

"Crash on the couch. Leave tomorrow?"

"Nope. Gonna head home. You stay here and enjoy this for both of us, okay?"

Stay with Dima. In his bed. Wake up in his arms. Lizzie bit her lower lip and closed her eyes on a rush of pure want. An exhale shuddered out of her chest.

Paul traced a finger over where Dima had held her throat. "We weren't too rough, were we?"

At least that was a topic she could discuss without a greed so swift it left her lightheaded.

Sex? Easy.

A heart full of forever? No way.

"You were just right. All of it, just amazing." She grinned big time. "And you? Something to write home about?"

"Oh, fuck no." He chuckled as he stroked a strand of hair off her shoulder. "But it was damn, damn good. Tell him that for me when he wakes up, yeah?"

"Paul..."

"You promised. This was a reprieve. A filthy hot reprieve. Now you have to fix this." He glanced down to where Dima's legs had tangled with hers. "Liz, how can you not?"

"I'm scared." Admitting it was like talking with crushed glass in her throat.

"Think about the alternative, then think about scared." With one last kiss, his lips warm and gentle, he stood away from the bed and got dressed. The same white tank, jeans, cowboy hat. Their sunshine was leaving. "I'll be back for Dima's big performance, yeah? I hope the waters are calmer by then."

"No repeat of tonight?" One last try. She forced herself to keep petting Dima with the same quiet strokes. Casual. Easy. Even though her pulse had climbed up from her chest and into her mouth.

"Fun time, remember?"

Lizzie understood the unspoken reciprocal. She and Dima weren't fun anymore. They were complicated. Paul was one hell of a smart guy.

"You deserve better than being used as a life raft."

"Don't you dare think this was some mercy mission. You

two have been an education." His lopsided shrug and endearing smile were so damn adorable. "I've never had any ideas otherwise."

She nodded, as tight on the inside as a rubber band stretched near to breaking. "Thank you, Paul. I hope the job goes well."

"Me too. Good night, Lizzie." He kissed his fingertips and touched them to Dima's shoulder. "And good night to you, you stubborn Russian bastard."

He tipped his cowboy hat and left. Lizzie flinched only a little when the front door closed behind him.

She snuggled into Dima's arms and closed her eyes, enveloped by their shared scent. Sex and sweat and satisfaction. Tomorrow would come soon enough, as exhaustion scratched behind her lids. She had a promise to keep and a partnership to save. Or more like, to mend and transform.

Sink or swim, Dima. We have to do this without him now.

As they lay there cradled and wrapped together, she realized—no matter how scary—that was exactly what she wanted.

Chapter Twenty

Dima woke in the middle of the night with Lizzie in his arms. They were spooned together on their sides, like a crescent moon. His hand was wrapped low over her hips, with her head pillowed on the biceps of his other arm.

It wasn't the first time they had fallen asleep together. They'd spent plenty of nights watching crappy rental movies in borderline seedy hotel rooms while waiting for the next day's competition. Nearly every time, Lizzie fell asleep first with her head on Dima's shoulder. He'd indulged in stroking her hair as he finished out the movies, mostly missing that she no longer poked fun at the poor kung-fu dubbing. Occasionally he'd fallen asleep as well. He would wake up completely twisted together with Lizzie, who slept like a goddamned log.

So waking with his thigh hugged between Lizzie's smooth legs wasn't new. That both of them were naked, with his cock pressed against her soft, bare ass... Yeah, that was new.

His dick woke up so damn fast.

The room remained dark with night and thick with the early season heat of a city summer. The comforter was long gone and only a top sheet twisted around him and Lizzie. Although Paul had left hours earlier, his cologne layered over the fainter smell of sex. What a fucking night that had been. In both the best way and the worst.

He'd fucked his Lizzie for the first time in a decade. More than that, the experience had gone beyond anything he'd imagined. Anything he'd instinctively thought could be there. What he had hoped for was nearly too big to think about, but the night had shown him the hard, stark truth. He was so desperately hungry for Lizzie that he wouldn't be satisfied with less.

Hiding his face against her soft hair did nothing but reawaken temptation. She was everything tender. Good. The light to carry him home. She challenged him in new ways every moment.

Although he'd be a lesser man without her, he was lost in this limbo between friends and lovers, between partners and goodbye.

She barely wiggled when he brushed the hair back from her temple and ears. From the side, her mouth was pillowed perfection. He loved the way she kissed, as if she invested every molecule in making him feel good.

Long, slow touches traced the arches and dips and hollows of her body. Her shoulder, where he draped his hands at turns. Her waist, which he held when lifting her over his head. Her hips—those lovely, devilish hips. Tonight every inch of her felt different under his eager hands.

They'd been transformed. The parts and whole, together and separated again. Just different enough that they didn't fit anymore.

She woke slowly. The sheet tangled around her feet was shoved down in languorous moves. She lifted her arm, hooking behind his head where he nuzzled her neck. "Mmm. I like that."

He chuckled against her skin. "Have I found the key to waking you in a pleasant mood?"

She uncoiled, pressing her shoulders back against his chest. "Want to give it a shot?"

He loved the hollow between her breasts, the resilient push of her stomach. She was open to him wherever he touched. So softly accommodating, even when he dipped between her thighs to the dampness of her pussy. She sighed and lifted her knee to give him better access. Each lazy dawn swirl of his fingers made her more lush, more ready for him. He spread wetness along her folds and caught her clit between two knuckles. Tender pinches earned him the quiet moan he loved so much.

Pulsing with sharp arousal, his cock was notched along the cleft of her ass. He thrust against her softness. She reached backward, her nails biting his hip with a little sting. He hissed as the sting all worked together, pulling him out of the dreamy, foggy place that was so much safer.

He couldn't stop licking her neck, grazing his teeth over her shoulders. Contact. He craved contact with her. How had he lasted through those endless, torturous months after her injury? Quiet apartment. Hands empty. He shuddered with the memory. Fumbling in the dark, he found a lone condom in the nightstand drawer and rolled it on.

She'd thrown an arm over her head and flipped onto her back. The dark meant he couldn't see the color of her eyes, but they glinted in a stray beam of light through the window. She extended a hand.

He laced their fingers together and held them up next to her head. The mattress gave little resistance. Their hands, wound together on the white sheet... He swallowed hard. The moment probably called for words, but he had none. No plans either. Just a hope.

Lizzie tugged him near. Her lips petted his with tiny sips. Small blessings, until he needed more. Surging, he took her mouth at the same time he took her body.

Pressed flat, his cock deep in the scalding warmth of her pussy, Dima knew. He knew how much he'd do for this woman, if she could bring herself to ask.

Because he loved her. More than anything in his life.

That didn't mean he could have her.

This moment was sex. Lovely, perfect sex filled with soft

words and kisses and hands that traced cold thrills down his skin. It was what he wanted.

It wasn't what he needed.

His hips worked steadily, thrusting into her. He framed her face in his hands. Tried to look into her eyes. She'd drifted away, her eyes half-closed and cloudy, her lips shaped into an absent smile.

He stroked damp hair back from her cheek. "Where are you, little one?" he said, as quiet as a spring breeze.

She sighed happily. "Here with you."

"And who am I?"

Her ankles lifted behind his ass, locking over him. Heels dug deep into his cheeks and gently parted that tender skin. Sensation rocked through his bones. Tingles gathered at the base of his balls. More and hotter and harder. He wouldn't be able to hold out much longer, but he needed an answer.

He tangled a handful of her hair, pulled her head back. The darkness tempted him. He could let loose so much, say too much. So he held back, kept his movements steady but slow. Those beautiful eyes flashed open.

"Who am I?" he repeated.

"Dima mine," she whispered. She stretched her hands above her head. Her breasts arched upward, begging his mouth. She was so beautiful, and he wanted to feast on that singular beauty, but he also needed her hands on him. Her touch. Her acceptance. He didn't know how to say that he longed to be her choice. "My partner. My best friend. My rock. My calm." The words blurred into a dizzy chant that went straight to his head.

He could float away too. Let all the softness and all the sensation drag him away until he didn't question, didn't look down the road. Didn't plan. Just accepted what he had. That ought to be enough.

The words spilling out of her mouth began to sound like taunts. He needed all of her, and he needed to be the man she loved. Not some near miss. It was more than he could take. The kiss he claimed was fierce. He pushed them up over the sleepy place where they had wandered together.

He slammed into her. Deeper. Harder.

She yanked her mouth away from his and came, voicing her pleasure to the dark in a rough groan. The tugs of her wet cunt on his dick pulled him toward orgasm. Pleasure jerked out his spine, loosened his joints. Took away the last of his senses.

He gathered her close. He tucked her head under his chin, the better to keep her from looking at him. Bad enough that his chest panted on harsh breaths. She didn't need to see what was undoubtedly written on his face.

He needed her love too. It wasn't ever going to be enough to love on his own.

He'd spent the last twenty years trying to earn his parents' love. Their approbation depended on his continuing to dance when that same career had disappointed them. Doing better. Being more. Rising higher. He didn't resent his parents, but neither could he put himself in such a lopsided position again. Dependence never led to love.

If she still harbored any doubts about his dependability as her partner, or if they looked down the road toward different professional goals, they didn't even have dance anymore.

Her hands petted his biceps. The wet swipe of her tongue glossed over his clavicles. "Salty." Her jaw cracked on a huge yawn. "We're going to have to shower before yoga and after."

Did she just assume things would go on as they always did? Holy Mother, he couldn't cope with that.

He kept stroking her hair and shoulders and the glorious slope of her back long after she'd fallen asleep. Streetlights shifted yellowed patterns on his far wall. A cab came and went, followed by a couple of giggling girls. The downstairs neighbors slammed a door.

The whole time Dima lay awake. Thinking. No matter the avenues and byways he traveled, he couldn't figure out how to fix it. How to keep and care for his Lizzie, without losing himself along the way.

He didn't remember falling asleep, but at dawn his eyes snapped open and he knew what he needed to do.

Lizzie slept half on top of him, including him in her usual sprawl. Her face was buried against his ribs, her arm thrown across his waist. One of her bare legs weighed across his thighs. Smooth skin rubbed over his knee. Pale blonde hair shielded her face.

It was like waking in heaven, but knowing he would be sent back to purgatory, as soon as she opened her eyes. She would smile and everything would be strained and uncertain again, except they might get to sleep together on occasion. Best when a handsome cowboy was involved.

He couldn't take it anymore.

She would stop following him soon. Because he was bound to fuck it all up. Hell, it was half the reason he wanted off the competition circuit. To go out on top, before the inevitable fall that had slowly claimed his parents. Before he hurt Lizzie's other knee. Maybe next time he'd bust her ankle or something worse—keep her from dancing ever again.

Lizzie had to suspect it too, even when dangling a tempting carrot in the form of Paul. She hadn't wanted him talking with Svetlana, so she'd enticed Paul into pulling him away. If Lizzie really wanted something more from him, she'd have made it happen. Maybe when he'd all but put his heart on that diner table. Perhaps she too saw an expiration date on their partnership.

Unwinding himself from that gorgeous pile of womanhood

was almost impossible. When he unhitched her hand from his hip, he thought her yawn meant she was waking up. He froze, because he was such a fucking coward sometimes.

Her muscles eased and she melted back into the mattress, letting him slip away. He pulled the sheet up over her shoulders. That was practically a kindness to himself, not her, because he wouldn't need to look at the perfect globes of her ass.

His instinct was to slide so easily into their old patterns. Yoga together, breakfast—all the little things that had constructed their life for so long. *No.* He'd already been living in a halfway land for too long. Putting his relationship with Lizzie above everything else made no sense when she didn't see him in the same way.

In silence he pulled on some clothes and gathered his wallet and keys. Leaving the apartment left him at loose ends. The city bustled around him, most people headed off to work, briefcases in hand or messenger bags slung over their shoulders. They all held coffee cups.

Dima shoved empty hands in his pockets. He wasn't needed at Club Devant until late in the afternoon. Loose ends was even an understatement. So he wandered. Against the swells of people, he headed downtown. He watched his sneakers track over the dirty, gum-spattered concrete.

He came to a stop, seemingly out of nowhere. He looked up and found the diner off the park. The place where it had all started to go wrong.

There was no halfway point on which to balance a life. Paul, for all his fun, had been a bridge—from the locked stasis of their old life, across to something new.

No one ever lived on a bridge.

And for Dima, there'd be no going back.

Chapter Twenty-One

Lizzie awoke alone in a bright triangle of sunlight. She blinked a few times, swallowed and groaned against the familiar dizzy hangover feeling of being dehydrated. Her mouth tasted like rotting mushrooms, and she really needed to pee. Too many petty demands on her attention, when all she wanted was to smile up at the ceiling and stretch her deliciously aching inner thighs.

Dima.

God, they'd been like comets. She wanted another ride. That meant getting up and doing the right thing. No more pretending that they were something they used to be. No more hiding from how much she wanted a future with him—more of a future than just dance partners.

She grabbed his bathrobe from the back of the door. Wrapped in his scent, she hurried to the bathroom to take care of those truly not-so-petty necessities. Brushing her hair before seeing him first thing in the morning had never been a priority. They'd been roommates too long for that sort of silly posturing, but she did the best she could with curls that had been mushed to hell and back. Her roots were showing. She smiled at herself, knowing how much Dima appreciated her new color. Time to make an appointment.

Make all these little changes. With and for him.

A shower would have to wait. She wanted to plaster her body along his back, snuggle up on that hard-earned frame, and kiss him on the nape until he needed to fuck her against the kitchen counter.

No thank you, sun salutation. Got an alternate workout planned this morning.

She found the living room empty. Standing there, feet bare on the hardwood floor, she stared uncomprehendingly at the pair of rolled yoga mats in the corner. The kitchen was empty too. Hell, it wasn't that big of a place.

"Dima?"

She hustled to her bedroom. Maybe he needed somewhere to stretch out that wasn't all over her. Maybe...

She already knew what she'd find. Her bed. Still neatly made—such a powerful contrast to his bed, which looked like it had been worked over by a tornado.

Cellphone next. No calls missed. No voicemails. No texts.

She laid her RAZR back on her nightstand and simply...sank. Down along the door of her closet, the terrycloth of his robe smoothed the way. Her knees collapsed in a slide that had no choreographed grace. Ice coated her heart. A fine tremble shook to the ends of her fingers and toes.

He was gone. He obviously didn't want to be found.

A powerful burn started in her belly and thrust into her throat. Sometimes she'd suffered the same roiling nausea before a competition, but Dima was always there to rub her lower back. He'd never touched anything else, heeding the hours she needed to prepare hair, makeup and fake tan to the outrageous extremes required of pro dance. The reminder—that Dima should be there, helping her through a crisis—only made her stomach pinch harder. The burn intensified until she staggered to her feet, barely making it to the toilet.

Kneeling there, her hair once again in sweaty disarray, she let go of weeks of bottled-up emotion. Maybe longer. Maybe she'd been holding in those sobs since her torn ACL slaughtered the healthy, vibrant animal that had been her old life. Hot tears coated her cheeks. She wrapped his robe closer around her shoulders and let every ounce of remorse and confusion find an escape.

But most of the time, close isn't good enough.

His whispered words from the night before came hurtling back into her mind.

That's what you don't get. I did think. Over and over.

She lifted her heavy head and scraped damp hair back from her temples. Her eyes hurt. Her chest ached. Shivering despite the heavy white terrycloth, she sank her nose into the soft folds. A deep inhale threatened a new round of tears.

I will never go anywhere you aren't eventually willing to follow.

God, how long had he been pulling them this way? Little choices. Small moves. And choices so goddamn huge that he should've made them with her.

How long had she been dancing her way to him in return? Flirting with other guys, telling him the details of every encounter, dragging Paul into the mix... She'd been replying to his every unconscious signal, when he'd asked for more.

He'd just...given up.

A sizzle of anger replaced the hard ache of hurt. She welcomed it, if only to momentarily numb the pain and sort through her confusion. She'd taken him for granted for too long. That much was true. The feelings she had been questioning and the indecision—all coalesced around the knowledge that losing Dima, as both her partner and her lover, would be the end of her happiness.

Yet she wasn't wrong in wanting him to open up. How long had he been motivated by the hope of becoming a couple? What was so damn hard about opening up about his plans, fears, dreams? She needed that. A true partner. It wasn't too much to ask. That he'd bailed without talking this morning was more than insulting. It was downright cowardly. She knew because she'd given in to just that sort of fear. Hearing him admit that he'd passed up Broadway to stay with her... Pretty terrifying.

Time to stop relying on Dima to make the plans. She couldn't trust them, not when his goals remained so stubbornly hidden. All she could trust was what she wanted and what she could get by working hard. That was the story of her career.

Then and now, she would have Dima when the hard work was over.

Lizzie stood, shaky and cradling her middle, and turned on the shower. Club Devant was the obvious place to start.

Two hours later, she entered through the rear door of the club and traded her jogging shoes for Latin dance heels. Hair tied back. Extra-large water bottle. Two protein bars that she hoped she could keep down. Eventually.

Time to get started.

She found Remy in one of the upstairs practice rooms. His hands were all over the new guy, Jack, whose head was tipped back against the bank of mirrors. The kiss Remy claimed along the other man's neck reminded Lizzie of the marks she must have left on Dima. She had yet to see them, although hers had been pretty obvious in the bathroom mirror. Proof that the previous night had not been some attention-starved hallucination.

She coughed into her fist.

Jack pushed away, while Remy only smiled. His hand was still firmly planted on the young man's ass as he made introductions.

"You're dressed for business, *chère*." His gaze traveled up and down Lizzie's body—not with any particular hunger. Instead he seemed to assess...and approve. He nodded once. "We'll finish this later, *non*?"

"If I let you." Jack slid Remy a rather undecided look, as if he really hadn't made up his mind.

Lizzie wondered how frequently the Cajun was rejected. Dressed in a formfitting black T-shirt and a ragged pair of jeans that still managed to cling to his ass, he was sexy as hell. She couldn't imagine it happened often.

The new dancer seemed to have other ideas. He cocked a hip and his head at the same time. "Frankly, sweetie, I don't think you're my type."

"Oh, I know that. But there's nothin' wrong with neckin'."

Jack had a huge smile, which beamed at Lizzie as he exited, gym bag slung over his shoulder. A pale purple workout shirt was strategically cut to drape over one shoulder. The muscle it showed off was defined and lean. "Have fun, Lizzie."

"Not the sort of session I'm after."

That got a laugh from him, big and melodic. Lizzie, however, was in no mood for levity. She shut the practice room door and sloughed her bag along the wall.

"So?" Remy said.

"I want to learn Jeanne's choreo. I'm taking her place."

"You talk to Declan about that, have you?"

"Not yet." She glanced at the camera in the corner. "He'll know soon enough. Let's go."

Remy unwrapped a slinky, lopsided grin and held out his hand. She took it. A quick pair of spins later, he held her with her back to his chest. He touched her neck. "He give you these, *chère*? Very pretty."

Lizzie's face flamed. Heart racing, she remembered Dima's hands there, cutting off her air, taking her to a place she'd never even imagined—one where he could hurl her into the stratosphere and keep her grounded at the same time. All the while fucking her absolutely mindless.

Hell if she was going to talk about that with Remy Lomand.

"Just teach me."

"Whatever you say, Lizzie." Another spin and she faced him. He framed her perfectly, his expression oddly serious. "Three dances: the bachata you already learned. There's also a cha-cha and a really slinky samba. You think you can do three before next Friday?"

"I can do all three before the end of the day."

His grin returned and he pulled her near. "If you hadn't noticed—but I'm sure you have—your boy Dima's a stern motherfucker. I don't want him ripping my balls off and hanging me from the nearest tree. If you push too hard, I won't teach you. *Comprenez-vous?*"

"Got it."

"Good. Now we samba."

"But this is close hold. It's for something like tango, not samba."

"You here to learn or backtalk? This is Remy's samba. And truth be told, it's got Dima's fingerprints all over it. Like your neck," he said with a chuckle. She tried to duck her gaze, but he grabbed her jaw. "You wanna show him what you can do. I know you do. So shut up and follow my lead. No more of this competition bullshit. I wanna know how filthy you can be—on stage, that is. Girl, you remember your bachacadas?"

Lizzie jerked free of his grip and lifted her chin, a scant inch away from Remy's. "I practically invented them."

"There's a girl. Hit it."

Two hours later, Lizzie was a dripping pile of goo. She hadn't worked so hard outside of a physical therapy room since...well, since the last time she'd danced with Remy—and with Dima. That had been something flirty and dangerous. This was sheer determination. Every impulse to correct her form and hold a clean, proper line was shot down. She fought for hot, gritty, full-on sexy. Basically, she danced with Remy the way she had fucked Dima. The promise of performing that way with her favorite partner was the reward she kept firmly in mind.

He'd wanted her passion. He would get every last thumping beat of it.

Remy propelled her into a cartwheel lift, then back down again with relative ease. She liked being able to trust him so quickly, even if she didn't readily catch his cues and body languages. Wrong man. Plain and simple.

Feet back on the floor, she prepared to go into the next sequence of body rolls.

Remy released her without explanation and stopped the music. "Goddamn, that's it."

She shook her head, wiped a glaze of sweat from her forehead. "What?"

"What's been missing from those two."

"Dima and Jeanne?"

"Sure as shit. C'mon. I'll show you."

Lizzie stood in the middle of the floor, her heart pounding for reasons that had nothing to do with two steady hours of dance.

"I meant it. Get your fine ass over here."

Rolling her eyes about as hard as she rolled her neck, she grabbed her water bottle and followed Remy down the hall. Her knee felt...all right. A little tender, but so was the rest of her. It actually blended in with the overall body shock of being back in positions that should feel natural. They weren't just yet.

Remy knocked on the door to Declan's private apartment. Once inside, Lizzie realized exactly why she'd been brought there. A huge bank of televisions, six screens by six, lined one entire wall of what appeared to be Declan's living room.

The man himself was sitting on his couch, feet up, with a cellphone and a half-eaten sandwich on the table next to him. A laptop was open on his stomach, which belied his casual clothing: sweats and a Club Devant Henley.

"Nice work so far, Miss Maynes," he said. "Glad to see you haven't lost your groove. In fact, it looks stronger than ever."

Lizzie flicked her attention back to the televisions, which displayed news channels, an old black-and-white movie, recordings of previous Club Devant dances, and a live-cam shot of each room in the building. Rumors circled that Declan was a bit of a voyeur and kept his business under close watch, but this was just overwhelming.

"Why are we here again?"

Remy nodded to a series of remote controls. "You mind, boss? I need footage of Maynes and Turgenev in Montreal last spring—their samba—and practice footage of him and Jeanne from yesterday."

With boggling speed, Declan was able to bring up the requested videos. He closed down the rest of the screens, which still faintly glowed a luminescent charcoal gray. Lizzie spun down the rabbit hole.

"Here," Remy said. His accent was thicker. Funny how he revealed more of himself when he was deeply submerged into his work. "Watch this, *chère.*"

The competition at Montreal had been a disappointment. Coming off their third world title, they may as well have had targets on their backs. Every couple had been gunning for them. The judges, too, had apparently decided on novelty rather than quality, giving their love to a Czech pair who played everything too by the book for even Lizzie's tastes.

Seeing a younger version of herself on film was like watching a ghost. Some other Lizzie Maynes. Deep tan. Stage makeup. Raven-black hair in a half up-do that still let her fling it and shake it. Dima was resplendent in form-fitting tuxedo-style trousers and a white dress shirt open at the throat. Through the catty politics of the circuit, they'd been shoved to the center spot on the floor. The cameras, and often the judges' attention, rarely strayed past the flash and sparkle easily found along the perimeter.

She'd been angry for this, their last dance in Montreal. No hope of winning—not after the previous rounds' marks. But there had been a moment. One moment. Searching for it on screen, she clasped her hands over her heart when it replayed. Out of protocol, and completely out of character, Dima had broken their formal pose to lean down and whisper in her ear. His breath had been a kiss, his words a benediction. "Let it go, little one. This one will be just for us."

They'd murdered that goddamn samba.

Remy whistled low under his breath, reminding Lizzie where she was. Not in Montreal, but watching herself on a wall of flat-screen monitors. Declan had crossed his arms, studying intently.

Drawn back to the dance, she marveled at how free they looked. Her and Dima. She'd been entirely soaked up by his eyes, that dark, magnetic pull. Every touch for her. Every bit of fire and sharpness for them alone. They'd made so much magic for two minutes that it had washed away the bitter taste of the bad weekend. Afterward, still in a buoyant, defiant mood, they'd gone out for totally forbidden French fries. They'd laughed and told the whole dance world to go take a leap.

He'd made it better.

Tears she'd thought exhausted that morning were gathering again. The night before had been about getting their fuck on, not getting enough rest. She was too tired for this pain.

"Remy, what is this about?"

"Watch this lift."

Textbook Maynes and Turgenev. Trust. Hellacious strength and momentum, but hiding those details until all that remained was sexy elegance. The best of the best.

"Shit, you're right," Declan said. He'd set the laptop aside, elbows on his knees. Only his eyes flicked as he examined the screen. "He's going to hurt himself."

"Please, guys. I'm tired. Can we get to the point?"

Declan only shrugged. He pushed a button on the remote. Montreal went into freeze frame, with her and Dima arched into a sensual body roll. Goddamn it. Another button pushed and the practice room footage started up. If watching the shadows of their old lives was difficult, watching Dima practice with Jeanne was torture. It was all she could do to keep snarky comments in her own head. Knees too wide. Weight not forward enough on her steps. She had a weird habit of using her flexibility in all the wrong ways. She just looked...loose.

No fire.

Then, the same lift. A two-hand grab that propelled Jeanne up over Dima's shoulders.

Lizzie recognized it too—the strain on his face. Dima never looked like that. The job of a male dancer was to keep his partner safe, show her off as a fabulous creature, and never reveal the difficulty involved in lifting her.

She frowned. "What the hell? He's doing all the work."

"I came to ballroom late," Remy said. "It's not my first language, so to speak. I didn't put it together until you and I were dancing. You trusted me right away."

"Best way not to get injured."

"That's just the thing. It goes both ways. I knew you'd be good for whatever I threw at you today, *chère*, so no worries. Bing bang boom, it worked. But I've been fighting this problem with those two for weeks, not seeing why it didn't work."

"Bad cycle," Declan added, his voice low. "He doesn't trust her, so he's doing too much of the work. He'll screw up his spine. She'll get freaked and hold back. They're going to wreck each other."

Lizzie stopped gnawing on her lower lip when she tasted blood. "Show me again."

Rewind. Replay. Same result. Dima was taking too much of the weight on his shoulders—quite literally. A man danced like that when he was inexperienced, which certainly wasn't the case. Or when he was holding back. Hell, maybe even when he was scared.

Of what? Good God, he was the strongest man she'd ever known. All his plans and his deep inner world...

Do you think I tore my ACL on my own?

She'd said it out of frustration. She certainly hadn't meant it. Yet what if, somewhere in his mind, he was still blaming himself? To hear it from her lips must've reinforced whatever hellish evil torture he stored in there. If he'd turned down Svetlana in the ER waiting room, maybe guilt had made his choice. Bad enough he was making decisions without consulting Lizzie, but to make them from such a bad, hurting state of mind?

All without consulting her. It was enough to make a girl pissed.

He was going to get himself hurt. In trying to atone for what had happened, maybe even to try and keep the new, less experienced girl safe, he was going to do his body serious damage.

"You going to join us, Lizzie?" Declan's stare was utterly controlling. He was a man used to having decisions made promptly. Her hesitation must be driving him batshit, but neither was she going to cave and make a choice when her heart was so badly bruised.

"I'd like to take Jeanne's place for Dima's next performance."

"Good. I'll have the promotions team make the change."

"Please," she said. "For the first show... I have a lot of

ground to make up with him. Hell, he might not even want to after...well, after some things of late. Can we just leave the billing as is?"

"You're trying to kill me, aren't you?" He said it with a slight smile. "All right, we'll leave it for now. Maybe you can knock some sense into him. While you're at it, make sure he signs that contract I gave him."

"Contract?"

"He hasn't renewed his stint here at Devant."

The floor fell away from Lizzie's feet. Dima, who booked their travel and their tour dates. Dima, who planned their meals a week in advance. Dima, who'd paid the bills since their first day living away from their parents. He never just *forgot*. No, his silence on that matter was a choice. He'd left her in the morning without so much as an explanation—another choice by default. Those two facts taken together in such close succession, and coupled with Svetlana's not-so-coincidental appearance the night before, shot cold chills down to her heels. The room turned stuffy and nightmarish.

"I want to get back to work," she said quietly, turning to go.

She'd made the right call in trying to step into this world with him, because the alternative was losing him forever. She only hoped she wasn't too late.

Chapter Twenty-Two

Even in the clinging, plastic dry cleaning bag, the dress was a menace. Dima hung it on the back of Lizzie's bedroom door and stepped back. He crossed an arm over his chest, held his chin with the other hand and simply stared at the dress.

Tiny. Red. Lots of spangles and beads and other adornments Dima had never bothered to learn. What he knew was that the dress barely covered her breasts. It arrowed down to satisfy the barest decency standards. In repose, the dress didn't look like all that much.

On her, though, it would be entirely different because of the way she moved. The ruffle that started at the ass would dangle down to her knees, as she shimmied hot enough to rival an open flame.

He walked backwards until his knees hit the stool she kept at her dressing table. His elbow hooked on one of the few empty spaces among the bottles and pots and sprays. The walls wheezed as the pipes strained and hissed to a quiet hum.

Dima ought to leave. They'd had three days. Three days without directly seeing each other. He hadn't even been sure it was possible.

After sleeping in every morning, she ran out the door with her dance bag over her shoulder. At night when she came in, she went straight to her room again. She didn't ask him to cook, didn't greet him beyond the bare necessities.

Not that he volunteered, nor sought her out in turn.

Because Christ, what would he say? *Sorry I fucked you and abandoned you the next morning.* What he'd been imagining for their future was impossible. She didn't see him as anything more than he'd been for the duration of their partnership. He just figured he'd beat her to the punch, before she realized what crazy, extreme places his head had gone.

However, there was no getting out of today, no matter how much he might wish.

He scented her first. That sugary wash of fragrance followed her out of the bathroom along with the warm, humid air. The door pushed open next, and there she was.

He held himself still, like posing on stage before unleashing the first step, but that didn't mean he was calm on the inside.

Lizzie wore only a towel.

A good-sized bath sheet, it concealed her from breasts to hips, even covering her perfect ass. Her exposed skin gleamed with dampness, and suddenly he dipped into a visceral, taste-and-scent memory of having his mouth on her cunt, of thrusting his cock inside her.

For only a moment, she'd gazed at him as if the sun and moon dangled from his fingertips.

She wasn't looking at him like that now. She stopped dead, her eyes going wide. She reacted more like he'd laid a nest of rattlers in her room. "Dima..."

"I knew you'd forgotten, so I had your favorite competition dress cleaned." He nodded toward the door.

Confusion scrunched up her nose. She shut the door, eyed the dry cleaning bag and dropped her jaw. "Oh no. The thing for Lionel's foundation."

He leaned his chin against his fist. The charity event in memory of late choreographer Lionel Woodruff drew luminaries from the entire dance community, not just in New York but around the world. To receive an invitation to perform was a marvelous honor. He and Lizzie had celebrated with a night on the town upon learning the news.

He sure as hell didn't feel like celebrating anymore.

"Yes, the exhibition. Which we agreed to last year. Before your injury."

Some bright flash sparked in her eyes. "Injury. I can't. It'll suck that we didn't give them much notice, but you know how these things work. They'll have three other options lined up."

"No."

She clutched more tightly at the knot of towel between her breasts. Her knuckles were white, but she still couldn't totally cover those pretty mounds. "Goddamn it, Dima. You don't get to *no* me. We're partners."

"Are we?"

He didn't need an answer. That was their problem. They were partners. Maybe less if she didn't even want to dance with him.

"Of course we are." Her chin lifted. "Which is why you don't get to lay down autocratic bullshit. I can't dance yet. Besides, we haven't practiced."

He boiled inside. Seethed and roiled. There were so many things he wanted. To shake her, to be able to live without her. To pull her down over his hips and toss that towel away. He'd fuck her until she was sweaty again and her head spun and she wouldn't be able to deny him anymore.

"We know this routine inside out. I bet you'd know how to dance it five years from now without a speck of practice. I don't know if your problem is with me or your confidence, but I'm not putting up with it."

"I don't have any problems," she blustered, but her gaze escaped to find the pile of laundry overflowing her basket.

"I know you're dancing every day." He stood. Troubles weighed on him so heavily, dragging his tendons into slow, jittering messes. Maybe it was the Russian thing to allow problems to depress him, but damned and the saints if a bottle of vodka wasn't a temptation. "I didn't understand that we were at a place where we had need of lying."

"I don't know what you're talking about." She shoved damp hair out of her face and gave him the wide-eyed look she seemed to think could convince him the sky was green.

He walked toward her, assuming she'd slip sideways and give up control of the doorway, but she held her ground. He ought to have known better. She might be his little one, but she'd always had a spine of titanium.

"After more than a decade, you think I don't know what you look like when you've been danced out? What your breathing sounds like?" He dipped his head low, until he was a mere lick away from her delicate neck. A single lock of her hair brushed over his cheek. He scooped it away, tucked it behind her ear. "As a matter of fact, it's almost identical to what you look like when you've been fucked to the point of exhaustion."

Her head jerked back so she could look him in the eyes, but she didn't go any farther. Red washed over the tops of her breasts, up over her pale throat. The barest purple smear there still lingered from his fingers.

She didn't seem to mind the idea of another round. She licked her lips and her eyes turned blurry, hazy green. If he wanted, he could probably kiss her, fuck her against the wall of her bedroom with her strong legs wrapped around his hips.

They would be exactly where they'd been before.

So he shut that part of him down. Again. Like he had for years, before he realized what he truly needed from her. His spine solidified, drawing him away from her sweetly scented aura.

"Get dressed. They're expecting us."

She stared at him blankly, as if she couldn't believe he'd backed down. Her mouth pulled into a pout. "I don't want to go all the way across the city wearing that."

"There's a car service coming for us in two hours. Think you can be ready in that time?"

"Of course."

"Fine." He managed not to throw open the door. Quite the accomplishment considering the tight set of his joints. He'd need to stretch for an entire goddamn hour before he could dance. "Let's see if you can follow through with anything without step-by-step directions."

With that, he snapped the door shut firmly behind him. His shoulders finally slumped under the weight of his tension and his fears. He let his head hang. He should have cancelled this demonstration, but giving it up would be tantamount to giving them up completely.

As much as he wanted to, he couldn't take that step—even if Svetlana's texts that morning had started to make sense. Back away from the pain. Make his own way. He could. As time dragged, waiting, he thought he might.

How could he, though, when one hour and fifty-eight minutes later, Lizzie emerged into the living room? He'd been passing the time on the couch, with one leg kicked up to stretch down the length. His smartphone was in his hand, open to an email from Svetlana—another entreaty to renew their relationship, in every sense of the word.

He stood and dropped the phone on the couch. All thoughts of Svetlana and a fresh start just...disappeared.

"Holy mother of God," he whispered.

The dress emphasized her lush femininity. Yet her strength shone from the straight planes of her stomach, solid arms, and the lines that created long ridges up her calves. And of course, red heels for dancing. He'd never known anyone so bold.

If she had wanted him, she'd have made it known. His Lizzie barreled after what she craved.

She held her hands out to the side. "Right on time and a work of art."

She'd said that before every competition.

Dima couldn't help it. He grabbed her hands. Three steps of a salsa later, a spin and a four count.

She laughed, her face turned up. "It's us, isn't it? We're back. We could take it back. Dima, we could still own it all."

The spot where his heart should have been slowly filled with lead. After letting go of her hands, he gathered the bags he'd set by the door. "Come on."

The town car downstairs was elegant and well upholstered—and quiet. No music played. Dima let Lizzie slide in first, looking out over the roof of the car. He felt her eyes on him, assessing.

He needed to slide in next to her. There was nowhere else to go. Even so, he was perfectly aware of the exact distance between them. Less than an arm's length, and yet enough space to fit another person.

Hell, maybe this would be better with Paul. He balanced them. His easygoing nature kept them from spinning too far out of control.

"Have you thought about it?" Her voice was so quiet. Not usual at all. "Going back?"

"I have."

He simply wasn't going back. The dances at Club Devant might be demanding, but performing there wasn't the same sort of life. Not on the road. Not pushing through even when he thought his shoulder was shot, fearing that anything less would mean missing out on the best floor placement the next day. Not practicing through exhaustion, or constantly adding new tricks just to keep up with the competition.

Tricks that ended with Lizzie sitting on the ground, clutching her leg, sobbing.

He could keep her safer at Devant. When his gaze dropped, it went right to the faintly pink line at the side of her knee. Her scar. He'd already failed her enough.

"And?" she prompted. Her fingers tangled in a bit of wayward beadwork. When her hips shook, the beads would emphasize the movement and make her look even more amazing. "Maybe just one more year. We'll take one more championship. You know we could."

"Certainly we could." He finally turned to look at her. She'd fluffed and feathered her hair. Her eyes were ringed with dark, dramatic shadow, absolutely amping up her desirability. "What the hell would we do with another championship? And why? Because four is a more magical number than three?"

"Because we *can*. Because how many other four-time world championship ballroom dancers have there been? The best of the best, Dima."

He rubbed a hand across the back of his neck. At least for this demonstration he hadn't needed to resume the fake-tanning thing. He'd been so awfully sick of that. "Let's not do this."

"Do what? Have an honest discussion?"

He wrapped his fingers around her jaw and tipped up her chin. "Honest discussion," he echoed, incredulous. "This is not honesty unless we include the fact that you were riding my cock not three days ago."

Her hands flinched toward her body. "I wasn't talking about that."

"Weren't you? Because what I'm hearing—what I'm always hearing—is that you'd like to go back to the way things used to be." He sighed, letting go of her smooth skin. He contained himself on his side of the car and looked out the window. "God, we can't do this now."

"No." Her sigh filled the car. "I'm starting to fear we never will."

Chapter Twenty-Three

On Dima's arm was the safest way to enter any dance arena, especially when faced with so many people who knew her parents. A prima ballerina from the age of twenty-two, Georgina Maynes was more than just a dancer. She was an icon who still fielded questions as to why Lizzie had chosen something else over "real" dancing. For some, world championships wouldn't change the fact that Lizzie had never performed with a company, let alone as the lead.

To her credit, her mother possessed a fantastically waspish tongue and cut any doubters down to size. She had always been supportive of Lizzie's decisions. When Dima's mother and father had started the spiraling nosedive that eventually led them to Boca Raton, alcoholism and obscurity, he had not been left alone. Lizzie's parents had taken him in as a son of their own.

None of that eased her nerves. This would be her first public dance since her injury. Everyone there would know it.

Sometimes, when her confidence before a competition was at a low ebb, she held Dima's hand. He would smile down at her—a so-soft smile that told her everything she needed to know. That he was right there. That the choices she'd made in her life were not only valid, but worth celebrating. That she would never feel like a disappointment because he would lend her strength.

She didn't dare look at him. The stifling tension in the hired car had been like acid to dissolve her outer shell. Plans she wasn't used to making seemed less certain when he gave her nothing but... No, *nothing*. Even blankness might be a small step closer to genuine emotion.

The Lionel Woodruff School of Dance occupied the entire second floor of a multi-use high rise in Battery Park, the monthly rent for which probably outstripped Lizzie's annual take-home. Up the elevator, out into the corridor, which was as sunny as the rest of the studio. Mirrors and one-way glass where there weren't windows. The bright midday light was strong enough to start a headache along her forehead.

Hot fear churned in her gut. She'd let this go too long. She would lose Dima, maybe even lose dancing. Facing the world without either would be a nightmare made true.

They came to stand before two golden pine doors—the entrance to the main studio room.

"Dima, Lizzie, so good to see you again," said the school's headmistress, Janet Peel. Sixty-something, excruciatingly thin and with a neck that seemed to go on forever, she had been a prima donna in her own right before taking up guidance of the school. "How's the knee?"

"Good as new." The smile was forced, naturally, but she was nearly in full performance mode. It wouldn't be difficult for much longer. "When are we on? Enough time to warm up?"

Janet consulted a clipboard and checked them off the list. "About twenty-five minutes. There's an afro-jazz troupe in there right now, then a pair of Lindy Hoppers."

Lizzie nodded and followed Dima to wait in the hallway with another half dozen dancers, all stretching, all wearing different styles of costumes. The foundation's annual event showcased dancers of radically varied styles, from classical ballet to krump. Donations funded a trust that helped underprivileged kids in Manhattan find a home in the world of dance.

She clutched Dima's arm a little tighter, probably giving away more than she wanted to. He flicked her a warning look.

A deep, sturdy, pissed-off part of her bubbled up. No tears

this time. Not even close. Those had been burned out of her after days of hard work with Remy. All that remained was the resilience that had made her a champion. He was not going to pull his moody shit in front of an audience, and certainly not one that was so influential in their community.

Back painfully straight, she met his gaze. She could give herself to him forever, if they got this damn thing right.

"You say you don't want to hurt me," she said, voice businesslike.

A flinch. His brows narrowed, just a little quizzical.

"Isn't that what you've always said?"

"Lizzie..."

"*Otvechaj*, Dmitri."

Answer me. Damn you.

His curt nod followed a slow inhale, as if he'd needed to consider his reply. A shiver of hurt slid down to her stomach, but she kept it hidden. No way could she be dressed in that outfit and not own the moment.

"Good. Then don't show any of this to those people in there."

"This?"

"Us. This crap we can't talk about."

"And if I do?"

"You'll get your wish from down in the car. We won't need to talk about anything because there won't be anything left to discuss."

She let go of his arm and looked through the window with a stunning view of the bay. Standing in that much sunshine, she should've been warm. Hell, she should be warming up altogether.

Fifteen minutes later, after stretching muscles thick with tension that had nothing to do with her injury, Lizzie heard their names called. Out of habit alone, she found Dima with her eyes. He was dressed in a pair of snugly fitted trousers that molded to every lean, toned inch of his thighs and ass. A cummerbund hugged his flat stomach. The heavily beaded red, black and gold chaquetilla accentuated his shoulders. Sleeveless and open, it left his chest and arms bare.

Out of the need to hold her own, she lifted her chin and didn't look away. If what they had was well and truly broken, she'd know it soon enough. They couldn't hide anything from one another when they performed.

She held out her hand.

He took it.

They were on. It was the first time in six months that they would dance in public.

God, it was like a life sentence.

Although Dima would lead throughout the dance, Lizzie, as always, was the first into the studio—their makeshift stage. Arrive with attitude, their coach had said for years. Arrive already performing. That meant she walked ahead and gathered up the stares, the coos, the clapping. Dima stalked behind her, a dark force at her back.

Dressed in red spangles from head to toe—quite literally, as her hair adornments and shoes exactly matched the gown—she knew how she must look to those two-hundred-odd bigwigs. All sex and attitude. Good. There was a certain comfort in being able to face those lions in full regalia. Roughly twenty tiny square inches of beaded armor on top, with a weighted skirt down the backs of her thighs to swing and twirl.

With a quick scan of the airy, high-ceilinged studio, Lizzie spotted all the bigwigs out in force. Because it was only a little past noon, they dressed in elegant suits and luncheon dresses. A few of what must be the school's best students, all teen girls except for two young men who looked like dead ringers for

Dima's Russian bone structure, sat together. Sweat still lined their smooth brows, meaning their performance had already taken place.

Lionel Woodruff's partner, a thin and exact black man in his mid-fifties, sat on a chair at center left that may as well have been a dais. A former soloist with the American Ballet Company, he was the public face of his late lover's legacy—a picture of dignity, grace and loss. Reporters and two television cameras ringed him and his collection of close associates.

Great. Maybe Declan would have the implosion of Maynes and Turgenev on film for his collection.

The music started, to herald the beginning of their famous paso doble, the one for which they'd earned perfect marks in Berlin to clinch their first world title. A lifetime ago.

That same music took control. In this dance, Dima was the matador and she was the cape. For the next two minutes, if at no other time, everything would be as it should.

From across roughly ten feet, they stared one another down. Slowly, they walked with exaggerated steps to meet in the middle. Dima's eyes blazed. He was in character, sure, but it was *real*. His passion and intensity. She'd been feeling waves of it for weeks, even as he tried his damnedest to hold it back. Now it pulsed from him in shimmering currents that sparked her inner desires. Fight back. Win. This was a dance of competition, and she would not be defeated.

Their first touch was...shocking. As if they had never touched before, not as partners or as lovers. Their bodies connecting. Hers woke up with a start, screaming for more. His skin. His fingers, although he held them taut and straight in proper form—not caressing so much as guiding. They clasped hands and broke eye contact for the first time, as if inviting the assembly to join in their conflict. Balanced just so, they extended their feet in a matched *développé* that tested their strength and flexibility.

Showing off.

Damn, they did it well.

Spinning Lizzie out of that position of control, he unleashed pure fire. So in command, so incredibly masculine, he led her body with practiced finesse. She became cloth, twirling and spinning at his merest direction. All the while his movements remained dramatic and larger than life. When she was free of his hold, Lizzie dipped into a low backbend, while Dima performed a graceful *rond de jambe* kick across her torso. Such velocity and control. She started in on a series of flamenco steps. His split leap ate half the distance across the floor, then matched her flamenco as he worked back to meet her.

Her lungs seared with heat. They could combust right there, right at that moment, doing what they loved, together, and she'd be happy.

Their hands touched again. Sweat. Dark eyes. Flared nostrils. He was more like an angered bull than a matador, as if their dance could finally bust through what bricks he'd stacked around deeper emotions. Arms locked, she backed away and away from his high, advancing steps. Lizzie escaped his pursuit, only to be caught by the wrist and coiled around his body like a cape. They came together in a controlled collision of pelvis to pelvis. She grasped his out-thrust hips. His hands reached overhead before bowing possessively low. The whole time, their foreheads pressed together, mouths open, breathing one another's fire.

The rigid strength of his frame was all the tension she required to gather momentum for the upcoming lift. But Dima overcompensated, just as she'd seen him do with Jeanne in the practice video. Instead of perching gracefully on his shoulders before sliding back down like a slither of silk, she nearly toppled. Panic gripped her heart and gave it a yank. Dima grunted only loud enough for Lizzie to hear. A swift readjustment of his hands kept her from falling, but the lift couldn't be saved. She curved down and through his legs in a classic snake twist.

Totally improvised. She wondered briefly who might be able to tell.

Yet there was no time to think, not while performing. Instinct and trust and long years of partnering were all they had. Those precious things brought them safely back to choreographed steps.

Along the floor, she made a plank of her body. Back arched, legs straight, arms stretched far overhead. Dima caught her by the back of the neck with one hand. With the strength of his arms and powerful core muscles, he lifted her to forty-five degrees and held her suspended while he maintained a deep lunge.

Face to face.

Although she'd never thought to kiss him at that moment, she was tired of wasting such opportunities.

Just a brush of lip to lip.

The unexpected contact was enough to widen his eyes and enough for Lizzie to grab one more salty taste of what she missed.

Anyone who disapproved in the middle of such a staid event could take a hike.

The dance wasn't over, and neither of them would think of missing the next count. Dima kicked a leg over and around in a full spin. He returned her to standing. She seductively arched her back as she twisted away. Dima pounced in a deep lunge and grabbed her waist. Chest out. Posture dominating. As if he had won this fight.

The dazed expression on his face said otherwise and put a smile on Lizzie's.

The music ended on a huge flourish. The applause roared

through the studio.

The spell of make-believe passion was broken.

Dima stood with the bearing of a beautiful, commanding prince. He held out his hand—just enough of an aid for Lizzie to smoothly twirl into his arms. They stood together as one before the cheering crowd. Not the most historic performance of their lives, but it was the most personally significant.

To the sound of more applause, they exited through a side door, toward the student dressing rooms.

Lizzie slammed them in together. "What the hell was that?"

"What? You kissed me!"

"I'm not talking about the kiss." She popped a fist onto her hip. "How's your back? You nearly busted it out there, like you've been doing with Jeanne. Or are you determined to do everything in a partnership alone?"

"It's been a while since I lifted you."

"Bullshit. You know what, Dima? I call bullshit on everything you've been pulling lately."

A furious scowl closed over his brow. "In that, I'm most definitely not alone."

"You know what? It gets old." A dam burst in her mind and all of her frustrations lashed out as frenetically as their dancing. "You make plans all the goddamn time. I know, because you drag me along with you. But I never get to hear the dreams behind them. You must have them in there somewhere, propelling all of your strategies, but I never get a glimpse of what must burn so strong and beautiful. Why would you want to hide that? From me of all people?"

Her voice broke. Emotion closed her throat but she swallowed it back. His shoulders had not lost their rigidity. Was any of this getting through to him?

"The best I get is weeks later when you suddenly look

happy," she continued, undeterred. It was now or never. "Then I know we've reached some secret milestone, some dream of yours fulfilled. You relax a little. Things are easy for a while, before the rollercoaster starts up again. It would be nice to be included. Do you even get that? I want to be included in the beginning when we decide together, and the end when you...Jesus, when you hold me and we share something amazing. You'd better know I'm not just talking about our dancing."

She dared to touch him like reaching out for a wounded animal. Ironic, considering his matador gear. He didn't pull away when her fingers found his.

"I'd like to know when you're scared too," she said. "It's hard being the only one."

His Adam's apple bobbed. "Scared?"

"I'm scared of us changing. I'm scared of getting hurt again. It's bad enough how our whole world got shaken up, needing to leave the circuit. I can't imagine what a worse injury would do. What if I couldn't dance again?"

She dared more intimate contact. The tight, thin skin along his low belly was hot. He breathed heavily, but Lizzie knew her own throbbing pulse wasn't because of the dance. Not anymore. He held as still as a statue other than the rise and fall of his magnificent chest. Dark eyes blazed.

"But you can't take the bulk of that guilt on your own," she whispered. "Any more than it was fair of me to accuse you." She took his face in her hands. "You didn't hurt me, Dima mine. I'm sorry for hurting you by saying so. It was an *accident*. If you think you can overcompensate in a lift or in any other area of my life...you *can't*. We're in this together, or bad things happen."

"Are we in this together?"

Lizzie swallowed. "You tell me. You're the one who hasn't

opened up."

A knock on the door shocked her back a few steps. Janet called, "It's an intermission, Lizzie. We wanted to introduce you both around. You coming out?"

"Of course. Be right there." She glanced at her partner, heartsick with worry that they'd shared their last dance. "Ask yourself who ran the other morning and why Svetlana's back in your life. Hell, why you haven't renewed your contract with Declan. Then be prepared to let me into that head of yours. I know we're both braver than this."

Chapter Twenty-Four

Until Lizzie was injured and staying with her parents, Dima had never realized how much life she breathed into their tiny apartment. No more salsa music pouring through the sound system in the living room. No more singing—badly—under her voice as she dusted and cleaned. No more late-night movies with her feet kicked up on the couch, eating air-popped popcorn.

That their place was equally quiet now settled like lead in his stomach. They lived together, but she might as well be gone. She stuck to her room, much as he stuck to his own space.

She looked at him, though—not like the three days after they'd made love in the dark, when they'd ducked each other like they were on the run from the police. No, she watched him silently.

It hurt worse.

Every day she went out to dance and he still didn't know where. She returned to the apartment with that special combination of exhausted and thrilled that came from working on new material. That she spent so many hours in someone else's arms wasn't the worst of it. He mostly worried she'd set her own path. That he'd lost her forever.

Because she'd been right the other day, at the Woodruff exhibition. He'd run. He'd always sworn that he would only take Lizzie where she wanted to go, but that didn't count when he ran blindly. All his talk about plans, all his maneuvering. He'd walked away from them all.

His goal certainly hadn't been the big dance tonight. He

and Jeanne weren't the partnership he wanted. He still hadn't signed the renewal contract, and Lizzie had been right about that too.

Even as he grabbed his dance bag from his room, then filled his pockets with wallet, keys and cell, he realized he was waiting. Listening. Searching for some hint of sound that said she was getting ready, though in her own sweet time. Because as awful as this strain was between them, he didn't know how to experience any important event without her at his side. She was simply, solidly always there.

As he walked past her room, he couldn't help himself. He stopped and knocked. The pause and silence stretched like saltwater taffy.

The door opened.

Right away, he knew the answer to his question. Low-slung jeans. A tight T-shirt with a Rangers emblem. Bare feet. Not exactly dress-code attire for Club Devant.

"You're not going."

Her gaze dropped somewhere near his throat. Tiny violet shadows draped under her eyes. Not enough to claim she was exhausted, but their presence was shocking in comparison to her normal vitality. If she was coping as poorly as Dima, then she hadn't been sleeping.

She idly thumbed a bit of nicked wood on the doorjamb. Funny, her close-trimmed nails were in full competition mode, glossed with a deep red color. "I'm tired," she said.

"Oh." He wanted to touch her. More than that, needed to. His skin pulled and tingled with flat-out desire. "Paul texted me. He's going to be there."

Fuck if that wasn't the dumbest thing he'd ever said. Terrified of admitting everything going on in his head—and his heart—for so long, he dangled another man in front of her, much as he had resented of Lizzie the night Sveta appeared at the club.

At least he'd severed that tie. Svetlana had called again, and he'd told her they were done. That wasn't somewhere he wanted to go. She didn't intend for them to proceed in a solely professional capacity, and he certainly wasn't prepared for anything more.

Not when he was so very in love with Lizzie.

He was beginning to suspect that was half the problem. He'd loved her even before her injury. For too many years to see clearly, he'd trusted in a deep, endless connection. And still, he'd been unable to keep her safe. Hell, she'd fallen right out of his arms.

Maybe it was shitty of him, but the fear wasn't so potent when he danced with Jeanne. Still there, but manageable. He only needed to pull her a little harder and guard her a little closer. Taking the weight of it was what the male partner did.

He couldn't imagine what he'd do if he let Lizzie down again. Break in two? Like his parents, once they no longer had the structure of their careers? Perhaps he would spend the next fifty years sitting on a plastic-wrapped sofa with a tumbler of vodka.

She seemed to regard him as some sort of planning god. Like if he had a goal, it automatically came true. That wasn't true. He'd failed plenty of times. Keeping that from her was to protect her from cruelty. It was better that he be the only one disappointed.

Her head tilted to the side, and she pursed her lips. "Was there something else you needed?"

If that wasn't a loaded question, he'd never heard one. The answer, however, was surprisingly clear in his thoughts.

He needed the assurance that if not even a single one of his plans worked out, he'd still be loved. Not for being the son trained to carry on aborted dreams, forced into dance lessons once his parents' career had hit its zenith. Not for being one half of the dance world's most successful pair. Just for being him.

He flinched. Shook his head. "Get some rest, lit—" He cut himself off, though the effort sliced blades under his tongue. "Lizzie."

He turned to go. She didn't make a sound. Neither did he as the door shut behind him.

Was this really happening? He couldn't believe it—that he was moving on to other destinations without Lizzie at his side.

Rather than walk, he took the subway to the club. The headphones in his ears weren't playing anything he'd consider his music. It was all Lizzie's. The independent musicians she loved supporting, the world-vibe stuff he could barely make sense of. At least it wasn't the empty noise of his own head.

When the plans were all gone, he didn't know what was left of him.

He slipped in the back door of the club, hopeful he'd avoid people until he absolutely needed to interact. By no stretch of possibilities was he prepared to flirt or schmooze or whatever the fuck Declan expected. He needed more quiet, to keep getting his head together. Hopefully there'd be plenty of that in his dressing room.

His room wasn't empty. A tiny sliver of light pushed into the hallway from the crack under the door. For half a second, he thought maybe Lizzie had come after all. If she'd taken a cab, she could have beaten him there.

Pushing open the door disabused him of that notion but provided a lovely distraction. "Paul." He dropped his bag on the counter. "God, you look good."

The blond man wore a black suit over a black shirt that was open at his neck. The white cowboy hat was the topper. Beat up and worn, it was the same damn one he wore every day. "That's good, because you look like shit."

Dima laughed, but he didn't have the energy to put much into it. "*Spasibo*. Thank you so much. Such a kind and polite man you are."

Paul shrugged. He'd planted his ass against the counter, but now he pushed off and held his arms open.

At first, Dima tried to give him a one-armed hug, since he thought he might split apart under the weight of his own worry if shown too much kindness. Paul wasn't having any of that. He grabbed Dima, arms wrapping around ribs and sinew, and squeezed tight.

Dima let his eyes roll shut. He let a long, shuddering breath work out of his chest. His head bent to Paul's shoulder for just a moment. He was exhausted.

But he didn't have all the time in the world. The show must go on. Plus, if he tried to bail, Declan would lead him on stage by the balls.

After pushing out of Paul's arms, he turned to the wardrobe in the corner. "It's good to see you tonight."

"I begged off work. Said my sister was sick." Paul plopped into the chair—the same one he'd been in when all this had started. He hitched the knee of his trousers between pinched fingers and crossed his feet. Cowboy boots, of course. "No way was I missing tonight. Where's Liz?"

Dima's shoulders snapped taut. He pulled on tight black pants and grabbed his shirt. "She couldn't make it."

"Damn." Paul's voice was laden with his usual concern. "I really thought you two would work it out."

Dima caught Paul's gaze in the mirror. Something hard and spiny jammed in his throat. His eyes burned. "I...I thought the same thing."

"It's over? For sure?"

He shrugged the shirt on. Started on a few warm-up stretches. "Maybe? I don't know."

To fully explain, he'd need to put everything out there all at once. He'd need to admit how much he loved her—all without a guarantee she'd return it. If there was ever a moment for fear of failure to rear its ugly head, it was now.

"You cannot possibly be serious." Paul's handsome features twisted into genuine surprise.

"What?"

"It's just... If I had any hope of a woman like Lizzie, there'd be no maybes involved. I wouldn't give up chasing her until I knew I'd won, or until I knew I didn't have a frog's chance in a snowstorm."

Dima chuckled as he stretched his quads. "What a way with words you have."

"Don't deflect. You know you're wrong. You've been a champion your whole life, and this is how you act when it really means something? Shit, Dima. Screw trophies and applause. This is Lizzie we're talking about. All you have to do is decide what you want."

"What the hell am I supposed to do?" The words burst from him in a flurry of released emotion. "Throw it all out there in front of her? Tell her what she might not want to hear? I've never been able to promise her anything other than trying my best. After all that's happened, you think she'll accept that? Forever?"

Paul looked so calm. Steady. Like he knew the way. "Ask her those questions. At least you'll know for sure."

Dima was shaking, but the possibilities blazed in his mind and in his heart. To know for sure. To know if he could trust her with all of him. What a relief that would be.

He caressed the back of Paul's neck. "You've been a very good friend. Both to me and to Lizzie."

"Damn right," the other man drawled. "You get all this worked out, ya hear? I expect at least a round of drinks out of it."

Dima couldn't help but grin. "I must say the idea of you slightly drunk has definite draw."

"You trying to butter me up and get in my pants? Because I'm telling you, there's actually a better chance of that if I'm sober."

His smile dried up. "I don't think... That is, until we get all this sorted completely..."

Paul reached up to catch Dima's shoulder in one work-roughened hand. "It was a thing and it's done. I had a great time. I won't ever forget you two."

"Like I said. A great friend."

Dima leaned down, claiming Paul's mouth. They exchanged so much from the simple meeting of lips. He framed Paul's head. Bristly buzz-cut hair brushed his palms in a slow-gathering tingle. Possibilities in one direction cut short, but at the same time he couldn't help the building excitement. Their kiss charged, with Dima's tongue sweeping into Paul's mouth. A happy end for a happy run.

They pulled away at the same time. "Yeah," Paul said on a smile. "Good stuff."

"Now out you go. I have a show to ready for."

Paul pushed up out of the chair and snugged his cowboy hat low across his brow. "You better kill 'em dead for your last show."

"I don't know. It might not be the last."

"Yeah?" Something hopeful lit Paul's bright eyes.

Dima still kept it simple. It was Lizzie he needed to open up to. No one else. "Yeah."

They agreed to meet after the performance. Dima paused

after he'd shut the door.

An eddying swirl of thoughts occupied his head. "Maybe...I have a life to ready for," he said to the empty room.

Because if Lizzie wasn't worth fighting for, he literally had nothing left.

He quickly ran through the rest of his prep. The stretches, his costume. When the time ticked down, he was right on his mark, at stage right of a dark theater. Fabian preceded him, microphone in hand.

"Ladies and gentlemen, rogues and bitches, here is our fabulous Dima Turgenev," Fabian cooed. The MC gave his customary spiel, but this time with a change. He'd not mentioned Jeanne.

Dima had only a half second to notice that before the music swelled. The dark on stage grew thicker. He latched down his emotions. He threw his shoulders back and posed his hands to the sides. The dance. There was nothing but the dance.

Then he'd be free to find Lizzie.

When an isolating spotlight snapped white, the blonde beneath it was decidedly not Jeanne. Seeing her had never made his blood charge or his stomach flip up toward his lungs.

This woman, however... Her arms writhed overhead, wrists together. Her face tucked to one side as she looked at him sidelong. Bouncy golden hair. Curves he'd worship for the rest of his life. A lushly pouting mouth with a tiny smirk at the edges.

His Lizzie.

Chapter Twenty-Five

Lizzie smiled. She smiled as if every other expression had been practice. She would dance as if every other competition had been a warm up for the rest of her life.

The lights were too intense to see Dima's eyes. God, she needed something there. In her heart of hearts, she wanted it to be happiness, relief, surprise. Anything to say that her small little plan—such an insignificant thing in the scheme of days they'd shared—would mean a future together.

The samba. Her favorite dance. Nothing outside of receiving really talented oral sex made her feel more like a woman. Just like that, she was back to thoughts of him. Back to the magnetism he could wield over her, strong as a tide, timeless as rhythm. Feeling pent-up and edgy, she teased the audience with a flirtatious ass wiggle. The opening permitted a few bars of improv, which had not been her thing about two weeks previous.

Until Club Devant, it hadn't been Dima's thing either.

He strutted to center stage and stood with his chest thrust back, his hips twisted toward the audience, as she prowled the black lacquer floor. The close hold she'd argued about with Remy was a blessing. It meant holding Dima, seeing him. Finally looking into his eyes and knowing whether her gambit would pay off.

His eyebrow quirked, nearly in time with the beat. "You're not Jeanne."

She pulled his white dress shirt out of his waistband. The buttons flew open with a single yank. Applause like a collapsing stone wall crashed around them. "And you're wearing too much."

"Lizzie..."

They'd already missed the start of Remy's planned choreo, but this was important. Slinking down Dima's bare chest seemed to entertain the hooting crowd.

Down she went, shimmying until her knees brushed the stage, then up just as provocatively. The beat was doing wicked things to her hips. Wickedly good things. She spread her fingers wide and made it her mission to touch every ab and rib and gorgeously stacked lat as she climbed.

A hard shudder shook his shoulders. He tipped his face to the ceiling, closed his eyes and swallowed thickly. Lizzie licked the hollow at the base of his throat, which incited Club Devant to near-riot levels of energy. It fed her courage and her muscles.

She nuzzled beneath his ear. He smelled of Paul's cologne, which made her smile against his hot skin. So many distractions. The noise. The lights. The overwhelming urge to move and just get lost in the music. She'd done that as often as she'd drawn breath.

This time, she had something to say.

"I'm not going anywhere and neither are you. This is forever, Dima mine." She pulled back into a slow body wave and flipped her hair. "Now let's give these people a show."

The man she loved—because oh, Christ, she loved him— had assumed the expression of a warrior. A hunter. He was after her.

They'd missed sixteen bars of choreography, but with one four-count of samba basic, they were back to it. Just like that. As if the tension and heartache simply dissolved into molecules of sweat. He pulled her groin-to-ass into four body rolls that circled the stage. Above her, alongside her, and as the foundation that kept her solid and safe, he was her Dima. Her partner and her lover.

They *danced* like lovers. Although he maintained the same ridiculously upright, graceful frame, Dima's hands...*owned*— owned her shoulders, her arms, her waist, until he twined their grips. He brought their torsos together. Breast molded to pecs. Belly pressed against belly. Never in competition had he been so bold. The incredulous expression he wore said he recognized as much, as if outside of himself, although that didn't stop the resurgence of his hunter's intensity. He grabbed with whole hands, his need sinking into her flesh as deeply as his taut, greedy fingertips.

Out of nowhere, he smiled. Bright. Beautiful. So near to bashful. The slight divot in his chin accentuated the lush fullness of his lower lip. Light cast shadows across his erect nipples. Muscles stood out in the sort of heavy relief that made artists grab the nearest paper and charcoal.

They didn't have Dima, his body and his heat. They weren't being blessed by his smile.

Lizzie laughed, threw back her head.

Game on.

Everything flared to life. Kicks sharper. Hips faster. Turns more precise. The lift they executed was textbook perfect, all sweet momentum and easy balance. The right give and take— and a cheeky pinch on her ass. Lizzie grinned like a maniac while giving her tits a quick shimmy. From that high vantage, atop Dima's shoulders, she caught a glimpse of a tall Texan wearing a suit and cowboy hat. Paul leaned against the bar, a customer tonight rather than an employee. She blew him a kiss.

Hands locked with Lizzie's, Dima brought her out of the lift with a dramatic death drop. She came to a stop with her nose mere inches from the dance floor, but they never got it wrong. She could've had an arrow tattooed on her wrists pointing to the exact spot held each time. A complete waste of ink. Dima had her.

Up. In his arms. Close hold, bodies practically fused. His heartbeat would feel like hers, like the rhythm of that dance. Eyes the color of midnight shadows glowed with triumph. Two synchronized body waves later, more applause hurtled out from the tables. The rest of the club became a blur of red and gold to match their costumes. She and Dima were exotic creatures camouflaged for such an environment.

She belonged here.

It was bone-deep knowledge.

The samba ended, followed immediately by the cha-cha. Every move became easier, more tuned to his. How could she have believed that competition dancing was all they had in them? Too many rules. Barriers. Expectations. She breathed this freedom deep into her lungs and shook it out with every kick and step and spin.

This was simply dancing with Dima, and it was *everything*. She put her soul into their union, drinking up his smile when it flashed. That they had discovered the cheeky playfulness required of the cha-cha was a minor miracle.

He twirled her into a stage curtsy with the finishing flourish of music. The inside of her knee reminded her that she wasn't perfect anymore, but that single misstep had allowed her to find an otherwise unknown spotlight. She knew what she needed for the future to be solid and good. He bowed right alongside her.

They crossed to stage left and grabbed the water bottles Fabian extended. "Friggin' fantastic," he said. "Damn."

Dima eyed Lizzie as his throat worked the quick swallows. Only a few. He had it down to a science, how much he could drink without getting a stitch in his side. Everything remained...him. Methodical and thoughtful. He screwed the cap back on the water bottle. Still watching her.

"Say something." She was breathless, but not entirely

because of the dance. Physical therapy had prepared her, and working with Remy had reminded her body what it needed to do. No, this was entirely different, like a defendant waiting for a judge's sentence. "Dima, please."

He backed her against the wall. Suddenly. No warning. Hands at her hips, mouth on hers. She wrapped her arms around his slick torso. Back and clavicles. Tight waist and firm ass. He had the same idea, rucking her skimpy spangled costume up her thighs.

Oh hell no. Not again. She found the presence of mind— barely—to shove against his chest. When that didn't work, she bit his lower lip. His growl of approval wet her panties in a hot rush. Good God, this was nuts.

"Performance," she said with a grin. "That applause? It's for us."

"They don't know the half of it."

Fabian tapped Lizzie on the arm. "Bachata. Then you two can get back to whatever this particular move is. Wish I had a big Russian stud to teach me."

"Find your own. I'm still working on this one."

Dima visibly forced calm into his lean body. His back bowed on a long exhale. Lizzie turned toward the stage, while he stood behind her and crossed his sleek, sweaty bare arms around her stomach.

"How's your knee? You up for round three?"

Hearing his concern, knowing how much guilt he took on himself even still, twisted in her gut. Some things would still take time to make right. Mostly by doing. "Yup. Followed by round four as soon as we get off stage."

He groaned against her temple. "Lizzie, I mean it. You sure?"

"Trust, Dima," she said in Russian. She twined their fingers together, and not-so-innocently pressed her ass back against his pelvis. "Besides, do you want this song to forever be the one where you saw me grind up on Remy?"

"Fuck no," he growled.

"Good. Because you don't have to break in this time. I'm yours."

When the lights went up, they were back where they belonged.

Dima spun her on the first count. His thick thigh wedged between hers as he bent her back into a long, sensual arc. He trailed his lips down between her breasts and danced a four-count with his body bowed over hers. All the while their legs kept time, their hips hitting stroke after stroke. It was sex standing up. Pure and simple. Since everything she and Dima had shared with Paul, and with the passionate undercurrents they'd only just started to explore, they found a hardcore groove.

The lights made Lizzie feel as if they were being watched—not while dancing, but while devouring one another in Dima's big bed. A need to be the center of attention had probably dragged her to the stage in the first place. It was a drug. She shared that high with Dima as he led and she followed.

She was ridiculously out of breath by the time the music concluded. Applause again turned Club Devant into a glittering madhouse. Everyone was on their feet, even Declan, who offered his praise by way of a slow clap and a marveled expression. Paul shook his head, equally stunned, but he followed it up with the grin that would rival the sun.

Whatever Fabian said about their departure from the stage was lost to her as Dima tugged her hand. He lifted his eyebrow in silent question. Lizzie waited until they found a dark, private corner to call him on his unspoken request.

She grabbed his face, fisting her fingers in his hair. "Dima.

I mean it. We can't keep putting this off. I need more."

"I know," he whispered, forehead to hers. "I promise. We'll make this right. I'm not letting you go."

Like inhaling helium, her body became lighter, floating in his arms. "I love you and I love what you just said, but it won't be enough."

He thunked her fists against his skull. "You want in here? Fine. But don't say I didn't warn you." With a curious blink, he straightened and looked at her with a slight frown. Total confusion. "You love me?"

"Very much."

"Lizzie, not just friends. I can't."

"Best friends. The rest too. All of it," she added, licking his salty shoulder and biting into the meat of his hard muscle. "Like I said that night. With us alone. You're my rock and my calm. I know I didn't say it right and you didn't hear it right, but I was trying to tell you how much you mean to me. All those pieces and facets. Are you hearing me, Dima mine?"

"My little one," he rasped.

Big hands cupped the back of her head and brought her mouth up for another kiss, this one long and indulgent. The pulse of urgency shone through at the edges as they rode the waves of a solid post-performance high. At least they started sweet.

It was exactly that. A new start.

Hip to hip, he revealed his excitement and his need. Lizzie tipped her head back to the wall...reveling. Dima was hers to hold.

"Love you," he whispered against her neck. "*Ja ljublju tebja,* my Lizzie. My little one. Can I tell you that now? Will you deny me?"

"Never again."

"I'm done too. I need you too much."

The words were a balm across so many hurts, the least of which was her tender knee. She dragged him closer. Maybe if they tried hard enough, they could melt skin to skin. Distance would never be a problem again. Inside one another was the only answer.

Tongues first, followed by his fingers sliding between her thighs. What a choice. Hear more of Dima's sweet words, hoping for them like wringing water from a stone...or keep touching.

"I dream," he said on a groan as her fingers found his prick. Maybe they could do both.

"Tell me?"

"I dream so big and so often that they scare me."

"Scare you? Dima, why?"

"Most of them are bigger than me. I'm not..." He shook his head. "I'm afraid of not being man enough to see them come true. The planning, Lizzie? All of my plans? It's the only way I know to keep the doubts at bay."

Chapter Twenty-Six

Dima had his hands on the prize. He didn't need anything but Lizzie. Pressed up against the wall, halfway down the corridor to his dressing room, anyone could come along and see them. He barely cared. He took her mouth again, not ready to hear her talk. Not yet. Too much more he needed to say.

"I've never told you because it's easier that way. If I'm the only one who knows the plan, I'm also the only one disappointed."

Her hand framed his cheek. "Do you really believe that?"

"I don't want to let anyone down." His mouth found the line of her throat. He licked since he'd been unleashed and he couldn't keep from touching her. "My parents depended on me, not that I managed to save them from themselves. You did too. Better not to disappoint you, of all people."

Her fingers gripped his cock, stroked through the material of his pants. "I still knew when you were upset. That you never talked to me about it... Dima, it hurt. I just want you. I want to know it all."

He couldn't do this in the hallway anymore. Grabbing Lizzie by the wrist, he pulled her along until they reached his dressing room. Right before he snapped the door shut behind him, he caught sight of Paul at the end of the hallway. For the moment, this was his and Lizzie's business. He snapped the lock shut.

Lizzie stepped backwards. On her lips she wore a hint of the grin he loved so much. Her chest jerked on harsh breaths, as if they were still dancing.

He supposed they were. There would always be dance with

him and Lizzie.

Warm and frightening at the same time, the word "always" unfurled in his chest.

She lifted her hands out to the side and wiggled her fingers in a tiny challenge. "Come on, Dmitri," she goaded in Russian. "Give me your biggest dream. The one you've never even said out loud to yourself, much less anyone else."

"Marriage." The word snapped out of him, burning his tongue, teeth, lips with its daring. He held down the shakes that threatened to follow in its wake. Instead he filled his hands with his wonder, cupped Lizzie's hips and lifted her to the counter. "Marriage to you. Be my Lizzie, forever."

Her eyes softened and her mouth went slack. "Oh."

He closed his eyes and lowered his forehead to her temple. The entirety of his body curled around her, shielding. Because even if she said no, he still needed to say it. "Marriage. Babies. A place of our own someday. Maybe a dance studio. Maybe a club like this. Who knows. But on the way, we'd stop by Hollywood and work there."

She laughed shakily. Her hands rose to the back of his neck. Fine tremors worked over his skin from the touch. "How could you keep all of that in? For so long? You dream so big."

"Don't you see? So many things to go wrong." He swallowed hard. "So many places I could still fuck it up. If you really need to go back to the circuit, something still to prove, we'll do that instead."

"I don't. I like the sound of your ride a hell of a lot better."

"You're sure?"

"Oh, yeah." She grinned. "I dare you to tell me tonight wasn't the best dance we've ever had. I'd be an idiot to give that up."

His gaze flicked over her features, landing on those steady

green eyes. "Lizzie, are you saying...? Will you marry me?"

"Absolutely."

How much he adored her faith in him, and how much it scared him too. He took her mouth with a hard, sweeping kiss that revealed everything he was still working up the courage to say. Those thoughts came out as whispers against her skin, as his mouth skated over her neck, her shoulders, her breasts.

"I've taken you for granted for so long," she said softly, her words sliding between them. "How could I not? Fifteen years of being safe and loved and completely understood. You've always been there for me. That didn't mean you always would be. When I think about you and Svetlana..." Her voice broke.

"I told her no." Dima gathered her close. "It wasn't even a choice, in the end. I'm yours, little one."

Their touches ramped so fast. More kisses. More hungry need to prove the words true. The press of her lips was drugging and heady, spinning him into the air. Leaps that never came down.

He rucked her skirt back up, shoved his pants down past his hips. A condom made a fast-scramble appearance. He pushed into her with one deep thrust. They froze. Lizzie's nails scored his skin. She hissed, and he slowly withdrew until only his head balanced in her wet sheathe.

"Dima mine," she breathed. Her eyes were hazy, but she didn't look away. Locked gazes. Her intensity worked down his spine.

He shifted her pelvis forward a fraction, until each of his strokes earned one of those fabulous, airy gasps. The next flurry of strokes turned gasps into moans. He covered her mouth with one hand.

"Uh-uh, little one," he purred. He couldn't keep the smile out of his voice, even if it made her shoot daggers at him. "You have to be quieter than that in my dressing room."

She tucked her fingers around his hand, pulled it off her mouth. "*Our* dressing room."

He chuckled, but it was strained by the effort of holding back his climax. "Yes, ours. Seems appropriate. This is where we started, after all."

"No more Pauls, though."

He hitched her knee over his elbow, jacked her higher. "Not without talking to me first."

She must have liked that, because her pussy clenched down hard on his cock. Her eyes fluttered shut, her face turned to the side, reflected back by the big mirror behind her. Her hands spread over his chest in absolute trust, letting him set their pace.

There, Dima lost his control. That trust. Everything he'd wanted and been afraid to ask for.

The moves turned jerky. Harder. Lizzie's pelvis lifted toward him. She groaned, low and soft when he fucked hard enough that her back squeaked against the mirror. She shoved her own hand in her mouth, the meat of her palm at her teeth.

She was slick and hot and perfect. Everything. Always. He couldn't hold it anymore. With his thumb between them on her clit, he amped it up again. The pleasure cut loose. She came only seconds ahead of him, scratching her nails down his chest and burying her scream against his neck.

He slapped a hand flat on the mirror, his orgasm cutting him loose at the knees. Tingles ran down his legs, shook out his arms. Burned through his body in a flash of *Holy Mother, yes.*

Only through the aftermath of soft kisses and straightening clothes did he realize their door was suspiciously quiet. Normally after a performance like that he would've been flooded with fans and dancers offering quick congratulations.

He pulled Lizzie's skirt back down over her hips. "Just to confirm... You're marrying me, yes?"

She smiled, so brilliantly. Lit up so brightly that he drank up warmth from even being near her. "Yes, Dima mine. I'll marry you."

"Good," he sighed, kissing her again. "But now..." He strode toward the door and yanked it open.

As he'd suspected, Paul waited outside. He looked back over his shoulder and grinned. "I've been shooing people away."

Dima laughed, clapping him on the back. "Thanks, my friend."

Lizzie appeared at Dima's side, tucking under his arm. God, she belonged there. With her arm looped around his back, tracing little patterns down his spine, she stretched up on her toes to kiss Paul. The exchange was less intense than he'd seen them trade before, but they still lingered like lovers. Such a pretty picture they made, two sunshine people. Dima didn't mind at all because once she was done, Lizzie snuggled back along his side. Her free hand spread flat over his stomach.

"Really, thank you," she said. "I'm not even sure I can list all the awesome."

Paul shook his head. "I'd have done it all over again in a nanosecond. There's just something good about the two of you together. And something *really* good about what you did to me." His grin was a beautiful thing. Tiny lines fanned out from his eyes. "You're out of time, though. Declan came by, said you have five minutes to get out there and talk to him."

"I'm surprised he didn't run upstairs to check his screens," Lizzie said with a grin. "Now, let's go wow 'em all."

"That's your job." Christ, how good did that sound? Because they were right again, the pieces of the puzzle finally snapping together in truth.

Dima followed her out to the main area of the club, Paul in turn behind him. His little one tossed up her hands at the entrance, striking quite a pose. Applause started in a wash and slammed upwards into a roar. From the back of the room came a rolling stomp of feet. Dima knew what he was supposed to do—cross his arms and look intimidating and solid—so he did so. Let her take this one on. She played up to the crowd, blowing kisses and doing a couple hip shimmies.

Eventually she pranced to where Declan held court. The man reclined with one of his usual girls at his side.

They didn't quite get there before Svetlana planted herself in their path. She sniffed down her nose. "You are not the man I thought you were, Dmitri. That dance..." She shuddered. "Completely crass." She skewed Lizzie with a glare made of daggers. "I am unsurprised considering your choice in partners."

Dima folded an arm over Lizzie's shoulders. "I'm unsurprised you think so, but I've everything I need."

"Broadway," she practically shrieked. "My backers are not going to stick around if I can't bring them Dmitri Turgenev."

Lizzie chuckled. "Oh, that's priceless. Nice one, Sveti. Well done."

Dmitri couldn't find it in himself to wish the woman ill, not after two years together. "I hope you find what you're looking for, Sveta. It isn't going to be me."

She shot Lizzie another evil look. "I hope you ruin your other knee," she hissed. "*Idi na fig.*"

With that, she flounced off through the crowd, a mass of fake hair fluttering behind her.

Lizzie flipped her off. "Does she think I don't know what she said? Go fuck yourself? Really? And she called *you* crass. Silly cow."

"Come on, little one." He took her hand. "This is a happy night."

She smiled up at him. "Hell yes, it is. Let's go make it even better." On she pushed toward Declan's table.

The man wore a pale pink button-down shirt open to his abs. "Quite the show. Congratulations on your reunion." The smirk on his mouth said he meant it in every sense.

Dima smirked right back. "It's about time," he agreed.

Declan snapped his fingers and someone stuck a clipboard in his hand. "You know what these are, right?"

Lizzie laughed. "I'm assuming they're contracts?"

He nodded, grinning like a maniac. He held them out, along with a pen. "Same terms as before for Dima, plus same for you."

She grabbed the clipboard. "I'm good with that. Dima?"

His mouth opened. Closed. He put his hand over hers. She came away from the main crowd with a tiny tug on her wrist, following easily. He bent his head so that she could hear him in the press of people and talk and noise.

Damn, this was still harder than he'd expected. His chest pulled shut on a rush of nervousness greater even than when he'd taken to the stage. "We'll sign, but with both of us on the line we can get more out of him."

"God, I love you." She beamed. "Plans?"

He nodded. Laughed a little. Because maybe this wasn't so tough. "I want enough for us to stick around, a year maybe? For both of us together, we'll get more money too. It'll be enough to take us through to audition season."

"Audition season?"

"In Hollywood." Her mouth tasted like his dreams. Thrilling. Their kisses pushed deeper, even though they were in the middle of a crowd. "Because I'm crazy, maybe? But we'll try."

"Together."

He traced his grip up over her arms, along her bare shoulders, until he framed her perfect face. That wide smile he loved so much. He rubbed his thumbs over her bottom lip. Kissed her briefly. "Together. Because nothing would be right without you. Lizzie, you are the sum of all my plans. All that I need. Forever."

About the Author

Katie Porter is the writing team of Carrie Lofty and Lorelie Brown, who've been friends and critique partners for more than five years. Both are multi-published in historical romance. Carrie has an MA in history, while Lorelie is a US Army veteran. Generally a high-strung masochist, Carrie loves running and weight training, but she has no fear of gross things like dissecting formaldehyde sharks. Her two girls are not appreciative. Lorelie, a laid-back sadist, would rather grin maniacally when Carrie works out. Her three boys love how she screams like a little girl around spiders.

To learn more about the authors who make up Katie, visit katieporterbooks.com and facebook.com/MsKatiePorter, then follow them on Twitter at @MsKatiePorter, @carrielofty and @LorelieBrown.

Lights, lovers...action!

Came Upon a Midnight Clear
© *2012 Katie Porter*

Born to old Virginia money, film producer Kyle Wakefield's conservative upbringing kept him in the closet. Only once did he venture outside: for a tempestuous teenage affair with Nathan Carnes. When Nathan's self-destructive streak landed him in prison, Kyle slammed the door on youthful hopes. Despite Hollywood successes, he still hides his true self.

He thought he'd moved on, until his production company hires Nathan and his Second Chances stunt crew to work on the London set of a big-budget action flick. Watching Nathan risk life and limb with fellow ex-cons looking for a fresh start makes it tough for Kyle to keep his desires hidden.

Thirteen years have passed since Nathan's teenage self-doubt led him to sabotage any chance of a future with Kyle. He's come a long way since then, but despite their explosive sexual chemistry, Kyle treats their attraction like a deep dark secret.

Their matched Hollywood ambitions and a pain-in-the-ass director make cooperation essential. As the London holiday season casts its spell, the two men find themselves on the verge of falling in love again—even as old secrets and pain keep them shackled. The only hope of unlocking their hearts is a Christmas miracle.

Warning: This book features a snowy London Christmas, sex on a pool table, a hot-and-dirty gay nightclub, and naughty references to candy canes.

Available now in ebook and print from Samhain Publishing.

'Tis the season for double seduction.

Checking it Twice
© *2012 Jodi Redford*

The only item on Jana Colton's Christmas list this year is Kevin Monahan. Preferably naked in her bed. The delicious, hunky chef has been resisting her forever, but she's pulling out all the sexy stops this holiday. Especially since his acceptance of an out-of-state job threatens to nix her quest to rock his boxers off.

Jana has always been Kevin's personal Kryptonite, but giving in to her isn't an option. Relationships are a four-letter word in his book. He cares far too much for Jana to let his emotional baggage ultimately break her heart.

With the arrival of his best friend, Nick Pappas, the balance of temptation shifts. From their past history of sharing women, Nick knows every dirty trick it takes to lead Kevin astray, and he's not afraid to use them. Particularly since Nick's convinced that Jana is exactly what Kevin needs to be happy and whole.

Their game of seduction quickly snowballs into something that feels an awful lot like love—in triplicate. But with Kevin dead set on leaving Michigan, there's a real possibility it could be a blue Christmas for them all.

Warning: This book contains an extremely tormented voyeur, a very naughty and not so saintly Nick, a liberal application of candy cane-flavored body paint, a buzzing butterfly, and enough raunchy fun on a sex swing to melt a snowman...or two.

Available now in ebook and print from Samhain Publishing.

It's all about the story...

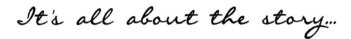

Romance

HORROR

www.samhainpublishing.com

9 781619 216402